MW01144727

Berman's Chosen

By Gretchen S. B.

Berman's Chosen
By
Gretchen S. B.

Gretchen S. B.

Acknowledgments

I want to thank all of you who read and enjoyed Berman's Wolves and have been waiting for this next book in the series.

I of course want to give a nod to "The Hubster." Although he hates to be mentioned, he deserves credit for all his support. Thank you for all that you do to help me make my dream a reality! I truly could not do any of this without you.

I want to also thank Lacie at Pelican Proofing for editing this book and for being so incredibly great about fixing this book so others could enjoy it. One last thanks to my Beta Readers for giving this book the last once over it needs.

Works by Gretchen S. B.

Night World Series:
Lady of the Dead
Viking Sensitivity

Berman's Wolves Trilogy
Berman's Wolves
Berman's Chosen

Anthony Hollownton Series
Hollownton Homicide

Delta House Series
The Doll Making Delta

Short Stories
The Tongue-Tied Hunter
Poker in Portland (Passion in Portland Anthology
2016)
Big City Bachelor (Highland's Fourth)

Chapter 1

Lyra died. Jack still couldn't believe it happened. He didn't know how the world had gotten so far out of control so fast. It seemed like only yesterday he was finding out Pack L attacked her. Even though it had been almost a month ago. It was the worst month of his life. Jack wasn't sure he'd slept more than five hours a night since Lyra's kidnapping.

When Lyra's aunt, Luna, phoned Jack to let them know she was pretty sure she replicated the suppressant mentioned in the notes they confiscated, Jack drove straight to Justin's house. He needed to be there. Not just as her alpha but as her littermate. He needed to be there for himself as well. He needed to know whether this was going to work; he knew if it didn't, they would have less than a week with her. There was no hospital they could take her to because of their condition. No hospital was built to handle werewolves.

When he pulled up to the house Luna had yet to arrive. However, Justin was there, as were Taylor, Ryan, and Hazel. The living room was encompassed in a heavy silence as they waited. When Luna and the Scotsman arrived there was no preamble or discussion, but none was actually needed. No one wanted to small talk. They were all there to see if this magical suppressant worked. So the Luna took out a rather large syringe and took a minute to find a vein. She then injected Lyra. Once she backed away they all watched Lyra's prone form; at first nothing happened. Then Lyra shot up into a sitting position, eyes open and unseeing and let out a pain-filled scream. Her body collapsed into a seizure stronger than Jack had ever seen the likes of before that. It shook the entire bed. The whole room watched helplessly. After what couldn't have been more than thirty seconds, the seizure stopped. All movement stopped, she wasn't even breathing. Luna and her husband ran to Lyra's body, trying to revive her. It was the longest ninety seconds of Jack's life. Lyra had then taken a shuddering breath and her body slipped back into a coma. Jack could vaguely hear Hazel crying behind him. Lyra died, and by some luck they had gotten her back.

Her aunt checked Lyra's vitals and declared everything normal, except for her not being conscious. There was nothing in the notes to let the woman know how long this would last. Luna suggested it might be better if Lyra was brought to the family compound, where she could be monitored full time. Jack had adamantly denied the request. Something in him felt if he let Lyra go that would be the end of it; he and his littermates would never see her again. He told her if the coma lasted longer than a week he would entertain the possibility, but until then she was staying with Justin.

That was three days ago. So far, no one else from Lyra's family had come to visit. Not even her brothers. Jack found that horrible and strange. If someone almost dies, you would think their family would visit them. But apparently not. The pack continued to stay with her, taking turns keeping watch; though no one mentioned it, no one wanted to leave her alone. Hazel still maintained Lyra could hear them.

Jack had nightmares about her dying every night since it happened. Shocking himself awake yet again, he looked at his alarm clock. It was only 5:30 in the morning. He didn't have to be at work until nine. But he knew he was not going to be able to sleep. Rolling out of bed, he felt maybe his time would be better spent going to visit Lyra. He didn't believe she could hear him, but knowing she was alive and not in imminent danger was enough; being. Being in her presence made him feel better. Yet it reminded him of how little control he had over the situation. But knowing she hadn't died was more important to him. Part of Jack couldn't believe their luck at saving her.

He got ready for work just as he would if he woke with his alarm at seven. But instead of heading to the studio he headed to Justin's. He walked in without knocking since he had a key to all of his littermates' homes. As he walked through the door, he felt bad. Clearly he had forgotten Taylor was there, sleeping on the couch. The other man woke, hearing him unlock the door and was sitting on the couch blinking at him.

"Sorry, Taylor. Just go back to sleep. I'm only here to visit Lyra before work," Jack said by way of apology, as he walked through the living room.

Taylor nodded before laying back down on the couch. "Gotcha."

Jack continued his trek up the stairs. When he got to the top, he saw Justin standing outside his bedroom door, blinking down the hallway. When he realized it was Jack coming up the stairs the other man gave Jack a curious look.

Jack showed him a tight smile then repeated what he'd said to Taylor downstairs, "Sorry to wake you up, man. I couldn't sleep and figured I would visit her before I head to work."

Justin nodded sleepily and headed back into his room.

Jack opened the door to the guestroom and walked in, shutting the door behind him. He got lucky; no one else was in the room with her. There was a chair next to the head of the bed. Jack sat down and watched his friend. He saw her hand lying outside the blankets. Before he knew what he was doing, he reached out to hold it.

Jack sighed. "I promised Hazel I would talk to you. Even though I don't believe you can actually hear me. You know I would really appreciate it if you would come join us in the land of the conscious. There are a lot of things we don't understand, and for whatever reason you seem to be the only one with the answers. Though I'm not sure what I can do to help you. This all seems way above my head. I wish there was some magical answer. Some magical antidote that cured you of whatever this thing has done to you. We don't have that. All we have is something to suppress the effects, or so we think. Even that seems to be a long shot."

Jack sat back in the chair. He could feel himself getting worked up and that wasn't going do them any good. Especially when he had to be at work in a couple hours. So he stared at the wall across from him, trying to rein in his frustration, worry, fear, and anger. Then he heard something that snapped his attention.

"Jack?"

It was so faint he wasn't even sure he truly heard it or whether he just imagined it. He looked down at the bed and Lyra's hand hadn't moved. Her eyes were still shut and her breathing slow and steady. He shook his head. He was imagining things now. Jack did not need to be hallucinating.

"Jack?" It was a little bit louder this time. Jack concentrated on Lyra's face and didn't move his eyes. "Yes, Lyra, I'm here," he responded, hoping he wasn't just hearing things.

As if by magic her eyes fluttered open; well, half open that is. After a second they were fully closed again. But her hand stirred in his. Something in him knew she was still at least partially awake.

"How long…out?" There was a huge pause between the first part and the last of the sentence.

Jack could only assume Lyra completed the sentence in her head, but her mouth wasn't quite working in tandem with her mind.

"When all is said and done, a little over a week, I think. You've been giving us quite the scare. We do have a lot to talk about but right now you need to be resting."

There was a very long pause and for second, Jack thought maybe Lyra had fallen back asleep. "Only aware... Before Luna comes... ask her... to lessen sedative... It keeps me asleep."

Jack felt his heart speed up. Could it be Lyra was ready to come back to them and the sedative her aunt was giving her to take away the pain was the only thing leaving her asleep? "Are you still in pain?"

"Tolerable," was all she responded. Jack didn't like that answer. But he wanted Lyra awake. "Okay, I'll let her know."

"Jack? You still there?"

Jack had no idea the process Lyra's mind was using to remain conscious. He only just answered her but her voice told him she thought it had been a while. That worried Jack a little bit. "Yeah, Lyra, I'm still here."

There was a long pause again. It took all of Jack's strength to not try and push her to speak. "Make Hazel stop crying. Annoying. Also… tell Dylan… no more elephant child… or I'll kill him."

Jack couldn't help but laugh. Here she was fighting some unknown drug and her priority was complaining about Hazel crying and something Dylan was doing. He couldn't help but wonder if her comment to Dylan was some subconsciously induced event. But he would bring it up anyway just to be safe.

"Can't tell you that… not allowed to," she said, her voice a little frustrated.

Clearly the conversation had continued in her mind when it hadn't in actuality. "Can't tell me what?"

Her hand gripped his and loosened. "Stop asking. You don't know what you're asking."

Jack felt himself get extremely curious as to what the him inside her head was saying. He could tell she was getting agitated, which was not what she needed right now. "Lyra, you need to rest. Go back to sleep."

There was a pause again and for a moment Jack thought for the first time ever Lyra did what he told her to do. But that hope was soon dashed. "Jack? You'll tell me everything that happened... when I'm awake, right? I hope you're real."

That last statement stabbed Jack right in the chest. His heart hurt for her. Lyra didn't know whether she was really talking to him or her imagination. He squeezed her hand. "Yes, Lyra. When you and I have our conversation, when you're awake, I'll tell you everything."

A ghost of a smile appeared on her face. "That's a pretty lie, Jack... Thank you."

Jack couldn't help but laugh. Even unconscious, Lyra knew Jack wouldn't be telling her everything. He didn't respond in hopes she would fall back asleep. Though part of him wanted to keep talking to her because he missed her, he knew sleep was more important right now. So he sat in the room with her another half hour and when she didn't wake up again, he gave her hand one last squeeze before leaving the room.

He didn't want to wake Justin or Taylor but he knew both men would want to know as soon as they could that Lyra had woken up. So he knocked on Justin's door loud enough that Taylor would be able to hear it downstairs. "You guys are going to want to hear this. I'll meet you downstairs."

He heard a grunt from inside the room and took that as an affirmative. Jack headed downstairs and into the kitchen. Taylor was already waiting for him, sitting on one of the stools. The coffee machine was running behind him. He looked up at Jack as he entered the room, frowning. Jack didn't say anything; instead he just sat on one of the other three stools waiting for Justin to join them. His heart was racing. He was the only one in the world who knew Lyra was awake. Part of him wanted to hold onto that knowledge and keep it to himself. More of him knew the others had a right to know. A few minutes later, Justin came down and sat on the stool next to Jack. When he had both men's attention, Jack spoke.

"Lyra is out of her coma." It was all Jack could get out at first. He felt himself choke up as he heard the words out loud.

Both men's eyes were riveted to him. Looks of surprise, shock, and joy filled their faces.

Taking a deep breath, Jack moved on. "According to her, the only thing keeping her sedated is what Luna is giving her every morning. Because the drug seems to wear off soon before Luna gets here, that is the only time she seems to be conscious of what's happening around her. Since that's early in the morning, none of us have thought to be around at that time. Which might be why none of us have noticed the past couple days that she's been like this. She asked me to tell Luna to scale it back a little bit. When I asked if she was in pain she said it was tolerable. I don't know what exactly that means, but I'm sure I won't like the answer. I still think Luna should know. She also said Hazel should stop coming in there and crying. That she found it annoying. She also gave me a message for Dylan." He looked directly at Taylor. "But I'm not entirely sure it wasn't a delusion. As she had trouble keeping track of our conversation and towards the end she could hear me talking in her head even when I

Gretchen S. B.

wasn't talking out loud. That being said, she said to tell Dylan to stop with the elephant child or she would kill him. Does that make sense to you?"

Taylor's eyes began to glisten as he pulled out his phone. He didn't answer Jack, but instead tapped the screen and put the phone to his ear. "Hey man." There was a pause. "No, it's not bad news. Apparently our girl somewhat came to and one of the only things she said was that she wants you to stop reading that stupid Aesop fable about the elephant or she'll kill you." There was another pause and Taylor smiled. "Yeah, count on our girl to threaten you even when she's on death's doorstep herself. I'll see you this afternoon. If you could let Graham know and the rest of the family, that would be great." There was a longer pause. "Bye, Dylan." He put the phone away and looked at Jack through glassy eyes. "Thank you, that means a lot."

Jack wasn't sure what to make of that so he simply nodded, then turned to Justin. "I don't know what time Luna gets here in the morning. But when she does, tell her this information comes straight from Lyra."

The look on his littermate's face told Jack he had given up all hope and in less than a minute Jack had restored all of it. In that moment Jack felt the burden of his position weigh on him. He was alpha, it was his job to keep them safe, and he wasn't able to do that. He couldn't even protect the ones that listened to him, not even from the pain. Suddenly he found it too hard to continue to be at Justin's house.

Getting off the stool he looked at both men. "If you could let everyone know what's happening that would be great. I'll be back tonight around seven."

With that he left. He wasn't able to take a good solid breath until he was outside. He felt himself sob a little. Lyra was okay. For now anyway, since there was no antidote. Simply a suppressant. But she was going to be awake. That was more than he could've hoped for. More than he dared hope for. He closed his eyes and just stood on Justin's front porch for a moment. He was so overwhelmed with the emotions coursing through him he didn't know what his next move should be.

He purposefully put Taylor and Justin in charge of letting everyone know, giving himself the opportunity to spending the next twelve hours like a normal person. He felt guilty for sloughing off part of his responsibility like that but it was for his own sanity. He wouldn't be able to work knowing he had to keep checking his phone. Something needed to change. There had to be something they could do to make it all stop. But Jack didn't have the foggiest idea what it was. Taking one last deep breath of the dawn air, Jack headed towards his car. It didn't matter if he was getting to work early. Whether it was his day job or as alpha, there was always work to be done.

Jack couldn't remember the last time a shift he worked felt so long. It seemed to drag on forever, knowing that as soon as he got off shift he was heading back to Justin's. Part of him wanted to say he was sick. That he needed to go home early. But he knew getting there early wouldn't get him anywhere. Luna came with her injections twice a day, once at seven a.m. and once at seven p.m. His getting to Justin's early wouldn't do any good. Especially since he had already put people in charge of letting everyone know.

Jack felt his phone vibrate before he heard the ring; pulling it out of his pocket, he was somewhat surprised to see the call was from Mathew. Not having a lot of time to talk, he put the phone back in his pocket, making a mental note to call Mathew back when he had a break.

An hour and a half later, Jack laid his headset down, took a deep breath and walked outside, being careful to stay under the overhang as Seattle had taken on a light drizzle. The weather, while normal, seemed inappropriate now that he knew Lyra was awake. Pulling out his phone, he listened to the message Mathew left him.

"Hey, Jack, I know you're most likely at work, but when you're off shift if you would be so kind as to pay me a visit at my pack office, there are some things I'd like to show you. I am inviting the other five pack leaders in question first before bringing it to our alliance in general. We seem to have dug up some information about who is pulling the strings of Pack L. Give me a call when you get this. Unlike you, I have a job where I can pick up my phone at any time." Then the message ended.

Not wanting to wait another four to six hours before getting the information, especially since his plan was to go straight back to Justin's house to see Lyra, Jack quickly put in the call to Mathew. The other man picked up after two rings.

"Jack, good to hear from you so quickly," Mathew answered calmly.

Jack was trying not to get irritated. It was all he could do to not yell "Give me the damn information!" but he answered as calmly as possible.

"Hello, Mathew, what is this information you have? Lyra is on the brink of waking up and I'd like to go straight there after work." He saw no reason to hide Lyra's progress from Mathew, especially considering Mathew might eventually hear it from Dylan.

"That is fantastic news… Jack, and I understand your sense of urgency; that being said, I think it will make more sense with visual aids, but suffice to say we found out four of the old lab assistants are working for the same, slightly-vague chemistry company under a Dr. Paul. I don't know whether you remember her or not, but Dr. Paul was one of the scientists working on our program; she was also one of the ones who felt we should be scientifically studied and replicated.

"We did enough research to conclude that she is definitely the same Dr. Paul. There seems to be an interworking, a web if you will, and we are not entirely sure if Dr. Paul is on the top of the food chain. Now that we have this information, I want to get the okay from the other six alphas to have them tailed to see exactly where they're working. To see if there is another lab other than this one they are officially working in and if so, what notes are there. I think if we can put them down, so to speak, it will go a long way toward putting much of our issues at ease. Though to be fair, we are not sure exactly how many other scientists are involved beyond Dr. Paul."

It was frustrating to hear; Jack was definitely relieved they now were headed in a direction that might be useful in their endeavor, but at the same time was incredibly frustrated to know that Mathew was right. He would need to stop off at the Pack M office to see this web in person before visiting Lyra at Justin's.

"I can be there between six and six-thirty," he replied.

"I'll see you then, Jack. Have a good rest of your day."

Jack mumbled a semi polite response then hung up. The next few hours were going to be horrible. They were already bad because he was looking forward to seeing Lyra; that is, assuming she had indeed received a smaller dose today. Now Jack would have to wait even longer and wade through more information than he would have before. Growling to himself, Jack headed back into the station.

He was the last one to arrive when he walked through the open door to Pack M's office. The other six people were standing, facing him but looking at the backside of a rolling standup corkboard.

Mathew glanced up and saw him first. "Oh, good. Jack, close the door behind you and lock it, would you?"

Jack did as requested before heading over and standing on the left side of the group, slightly behind so he could take in the whole board. It looked somewhat similar to the family tree diagram Jack was made to do in middle school. The bottom of the tree was all of the lab assistants, four of which had strings connecting them to Dr. Paul and a company called Cell Corp; on. On the strings were notes with thoughts between each. Then there were strings to two more that worked for some other company that was a subsidiary of Cell Corp; there were notes on the projects they were working on. Three of them worked on projects under the supervision of Dr. Paul; the other half had question marks above their picture. On the same level as Dr. Paul were two more squares with question marks. Those three squares shot up to another question mark above them.

Mathew cleared his throat to let the group know he wanted their attention. "As you can see, we only have a little more than half of the information we need as of yet. Right now, we know at least half of Berman's lab assistants are involved in some way. We know about Dr. Paul and from what information we've gotten—which isn't much since we've only just begun digging—there are at least two doctors working with her on this project and she clearly answers to someone, so we assumed these other doctors do as well. We could be wrong about the shape of the hierarchy; I have people looking into it and trying to see if they can look through her emails to get more information. Two members of Bishop's pack, who actually are experts when it comes to this kind of research, are working to get us access into any of these people's emails so we can track down everybody else involved. My understanding is we are looking at two or three days max. But because we're working on the assumption that they are being careful, we would like everybody's okay to send a few of our own to tail Dr. Paul and several of the lab assistants, in order to find out if there is some other location they're doing their research at. Mainly the place they took Lyra when they stole her away several months ago. I think if we can find that location, we could probably find their headquarters, because I can't imagine the two locations are far from each other. We also have printed up copies of the web you see before you so you could each have a two foot by three foot version of this. That way, should something happen to it, everyone has the information. So, what is everyone thinking?"

There was quiet, as if no one wanted to be the first to speak before the alpha from down south, whose name Jack couldn't remember, folded his arms. "Boone is particularly good at this kind of thing. I would suggest we use him to track because he's harder to lose than most. Whether you decide to use him or not, I think tracking these people to try and find a location is probably our next best bet since you already have somebody on tracking the emails."

There were mutters of agreement from the other alphas. Jack couldn't really see a reason to not have these people followed; it was their best bet to keep their people safe.

After a few moments when no one had anything else to say, Mathew gestured to the table behind him to a pile of rolled up posters. "All right, if nobody has anything else then feel free to grab a poster and go about what you were planning to do this evening before I interrupted. I will let you know what comes of the emails, as well as contact any of you who may have a werewolf that would be good at tracking, or. Or if you'd like to stay after and volunteer someone, that works, too. The goal is to have people tracking them within the next day or two; that way, hopefully, everything will fall into place at once."

Jack snatched up one of the posters before bee lining out of the office. As much as he wanted to stay after and hear more about who exactly would be going to spy on the lab assistants and Dr. Paul, he needed to see Lyra more. He needed to be with his pack. Once he got out of the pack office buildings, he broke speed limits all the way to Justin's house.

His frustration was increased when he arrived and found he had to park a block down the street. He made quick work of walking there, but he was still a little annoyed. When he opened the door he wasn't entirely surprised to see the front living room half full with people. On the side of the room closest to the back of the house were Seth and Justin. Front and center was Graham, having a screaming match with the Scotsman. Behind the Scotsman was Luna, frowning. Standing a little out of the way, but between the two of them, were Dylan and Taylor. The first person to notice that he'd come into the room seemed to be Taylor.

The other man's eyes widened and he exhaled before hollering over both the Scotsman and Graham. "Both of you, shut up! Jack is here. And he can confirm what Luna plans to do."

All eyes in the room turned to Jack. He wasn't too thrilled about it, but he didn't show it. Making his face stoic, he folded his arms over his chest. "What's the problem? Why is no one upstairs with Lyra?"

Graham turned and focused his anger on Jack. "Luna says she is on your orders." The last word was dripping with disdain. "To lower Lyra's dosage of painkilling meds."

Jack glanced at the Scotsman; the other man rolled his eyes before turning to Jack. "I've tried to tell him several times why; all the young buck seems to want to do is interrupt me. Would you be so kind as to tell him why we are lowering her dosage? He doesn't seem to want to listen to anyone else."

Jack let the disgust show on his face as he turned back to Graham. "She spoke to me this morning. She asked for the meds to be lowered. She claims it is the only thing keeping her asleep. That she is most awake before Luna comes for the injection. That's why she's lowering the injection, Graham. I'm sure somebody mentioned that to you before now."

The other man growled, "I don't believe you." He was clearly seething and irrational.

Jack had enough. They had enough problems without infighting as well. "Get out." He lifted one of his arms and pointed to the front door. "I have had enough of this. You've officially made yourself a nuisance. You are now causing problems and are counterproductive to Lyra's care. Get out. I do not want to see you in this house again. Have I made myself clear?" Jack folded his arms again.

Graham's growling grew louder a split second before he lunged at Jack. Before Jack could get into a fighting stance, the Scotsman grabbed the younger man by the collar of his shirt. Jack wasn't sure how he did it, but he was able to hold Graham and all his werewolf strength at that. The older man shook Graham until he stopped growling.

"You'll be doing what Jack tells you. Or I'll inform your father how you are hindering your cousin's care and how you've challenged Luna's authority. You and I both know how he'll take that."

Jack wasn't entirely sure how it worked, but Graham went limp with his feet an inch off the ground. The Scotsman let him down and Jack moved out of the way as Graham left the house, slamming the door hard enough on his way out that the wall around it rattled a little. The entire room seemed to breathe a little deeper with Graham not there.

Jack looked from his littermates to Taylor and Dylan. "Off the deep end?"

There was silence for a couple minutes as glances were exchanged. Luna smiled at Jack before taking her bag and heading upstairs.

Dylan cleared his throat. "Honestly, we're not entirely sure. Once he has an idea he won't sway from it. I think he's afraid to hope that his cousin will come back to us. But I don't know for sure. He has never exactly been the most rational of people. Especially where his family is concerned." The younger man shrugged.

Jack believed Dylan thought what he was saying was correct, but Jack didn't buy that as the whole summary of the problem. He left it alone because Graham wasn't really there or of the mindset to explain himself.

Sighing, Jack sat down on one of the two navy blue couches in Justin's living room. He was simply going to wait until Luna came back, then ask her about the progress her people had been making on the antidote. As well as the new level of sedatives she would be using now that Lyra had requested less. He didn't really feel like engaging in further conversation about Graham; he really didn't feel like talking about much of anything at the moment. When the others in the room seemed to be watching him, Jack leaned back on the couch and closed his eyes, effectively cutting off any conversation that might have ensued, making it clear he didn't want to speak to any of them. He knew that was rude, but he couldn't help it. The last couple weeks had been trying and Jack just didn't have it in him to placate anyone.

Jack had no idea how much time had passed when Luna and the Scotsman came back downstairs. When he heard them coming, he opened his eyes to watch them. The Scotsman looked sad and Luna had tears in her eyes. Jack finally stood as they came to stand in front of his couch.

"I gave her less. I only used about seventy-five percent of the usual dose. I'm doing this on your word, Jack. I'm really hoping this works. I would give almost anything to have my niece wake up." The older woman continued to look at Jack for a moment, glassy-eyed, before turning and leaving the house. The Scotsman was not far behind her.

Taylor turned to Justin. "With all due respect, man, I think it would be a good idea if you or I slept in the same room as Lyra tonight. Or at least took turns watching her. Just in case something happens or in case she wakes up. How would you like to handle this?" Taylor's tone was flat, but there was a hint of hopefulness to it.

There was some shuffling and Jack's attention was drawn to Seth. "I think the best plan of action would be if the three of us split six-hour shifts. That way we are with her through the night and one of us is watching her after the second smaller dose is administered."

Just as Jack opened his mouth, Dylan beat him to it, "Please let me help. I need to feel I'm doing something." His eyes were on Jack when he said it.

Part of Jack's chest hurt watching the pain in the younger man's eyes. He felt a part of him give a little. "Fine. But I want at least one person from Pack F here in any given time. If her status changes at all, I better be getting a phone call or I am ripping all of you a new one."

He was rewarded with Dylan's beaming face. "Thank you, Jack." There was so much sincerity that Jack had to look away.

When he turned back, Dylan's face was solemn. "I texted the other alphas today, updating all of them on Lyra's condition. Odds are they are going to want to have a multipack meeting to see if there's anything that can be done here. Frankly, I don't see what could possibly happen, but any help we can get right now would be good. Any ideas right now would be welcome." Jack ran his hand through his hair. He didn't want to leave yet. He wanted to sit with Lyra awhile, just in case by some miracle she woke up. "I'm going to sit with Lyra. You can figure out your own schedule and whoever's going to relieve me can come and do it at eleven."

He didn't give anyone a chance to start a discussion. Instead, he maneuvered himself around all the furniture and headed up to the room Lyra was in. Even if it meant her not waking up, Jack thought maybe the silence and not having to deal with people would help him think. Help him think back the anger, the fear, and the frustration and find a plan.

Chapter 2

Lyra was foggy; the fog was so thick she couldn't see through it. It'd been a long time since she'd seen a memory at all. But she had had a new experience. She was almost positive she had a conversation with Jack. She didn't know how long ago it was, but she held on to the hope that it really happened. Because if it hadn't, then it would mean she was trapped here in her head, slowly dimming. If she'd spoken to Jack then maybe, just maybe, things would be okay.

All she kept thinking about was if he would go talk to her aunt. If he would tell Luna to lower the dosage. Or if he would think she was delusional and not have it done. She had no way of knowing until whenever the next dawn was. If she was less groggy, more in control of her own body, that would mean he'd listened to her. Otherwise, it would be the same trapped feeling she had every morning. She needed to take the opportunity to think. She had to find a way out of this for everyone. She knew the best thing to do would be to speak to her uncle. To ask for asylum for all of Berman's wolves. But she was unsure whether he would grant it. It would take some heavy maneuvering on her part. She couldn't do that from inside her own head. Lyra had to concentrate on waking up. Then she had to convince Jack to let her go back to the family estate. She knew the first would be much easier than the second.

Then she heard it. The shuffling. She had heard that same shuffling right before her conversation with Jack. She concentrated on trying to move her consciousness towards it. Had she been awake she would have broken into a sweat. Then she strained to listen.

"Lyra? Can you hear me? If you can hear me, now would be a good time to wake up." It was Taylor.

Part of her was a little disappointed that it wasn't Jack since she had to talk to him. But a larger part of her was relieved because she could talk to Taylor without having to hide anything.

She focused everything on getting her mouth to move. "I… need… to ask uncle… for asylum." She swore her mouth had moved and her voice came out, but there was silence; she started to become frustrated. If she couldn't make her body move, how was she supposed to wake up? As her frustration began to build, she was finally rewarded with a response.

"I see, even in unconsciousness, you and Graham have ended up at the same conclusion. He has been working on his father for over a week. He's almost convinced him to have a meeting. If we could get you up and moving to see him, it would swing the idea over the fence. How are things going in there? Honestly, is that even a possibility right now?" he asked, his voice full of concern.

Inwardly she smiled at his concern but she knew outwardly her face stayed blank. "I have to. No other way. Tell him… telephone call. I want to meet with him two evenings from tonight."

Even slipping in and out of consciousness as she was, she could hear the hesitation of them asking for asylum. And he certainly didn't like the idea of Lyra going back to the family compound so soon, but Taylor was smart. He would know it was in everybody's best interest. She waited for what seemed like hours for him to give some type of response.

When he didn't, she pressed on. "Tell Luna… half dose. Then half dose again."

"Lyra, is that a good idea?"

Lyra felt sleep dragging her back and her body was growing more lethargic. Talking was hard.

She didn't wait to see if he had anything else to say; instead she let the darkness take her again. It didn't bother her this time because she knew if she could just get her ducks in a row everything would be fine. She was positive between them, she and Graham could convince her uncle to give the wolves asylum. He had to. There was no other way out of this with everybody, even most of everybody, alive. Without waiting for him to respond, Lyra let unconsciousness take her. This time when she went into the black she wasn't at all concerned. She knew she was coming back. She knew if she worked hard enough, everything would be okay. Or as okay as things could get being a werewolf.

Chapter 3

Taylor didn't like what he was about to do. When he heard Luna walking down the hall towards him, he steeled himself for it. He thought Lyra getting a smaller dose of the sedative was a bad idea. She needed to rest. She needed to recuperate. But he understood that she felt responsible for her pack. To an extent he felt the same. Hell, he'd even told Bishop the truth weeks ago. The other man had handled it better than Taylor would've expected.

As the woman opened the door she looked at him with surprise. There was a moment that she studied his face. Then her eyes narrowed as she placed her bag at the foot of the bed. "Why do you think I'm not going to ask about whatever has that expression on your face, Taylor? You are not that good at clearing your expression yet."

Sighing heavily, Taylor rubbed his face. "Because I don't like the idea. But I'm concerned that it might be the best option available to us." He took a deep breath before pushing on. "Lyra wants you to give her a half dose of the sedative. And then tomorrow another half dose. Don't get me wrong, she means half of the half tomorrow. And she doesn't want you to stop lowering it until she's awake. She has this idea in her mind that she's going to go to her uncle and ask for asylum for all of Berman's wolves."

As he watched, Luna stepped back, almost stumbled, into the other chair. Her eyes and mouth rounded in surprise. "Does she really think that's a good idea? I can't imagine the counsel would respond well. I mean, I see the merit, but it opens a whole can of worms. Not to mention the repercussions for lowering her sedative. I have no way of gauging how much pain she's in. Or what that drug is doing to her. Having her sedated… It doesn't matter." She stared off past Taylor's shoulder, clearly in her own thoughts

He could almost see the battle within her as she tried to decide whether to do the requested or to keep her sedated. A minute went by, maybe even two, before she looked at Taylor again. "I'm no closer to finding an antidote. That's not entirely true. I'm closer than we were a week or two ago. But it's going to take a good month or two before we even have a viable option." She frowned.

Sighing deeply, Luna stood up once again and then dug through her bag. As Taylor watched, she prepared the sedative. It wasn't quite half a dose. If he had to guess, Taylor would say it was sixty percent of one. As if Luna didn't have it in her to quite lower it that much. Not that he could blame her. No healer would want to put their patient in pain.

Once she finished and began checking Lyra's vitals, Luna looked up at him. "This would be so much easier if it was done in the old days. All this new tech and science is making my job so much harder. There's so much I don't know. That's never been the case before. Lyra is going to have an even harder time when she takes over for me. I worry about this new world order we are in, Taylor."

The rest of her visit was done in silence. Both of them were thinking about her words. Taylor agreed with her. They had a rocky road ahead of them. There was no smooth end in sight. They were no longer safe. Or as safe as they could ever be. Warring families never made their lives exactly safe, but at least they knew what to expect. Between Pack L and their cohorts, the rogue scientists, and this new drug, there was just so much after them. Odds were against them.

Taylor made sure to smile and inclined his head to Luna and she laughed. Once she was gone his mind drifted again. He knew as soon as the lighter dose of sedatives kicked in and Lyra was able to be conscious, he would be wrangling Graham and Dylan in to talk about a strategy of approaching Graham's father. It was not an idea he was looking forward to.

"Stop it. Just grab Graham and get over here," Taylor growled.

He felt Dylan stiffen over the phone. "Is everything all right?"

Taylor couldn't help but snort. "Is anything ever all right? Everything is as fine it's going to get. Since Luna's visit this morning, Lyra is more awake. You can tell she's in pain, but she's insisting on getting stuff done. So if the two of you could get over here quickly then she can rest and we can get this whole thing over with."

There was silence for a moment. "Why do I get the feeling I'm not going to like this?"

The laugh bubbled up in Taylor's throat before he could stop it. "Funny, that's exactly what Luna said to me this morning."

"That doesn't help me any. In fact, that makes me worry more. We'll be there in about a half hour." Dylan hung up.

It was only four in the afternoon. Taylor was the only one at the house. While this went against Jack's express orders, there was simply no one else who could be there that time of day. Everyone was working. It gave him the opportunity to get Graham and Dylan to come by so they could hear Lyra's plan. Both Cole and Ryan had spent a good chunk of their days at Justin's house this week. But both of them coached football for rival high schools. This week marked the first day of tryouts; therefore. Therefore, neither of them could afford to be there.

Taylor shook his head and slid his phone back into his pocket before smiling down reassuringly at a very exhausted Lyra. She didn't look good. There were bags under her eyes and she was thinner than he had ever seen her. He was pretty sure she was in pain from the tightness around her eyes. But he knew she wouldn't say anything. Not only were they raised to not complain about pain, but he knew Lyra wouldn't mention it for fear Luna would come back and sedate her more.

"Frowning that hard is not going to help us any. It's also not going to give you the answers to the universe. If you really feel that you need to scowl at something, stop looking at me," Lyra said.

The ghost of a smile slipped onto his face. It was good to have her back. When she had died it was as if the world stood still. He couldn't believe it was actually happening.

"Graham and Dylan will be here in about a half an hour. Be honest with me. Are you even up for this? Can you physically even hold yourself up?"

Infuriatingly, Lyra just shrugged. "I won't know until I try. I don't think I have the energy to do it today. Maybe tomorrow. But we can't meet with Graham's dad any later than next week. You and I both know that if we don't get in by then for an audience, we would have to wait another three weeks. He would be too tied up in family business to deal with anything else."

Taylor nodded. There was a family meeting that went on every month. They had to get on the docket, so to speak, before that meeting. If they were on the docket afterwards they'd be less likely to get anything done, because family issues would take precedent. The last thing they needed right now, with all the people after them, was to be set aside by the family who just might have the resources, connections, and know-how to protect the werewolves.

"How are things with the family right now? I can't imagine they're very happy about me staying here," Lyra asked.

Taylor scoffed before he could stop himself. "It's about what you'd expect it to be. They are unhappy that you are not under their care. But that is the agreement they made. Luna can take care of you so you're getting almost the same care you would if you were home. But someone somewhere has forbidden anybody in the family from coming to visit you. I am not entirely sure why, I just know that's the case. Which seems insane to me, but there you go."

Lyra frowned. "This is getting ridiculous. We really need to talk with Uncle."

Sighing, Taylor leaned back in his chair. He agreed to an extent, but he also knew the danger that could come from the two groups mingling. He would, however, go with whatever Lyra and Graham decided. That was his place in their little chosen family; he was a peacemaker and a good soldier when needed. Taylor just hoped they were not walking everyone toward mutual destruction.

It took Graham and Dylan almost an hour to get there, thanks to rush hour traffic, which made Dylan nervous because it meant they would only have a half hour to discuss the problem at hand before Seth would be there. The other man came straight from his work and would not leave until Justin or Jack was there. Plus Graham had gotten himself kicked out, so they wanted to clear him out before anyone knew he had been there.

Taylor was pretty sure Seth didn't trust him. If the tables were turned, Taylor was pretty sure he would not have trusted any of them from Lyra's childhood either. They kept so many secrets and shared none, just like they were raised to do. In doing so they were partially endangering all of the other packs. Ultimately though, that was what Lyra wanted to talk to the others about. She wanted to break their silence. She wanted to tell the truth— most of it, anyway—to their little corner of the world. They would face major opposition, seeing as no one had done such a thing in recent history. But that was why Lyra wanted to meet with Graham, Dylan, and Taylor; if they really wanted to move forward with this, they would need a united front to show Graham's father and his counsel. The thought of the consequences for what they were about to attempt terrified Taylor; if this went the wrong way, or the wrong people disagreed with them, they could find themselves in a very bad way. He knew the way Lyra and Graham saw it. They didn't have a choice if they wanted to save the lives of the people they had grown so close to. If Pack L and these other scientists continued to come for them, eventually they would win without the family's help; there was no use pretending otherwise.

Shaking his head to clear his thoughts and concentrate on the present, Taylor sat in one of the two cream-colored chairs that matched the couch Graham and Lyra were sitting on. Dylan sat across from him in the chair closest to Lyra. Though they were all happy to see Lyra up and around and coherent, all of their expressions wore the same grim mask. They all sat in silence for several minutes before Lyra finally spoke.

"I would like to ask how the family's doing. I want to know why I haven't heard any of their voices as I have yours and the pack's, Where the order not to visit came from, but I know we don't have time for that. Seth will be here soon and we need to have this decided before he gets here. I have a sort of sinking feeling that we might not all agree on this. Graham, Taylor tells me you've already spoken to your father about this? What was his reaction when you broached him about the packs going to the family council meeting?" Lyra had leaned forward on the couch as she asked her question. Taylor was pretty sure she didn't even register that she was doing it.

Attention turned to Graham; the other man leaned back on the couch, resting his head along the top, and closed his eyes. "When I finally told him what had been happening over the last month he was very amenable to bringing them in. .Only he did say, however, that he thought it would be best to only bring in the seven packs that this problem involved. Father wasn't entirely sure he could convince the council to do more than that. Hell, he wasn't entirely sure he could do that. To be completely honest, I don't think he would've agreed to help us if Lyra hadn't been attacked. He has always had a soft spot for you." As he said the last part, he turned his head and opened his eyes so he was looking at Lyra sitting next to him.

When Dylan cleared his throat, he wasn't looking at the group at large but instead seemed to be picking at some invisible thing on the arm of the chair. "How exactly does he want to do it? I mean, I assume there would have to be some big family meeting for something like that. Not just us roping in however many people and corralling them in the council's chambers."

Graham frowned as he turned his attention to the other man.

"He didn't seem entirely sure. He was worried about having an all-family meeting, though he seemed to be leaning towards that. I think an all-family meeting would work in our favor because there would be more people cheering for us, so to speak. Honestly, what I think we should do is when Dylan and I get home tonight, I will corner my father and maybe one or two of the council members, then get you two on the phone so the four of us can try and talk them into officially moving on the idea. I really think it is in our best interest to move quickly here. We have no idea what their next move is going to be and I can't honestly believe that we set them back by blowing up those warehouses."

Lyra turned on her side of the couch so her back was against the corner, giving her a better view of Graham. "So what I'm hearing is that your dad likes the idea and the council doesn't. But he thinks he can at least swing getting all of us there so that we can win the popular vote, making it hard for the council to say no. Am I right?"

Graham simply nodded in response.

Lyra gave a heavy sigh. "Okay then, set it up. We'll do whatever your father thinks is necessary to get this done. Here I thought I would have to go see him in person; I would be lying if I said I was not relieved that we can do all of this over the phone. I think it's important we show a united front, which means I need two or three days before I'll be okay to go and show a strong front to the family."

"That's fine," Graham answered as he stood rather swiftly. "I'll need that much time to contact the other three weres and let them know what's happening. I'll call Taylor's phone when I have my father alone. That might be less conspicuous than calling him into the room. We'll talk to you guys later." Then he hesitated before turning to the other side of the couch and bending down to hug Lyra from where he stood in front of her. If they had been normal humans, Taylor would not have heard what he whispered in her ear. "I can't tell you how good it is to see you alive and awake. This whole thing has been killing me."

Taylor hadn't said anything about Graham's blowup with Jack. He hadn't felt that Lyra had recuperated enough to be hearing all that happened when she was asleep. He knew at this point her anger and frustration might be counterproductive anyway because you never knew with Lyra whether she would be able to ignore it and wait until everything was done or if she would blow up and sabotage this tentative peace they were trying to build. No, he had told himself he would leave it to one of her littermates to explain to her. He watched Graham give Lyra one more tight squeeze before standing back up in front of her and turning his head to Dylan.

"Let's get out of here before someone realizes we were here in the first place." With that he turned and headed to the door.

Dylan leaped up, giving Lyra his own quick squeeze before heading out behind Graham.

When both men were gone, Lyra returned her attention to Taylor. "Well, that was better news than I thought. It's good to know that Graham has been working on his father this whole time I've been out and that we agree on this thing. I can't imagine how much damage there would be if we were on opposite sides. That being said, I don't know why they came all the way out here just to tell us that. I think a phone call would've been completely sufficient and would've used less time."

Taylor laughed, although it was more of a scoff than a laugh; he couldn't help it. He shook his head at his longtime friend. "I know it seems strange to you, but they wanted to see you in person to sort of know that you were alive. Seeing is believing, you know."

Lyra frowned and watched him for a few seconds, as if she was trying to contemplate what he said. He watched as her mind chose to change the subject instead. "At first, after Luna gave me whatever it was she gave me—not the suppressant, but before that—I relived memories. There was no true rhyme or reason to them, but they were backwards chronologically and I couldn't help but think of it as a warning that things were going to end. It was frightening and comforting at the same time. Getting to see those I care about as the last things I see on Earth somehow made it okay. But then something happened and I was jolted back, but I knew I'd been gone. Did I die?" When she finally got around to asking that last question she tilted her head up and her sad, inquisitive eyes looked right at him.

It felt as if she'd punched him in the stomach. He had been with her almost the entire time since she'd been awake, afraid something would happen should he leave her side again. Part of him was surprised no one had mentioned it, though he would've known if somebody had. The other part of him was horrified that she had been aware of being gone.

She swung her legs up so that she could put her knees to her chest. "I see. I can tell by your face that the answer is yes. How long was it? I mean, I know it couldn't have been too long because…" She trailed off as if she wasn't sure she wanted to finish that idea.

"I think it was about ninety seconds."

She looked at him a moment before nodding but didn't say anything else. The two of them sat in a contemplative silence. For how long, Taylor didn't know. He could tell from her face she had questions she wanted to ask but wasn't sure if she wanted to know enough to actually state them out loud. He watched as she set it aside when they heard Seth walking up the porch to the front door. He watched her body language change: she untucked her legs, put her hands in her lap and turned so she could face the front door as her littermate barged through it, slamming it behind him.

Seth dropped the backpack he had been holding and dove on the couch so fast that Taylor would not have seen it if he had not been used to watching movement at werewolf speeds. In what seemed like little more than the blink of an eye, Seth had Lyra in his arms in what appeared to be a bear hug just tight enough that it was probably a little uncomfortable.

"Lyra, I have never been so happy in my life to see your snarky butt. I'd say you gave us quite a scare but I think that that's an understatement. How are you feeling? There was some discussion over whether they should be giving you heavier drugs. How much pain are you in?" He pulled her away so he could look directly into her eyes as he spoke. His eyes were narrowed as if he was trying to search her face for the answer to his questions.

Lyra smiled gently and patted Seth's arm. "How about you put me back on the couch, then we can hold a conversation as if we were normal people."

Seth did the opposite: he pulled her in tight again, holding her for several beats. Taylor could see the relief on the other man's face and was sure his expression had mirrored it earlier in the day. Then, almost reluctantly, Seth put her gently back on the couch before sitting in the seat Graham had vacated.

Taylor wasn't at all surprised that when Lyra spoke, she stepped right over her littermate's questions. "How is everybody holding up?"

Seth frowned. "About as poorly as you would expect. Actually, I take that back. For whatever reason Justin was convinced that you would come back to us. He seemed to never think you were going to die. That is until..." It was as if the other man couldn't bring himself to finish the sentence.

Her eyes softened as she looked at her littermate. "I know, Taylor just told me and to be honest, it hasn't quite sunk in, but I can't imagine how hard that was for you guys to watch." She reached out and laid her hand on her littermate's thigh.

The caring and love Lyra had in her eyes as she looked at her littermate made Taylor's chest hurt. He cared for his pack. Bishop was a good and honest leader, which was why he had told Bishop the truth about the family secrets. He felt dishonest keeping something that important from a man who was simply trying to do the best by his pack. Bishop had been sworn to secrecy and he had not even told Victor the truth about the family. Taylor couldn't imagine the toll it was taking on Lyra to keep these secrets from people she cared so deeply for. He might be upset if something were to happen to Bishop, but it would break something in Lyra to watch something happen to her littermates. Watching the exchange only solidified Taylor's belief that the family needed to grant the packs its protection.

Seth gave his littermate a small, sad, almost defeated smile before placing his hand on top of hers. "Yes, it certainly has not been easy. I think the argument—well, that's an understatement—the fight between Graham and Jack made matters worse from the get-go."

Taylor winced as he watched Lyra's eyes widen and she drew back her hand. "What do you mean Jack's fight with Graham?"

Her words slithered to Taylor's ears like a venomous snake; nothing. Nothing good was about to come from Seth's next few words. He watched her eyes break from Seth's for a split-second to look at him; she gauged his reaction and looked back at Seth.

The other man straightened slightly before cursing. "Lyra, I thought someone had already told you. But of course they wouldn't have, you just woke up. Long story short, they got into quite the raging fistfight about what to do with the information they found on the suppressant in the warehouses. Graham has basically gotten himself on everybody's list, so to speak, because of it. Taylor here was almost the only thing that stood between an all-out brawl."

Lyra's eyes narrowed, her lips thinned, and she crossed her arms over her chest. She looked from one of them to the other before speaking.

"One and/or both of you are going to tell me right now what exactly happened while I was out."

Taylor exchanged glances with Seth; he was pretty sure the expression he saw on his face was exactly what was on his own. Neither of them wanted to be the one to update Lyra on what had happened since she had been kidnapped after her plan went south. But Taylor knew that if they didn't tell her now and she found out about it later, she would be pissed and she would probably, counterproductively, take it out on one of them. He took the opportunity for what it was and started by expressing his anger at finding out that she had been kidnapped. He knew out of the two of them he was most likely the best to explain the situation to her, as he not only had a better grasp than Seth probably did, but he knew his and Lyra's friendship would survive it should she get upset. He had no idea about her and her littermate.

It took much less time to explain the whole situation to Lyra than Taylor thought it would. He watched her expression carefully as he spoke; every once in a while Seth would interject something that must've happened when Taylor wasn't there. Lyra was trying to keep her face blank as much as possible throughout the story, but there were moments where she failed. Her concern for what happened at the warehouses seeped. She clearly disapproved of the plan, but she didn't say anything. She frowned further when Taylor informed her of what he had been told about the family not being able to visit her. The look on her face as he finished was a concerned frown. She wasn't trying to hide that expression; she clearly wanted them to know what she was thinking.

"I don't like any of it. For the moment, I'm just going to ignore the fact that Graham basically assaulted Jack and that Jack was being a little sluggish about the whole thing and also the fact that everyone endangered themselves by going into these unknown warehouses totally unarmed and unprepared. That was just stupid."

She opened her mouth to continue to speak but was interrupted by Seth.

"Don't even start, Lyra. You are not as naïve as all that. You know very well we went in there looking to help you. There would be no other reason for all of us to endanger ourselves like that. We wanted to protect you, to help you find some sort of cure. And yes, not all of us really thought that we would be able to find a cure for you, but something did come of it. Don't try and convince any of us that it was a bad idea, because it wasn't; it got us you and ultimately that's all anyone's going to care about." Seth sat there staring at his littermate for several moments.

It was as if she wanted to argue with him but knew better. Taylor was genuinely surprised when

Lyra did not even attempt to argue. It was so in her nature to be contrary that it hadn't even occurred to him that she might not fight with her littermate. He just stared at her, watching as she processed what Seth told her. He didn't know whether his old friend was thinking about arguing or if she simply didn't have a response; whatever the case, it was longer than he thought it would be before she spoke.

"No, you're right." She honestly sounded defeated. Perhaps defeated was too strong a word. She sounded and looked resigned. The expression almost aged her. There was a moment on her face when every secret and every lie and every struggle they had been through was etched on her face. Their little Luna was more careworn than they had imagined. In that moment Taylor simply wanted to wrap his arms around her in a hug to let her know that even though times were horrible, at least she didn't have to go through it alone. That was just it, though. To Lyra it would feel as if she was doing it alone. She would feel as if she had to protect everyone, even those that didn't quite need her to do any kind of protecting. That was just who she was. Then the expression was gone from her face and a blank, almost bored expression took its place. "Is Jack coming by tonight? I need to have a talk with him."

Seth and Taylor exchanged glances. Jack was indeed going to show up and there was nothing they could do to stop it, but it was as if both of them had the same thought at the same time. Perhaps it wouldn't be in anyone's best interest if Lyra knew that ahead time. It was almost nonsensical to think, but Taylor couldn't help it and he knew Seth was thinking the same thing. Taylor closed his eyes before turning back to Lyra.

"Yes, Jack will be here tonight, but I don't think he'll get here until seven-thirty or eight o'clock due to a filming schedule, I think he said."

Lyra nodded and looked somewhat relieved. "Good. That'll give me time to take Graham's phone call and get everything squared away before talking to them."

"You telling me you're going to get Graham's side of the story before you get Jack's?" Seth sounded irritated and as if he was holding back just a little bit of disgust.

Taylor knew better though. He knew the phone call Lyra was talking about was with her uncle. Lyra was letting him know that depending on how the conversation with her uncle went, she would be breaking the news to Jack about the family. Jack was not going to take it well. Taylor didn't know Jack well but that much he knew. Tonight was going to be a very long night. Knowing that, Taylor heaved himself off the cushion he sat on and turned to Seth. "I'm getting the distinct impression that this will be a long night. I'm gonna go grab coffee from Bigfoot Java for the lady and myself. Would you like me to pick you up anything?"

Seth curled his lips slightly before he spoke.

"No, thank you, I don't really take any kind of overdone coffee. If I want it I'll just make it in Justin's machine later tonight, then I'll have a whole pot."

Taylor nodded even though he didn't quite understand Seth's disgust. But he wasn't in the mood to get any more information so instead he turned to Lyra. "The usual?"

Lyra smiled, though it didn't quite reach her eyes. "Please."

Taylor didn't bother to say anything else; he simply headed out the door to his car.

Chapter 4

Lyra's heart was roaring in her ears she was so nervous. Though she knew that she had every right to be nervous when she saw Graham's face pop up on her phone in an incoming call, she couldn't justify just how shallow and quick her breathing became. She smiled as she sat and flashed Seth her phone so that he could see that she was about to take an incoming call from her cousin. He frowned at her but didn't stop her from wandering back upstairs to the guest bedroom.

Once she had dashed up the stairs, she hit the screen to answer the call. "Hold on a sec while I make sure I'm as private as I can get," she whispered into the phone before bee lining to the extra bedroom and then locking the door behind her. She then sat on the bed, near the very top, so that she was as far from the door as she could get. Her hearing was good enough that she would've heard if somebody walked up to the other side of the door, which meant that she would be as secluded and private as she could get. While Seth's hearing was good, it wasn't as good as Ryan's, so for the time being she could at least keep this phone conversation between herself and her cousin.

She took a deep breath. "Okay, give it to me straight—what's happening?"

There was a masculine chuckle on the other side of the phone; it was not her cousin. "It is quite the relief to hear your voice. I have to admit the put-out inflection that comes with your words is quite amusing, Niece."

Lyra's heart had begun to slow a little bit, but hearing her uncle's words made it rev back up again. Either her uncle had taken the phone or she was on speaker. And with the language he was using, and by using her title and not her name, she knew there were other people in the room that she couldn't speak frankly in front of. This was not good news. She took a beat to calm herself as much as possible before responding; it would not do to embarrass herself further in front of whoever else might be in the room.

"My apologies, dear Uncle, I did not know I would have the pleasure of speaking with you this evening. I am most grateful that you would take time out of your busy schedule to speak with me." It was as diplomatic as she could manage on such short notice. She only hoped it was enough to appease whoever happened to be in the background. Because even if she wasn't on speakerphone, odds were someone in the room could hear the conversation.

"My little Luna, in case you hadn't already caught on, you are on speakerphone. In the room with me is your cousin, obviously, as well as your father, your youngest uncle, and head council member, Richards."

There it was. There was the other shoe. Knowing the situation should've calmed Lyra's nerves, but instead it kept her adrenaline pumping and her heart racing a mile a minute. The family was run on a council that was by no means Democratic. You worked your way onto the council, whether by schmoozing and making friends or intimidation and fights. Her understanding of

Richards was that he'd made his place based on the latter. If that wasn't bad enough, he was on loan from another family as a show of support. So he had not even earned his way onto her family's council, but instead earned his way onto the Ruiz family council out of California. He was on loan to them for six months, just as their councilman Conrad was loaned to the Ruiz family. It was a sign of respect and peace to loan out your people to other families and while Lyra was happy and proud that her family was on decent terms with several other local families, now was not the time to have one in the room. It was a well-known fact that the council members from other families reported back to their main family as a sort of understood spy. Lyra had no idea what Richards had done to get himself in that room.

Thinking as fast as she could, Lyra switched gears; perhaps there was another angle she could go at this with. "Greetings, Council Member Richards, I am so sorry to have interrupted whatever business you had with the members of my family. It was simply that upon Graham's arrival back at the compound, I wished to speak to my relatives, as I have not been well enough to see or hear them in quite a while. I did miss them, but I certainly do not want to interrupt your business and will instruct my cousin to take me to my brothers and my mother while you wrap up whatever issue may be occurring. He can come back and I can speak to my father and uncles when you are finished. Again, I am so sorry to have infringed upon your time." She was sweating. She could feel the slight dampness on her forehead and on her upper lip. She was silently praying that her cousin had not burst into the room and divulged their plan. The last thing she wanted was for the other families to think hers weak because they would be bringing in extra people who had no knowledge of the way the family worked. Especially considering they had not even been approved yet.

The soft, lightly accented voice that came over the phone told her it was not one of her relations that responded. "Little Luna, your and your cousin's excitement is more than understandable. I must admit I was a little alarmed when Graham burst in here and handed the phone to your uncle. At first I thought something dire had taken place but I am glad to see, well to hear, that you seem well. While I myself do not know the joys of having a large extended family, I feel for you and will take my leave now and will simply take up this appointment with your uncles and father later this evening. Again, little Luna, it is wonderful to hear your voice; I'm sure it will go a long way to soothe your family a bit."

Before she responded, there was some shuffling so Lyra kept her mouth shut; she did not know what room they were in and that would make a large difference in who could hear her if she spoke. There was some shuffling and mumbling on the other side of the phone. After a minute or two, she heard her uncle's voice, though it sounded as if he was moving while he spoke.

"Son, you are lucky that your cousin is better on her feet than you are. You are not too big for me to give you a beating. Honestly, barging in here like that, we could've been in here with anyone." The exacerbated tone made Lyra feel relieved she wasn't the one on the receiving end. There was a heavy sigh as she heard a door open and shut. Presumably they were headed to a more secluded location.

"Lyra, honey, how are you? All politics aside, your mother and I have been worried sick about you. And while I understand the politics, it has been killing us and your brothers that we could not come see you. That must change soon. You and I both know your mother will not settle down until she can see you and hold you in her arms. We will never be able to convince her that you are even remotely safe until then. At this point I feel the same way."

Lyra felt her eyes begin to sting as she heard her father's voice. It was a sheer force of will to stop herself from crying. In the stress of all that was going on, being able to curl into the arms of her parents and to feel safe again seemed the perfect fantasy. But she knew it would be a lie. Her parents' arms couldn't keep her safe from what was coming and it was that thought that kept her from crying. Crying would get her nowhere; it would not save anyone and that was, after all, what she was trying to do.

"It's really nice to hear your voice, Dad. You don't even know how nice. But I can't come home yet, not until this whole mess is over. I know Jack won't let me stay there until he's convinced it's safe, which probably won't be the most sellable of ideas at the moment. And we all know that until we're out in the open about the family, humoring Jack and the other packs is the best way to stop them from stumbling onto our secrets."

There was a long pause this time. Just as Lyra was beginning to think they had been disconnected, Graham's father's voice came over the phone. "Ah, and that brings us to the purpose of this call. I'm going to go out on a limb here and assume that you feel the same as Graham does. That we should bring several of these packs of yours into the fold where the family can help protect them."

Even though it wasn't technically a question, Lyra felt as if she should answer anyway. "Yes, sir."

"It just so happens your uncle and father and I agree with your assessment. While I do believe it will take some convincing on the part of the council, as most of them do not have skin in the game, I do believe our best bet is to hold a family meeting. If we can get the popular vote and the family behind us, the council will feel forced into going the way we wish them to. I truly believe that is the only way we have even a remote chance of making this work. How soon do you think you will be well enough to attend a family meeting? I do believe we will need all seven of you here to really swing this and we all know you are the most persuasive out of everyone."

Lyra didn't even have to hesitate. "Two days. I really think that's what it will take to get me in enough shape to be able to stand there and take a beating, verbally that is, from a family meeting."

There was something in the quiet that came over the phone that told Lyra they were probably exchanging glances to decide whether to call her a liar or argue that she needed more time, but she was ready to argue for those two days; they needed to get this done as soon as possible.

"Fair enough; two days from today we will be holding a family meeting on the compound. All those who can be in attendance are required. Graham, you are in charge of contacting the rest of your cohorts and making sure they can make it. And tell them to bring the rest of their packs with them; it will be a tight squeeze with all of us in the meeting chamber, but I truly feel it is necessary to put as many faces to this problem as possible. We will see you in two days, Niece. Recover swiftly." That was all the goodbye she got as she heard the line go dead.

Not that she had expected more or any kind of sentiment. Her uncle was a pragmatist in that he understood when there was a problem, it took precedent. It was what made him a good family leader and she scolded the part of her that was a little sad at the lack of handholding. Shaking her head, she let her phone slide onto the bed, shutting her eyes and taking a deep breath as she leaned back against the wall. She just needed to breathe. She just needed a moment to herself to calm down her heart and her breathing. She needed a moment of calm silence, where she didn't have to think about the problem at hand or the problems that would be happening soon. She just needed a moment to sit in silence before all hell would break loose. At least she had two days to prepare for part of it. If only she had two days to prepare for the bombshell she was about to drop on Jack.

Jack would forgive her for keeping secrets, but he certainly would not be forgiving her anytime soon. This was going to cause a rift, one they really didn't need right now, but there was no way around it. So she would spend the next hour or two worrying and stressing over it until Jack finally got there.

Jack didn't arrive at Justin's house until just after eight, but it seemed three times as long to Lyra. When he finally arrived she was almost relieved. Relieved that this nonsense would finally be coming to a close, that she'd be one step closer to getting this over with. It didn't help matters any that he looked so relieved and happy to see her awake. As soon as he walked in the door, he set his backpack down and came and hugged her on the couch. It was a tight, all-encompassing hug and she could almost hear the shudder in his chest. It made her own chest hurt for what she was about to do to him; she felt her eyes begin to sting and she fought against it as hard as she could. It seemed a long time before he finally let her go and stood up in front of her, and it took all of her might to keep her face a pleasant blank.

"It's good to see you too, Jack. Although I hear all sorts of craziness happened without me." She tried to give a soft smile, but it probably looked more like a grimace.

As she watched, there was a spark in Jack's eyes, but it faded quickly. "Let's not even get started on your conduct that got us in this place to begin with, Lyra," Jack said, his voice ever so slightly playful.

Lyra pushed herself off the couch and swiped at the forty-four ounce vanilla and cinnamon latte Taylor had come back with after his trip to Bigfoot Java. Though she hadn't needed the extra buzz, as adrenaline was already coursing through her system;, having the coffee was still a comfort to Lyra. Her standing up had forced Jack to take a step back and his expression held confusion.

"Before we get into pointing fingers, I think you and I need to have a private discussion as littermates and as alpha to pack member."

Wariness snapped into Jack's eyes, replacing everything else that had been there before. "All right then." His voice had been almost dangerously neutral.

Lyra turned on her heels and went the long way around the coffee table, knowing Jack would follow her all the way to the extra bedroom without saying anything else. The living room was full of inquisitive glances, as a good number of their pack members, and Taylor, were all sitting on the furniture and the floor. None of them seemed to have the courage to ask what was going on outright and instead just shot glances across the room at each other. Not that Lyra blamed them; a private conference was so out of character for her. That in and of itself told everyone in the room that it was ominous.

The two of them wound their way through everybody in the living room and up into the extra bedroom in silence. Once the door was shut behind Jack, Lyra plopped down on the bed and scooted all the way to the top so that she could sit leaning against the wall. Jack stood almost aggressively in the middle of the room, at the foot of the bed, arms crossed and frowning.

"Jack, you want to sit down for this," Lyra advised softly.

Jack's arms fell from his chest and one raked its way through his hair. "Oh, come on, Lyra, we just got you back. Do you really need to be giving me bad news now? Unbelievable. This would only happen to you. No other pack mate would give me this kind of trouble." As he spoke, he plopped down in the chair that was still stationed near the head of the bed. This put them out of touching distance, but they weren't necessarily across the room from each other.

Lyra gave him one last long look before devoting all of her attention to the coffee cup in front of her. She began picking at it with her nails, wishing Taylor had gotten her a smaller size so that she could have picked at the paper cup. The forty-four ounce cup was all plastic and gave her nothing to fiddle with. Lyra took one more extremely long breath before heading in face-first.

"I'm sincerely hoping that what I'm about to tell you is something our friendship can survive. It is my deepest darkest secret, but I can't keep it a secret any longer, not the way things are going."

There were several soft curses next to her but nothing more; he wasn't trying to interrupt, just vocalizing the stress that hovered densely in the room.

"I'm just gonna come out and say it and then answer any questions you may have. I feel like I should have more finesse about this, but I honestly couldn't finesse to save my life at the moment. You know how my family is crazy and you've never been able to come to my family's house."

Though it wasn't a question, she looked at him anyway. Jack gave a hesitant nod but stayed silent so she would continue.

"Well, as you suspected there's a reason for that: we almost seem to be like the mob. I mean we're pretty close actually when you really think about the comparison. Anyway, you know how the change has always been really easy for me. Outside of the first month, if not a little bit before, I haven't had a problem."

Another nod, much slower this time.

"Well, the two are actually related, almost ironically." Her heart was racing so fast and her breathing was so rapid that her words were coming out breathy, as if she had just run for miles and was trying to speak. Each word was its own difficult message; all she could see were dozens of words ahead of her and each one was going to be a struggle to try and get out.

"There's such a thing as real-life werewolves outside of the science experiment. My family is one, I guess you would call it, pack. We don't call it packs, we call it families, which is why we call our groups packs; it's kind of ironic. In reality, the people that are born werewolves call themselves families and my uncle is sort of the head of ours.

"That is why it has been so easy for me. I've been doing this since puberty, a little before when the change actually started, but now I'm stronger than I was.

"There are some minor differences between the way we change and the way you guys change.

And you know all seven of us that the scientists wanted to kidnap? All were actually born werewolves and I think that's why they wanted us. They figured out that we all had different test results; mainly because we didn't know how to hide it in the beginning."

"I think that those changes on the tests they saw made them want to kidnap us. Either they knew all about the real world werewolves and this was the opportunity to study them, or they just noticed we were different and they want to know why."

She had sputtered that out in one quick sweep. It felt like it had only been in one breath even though she was sure her shallow breathing had punctuated each word. She was terrified to look at Jack, as she had just dropped the bombshell of a lifetime, but she knew that looking at him was the only way to see his response. Slowly, almost as if she was in a horror movie, she turned her neck and wasn't surprised by the shocked fear in his eyes. His mouth was agape as he stared at her. It made Lyra itch to yell at him to say something, but she knew she had to give him the chance to process everything on his own.

They sat in silence for what had to have been almost five minutes; just staring at each other before Jack started cursing loudly, leaped from the chair, and started pacing the room. Curse after curse after curse, he grew louder and louder until he was almost shouting. Lyra knew Taylor would stop anyone from coming up to bother them, but if Jack continued to curse at that volume much longer, people were going to get even more suspicious.

Finally, after Lyra didn't know how long, Jack stopped cursing and simply paced back and forth. It was more of a stomp than a regular pace; finally he stopped at the foot of the bed, turned to her, and slammed his arms hard enough on the mattress to make the whole thing lift and come back down.

"This is freaking unbelievable, Lyra. No, I'm not saying I don't believe you because you wouldn't make that kind of thing up, but the fact that we've been struggling for years and I'm only now hearing of this is horrendous. We have been friends for more than a decade and yes, this is a big secret, and I am unbelievably hurt that you wouldn't tell me. Intellectually, I can understand why you wouldn't. I'm just going to skim over the fact that you probably told Hazel all of this, which makes me more angry. Just please tell me that I am not the only littermate in the dark about this?" It wasn't really words as much as everything came out as a growl.

Lyra had spent enough time around alpha dogs to know better than to make any sudden movements or challenge him in this state. He was completely in his right to be mad at her and while part of her wanted to get mad back just on principle, she knew she didn't have the ground to stand on, so she sat on the bed, clutching her coffee as tightly as she dared. She looked back at him and responded very quietly. "She is the only one who knows, and I didn't tell her until we lived together in college because turning into a wolf during the full moon every month is a really hard thing to hide longer than one quarter."

For whatever reason, Jack seemed to take comfort in that and she watched his face change as he worked at calming himself down. The sight of that made Lyra's breathing calm ever so slightly but she didn't move; she didn't dare catch his attention from where it was on the bed.

He didn't look up at her again as he spoke this time, "Why are you telling me this now? As you and I both know we could've gone our whole lives without you telling me this. What makes now so special?"

The anger and hurt in his voice made her throat close a little bit but she knew better than to not answer. "My cousin and I have been petitioning the family, or will be petitioning the family, to take the packs under the family's protection. Our family has resources that we do not and despite all the connections that Mathew might have, my family's reach is much farther. If we can convince them to take at least the seven packs with born weres under their wing that gives us an edge on the scientists. And as of an hour or two before you got here, my uncle tentatively approved a family meeting to discuss whether the packs will go into the fold or not. Because of that, I felt it would be wrong of me to spring that on you the night of. I do have some conscience, however little it may be. At least now you have two days' notice and whether or not you tell the rest of the pack the truth is up to you. You're the alpha, you make the decision, but the more of us that can show up at the family meeting, the better."

"Gee, thanks for actually putting the ball in my court at some point. As if I'm going to choose to spring this on our people the day of the meeting."

Lyra watched as Jack physically reeled himself back in after snapping at her. She knew he wasn't actually going to apologize, but would stop himself from snapping again if he could help it. "Okay, you said there were a few differences between made wolves and born wolves—what are those?" Jack asked, as he slowly and deliberately made his way back to the chair he originally sat in. He stared at her point-blank, his eyes boring into her. There was nothing friendly about his expression, but in Lyra's book, if he was at least talking to her there was hope.

"The biggest difference is the change. We all change smoothly—not from the beginning, but with practice. Anyone ten years or older can smoothly transition with clothing on. It doesn't mean that they always do it, but they can. You can tell the strength, I guess you would say, or the power of a born wolf by when they can change. A born wolf can only change three days before the full moon and three days after. It's unheard of for anyone to be able to change before or after that period. You'll remember when we had that meeting with Dylan and Taylor in the office and I just changed my hand. We were a full week and a half after a full moon; as a born werewolf that should not have been possible. I was asking them if they were able to do that as well. Changing only part of your body is another way that we differ; I have not seen any made werewolves be able to do that. Where with born werewolves it's just a sense of practice and ability. Not everyone is strong enough to do it, but in order to do it smoothly you have to practice. Born werewolves are stronger and faster than made werewolves just as a general rule. While Cole could beat me out of sheer strength, if there was a born werewolf his same size the born werewolf would win, hands down.

"The last thing is a bit of a doozy. Certain born werewolves can do, I guess what you would call, magic. It's not really an accurate term, but it's the closest I can think of. There are certain bloodlines in the families that possess a certain amount of healing magic. They're sort of the doctors for the family. They have a natural proclivity towards the medical arts and once they are discovered to have this gift they are raised from a young age to assume that position in the family."

Jack held up his hand to interrupt. " Luna, your aunt. Is that why they call you little Luna? Are you the next in line for that position?"

Lyra nodded and took a long sip of her coffee that was now starting to grow cold. "Yes, but I can't heal the way she does. I can do little things here and there, but there can only be one Luna or Lunar—if it's male—per family, and there is a ritual that goes along with it. And when I say family in this case, I mean bloodline. Since my aunt has that fully covered, my powers will not develop. She has to choose to give up her gift in order for it to come to me, and there is a ritual that can last up to six months as a training process that needs to be gone through in order to pass on the power, or my aunt needs to die and then all of the power will rush to me. The second is not ideal but has happened. And it's not really magic in the traditional sense; it's almost like luck. I guess we tend to have photographic memories so that we can remember an entire Luna's medical book for herbs and things like that. There is a little bit of magic in the energy; really we're harnessing the family in order to heal that member, using the family as a whole's connection to that person. If they're not connected to a family, or it's not a very big family, it's harder to heal them." Lyra fiddled with the lid on her cup, flipping it on and off. "That's about it, I guess."

"You realize that is a lot of information to just dump on me, right? This is life-altering information that you're just putting at my feet. This is a lot to take in. I don't even know where to really start. Other than the fact that this was kept from me for so long, the thought that my mind keeps circling back to is could Berman have known about the born werewolves and been trying to create his own version? Or are we operating on the idea that this is surely a coincidence?"

Lyra kicked out her legs so she was going from a cross-legged position to having her feet out in front of her, and began shifting her feet forward and backward to stretch her hamstrings. "Honestly, we don't know. My family and the council that run the family have discussed it round and round and nobody's. Nobody's come up with any sort of definite idea. Side note, I should probably tell you the council is the ruling body for each family. There is no set number of seats on the council, so there could be as little as three or as many as a dozen. Well, baker's dozen really, because they always have to have an odd number. They make all the decisions for the entire family, which is why my uncle wants to have an entire family meeting; he's hoping that the family wanting to help us will influence the council into making the decision. Really no one has any idea whether Berman met a werewolf at some point accidently, which is incredibly rare, or if he merely read too many fiction books growing up and felt he could do better. We just don't know."

Jack watched her for several seconds; the frown on his face spoke volumes. "Okay, so the mythical werewolves are real and they are stronger, faster, and better connected than us and several of them stumbled upon this man-made werewolf mess and are trying to get the other werewolves to help us deal with the situation we find ourselves in with the scientists. In order to do so, they want to wrangle all of us made werewolves up to a meeting, where we we'll be outnumbered by the werewolves that are stronger and faster than us, to try and convince them to help. No offense, but from a logistical standpoint this sounds like a very bad idea. You and Graham have come home with bruises and scratches and things like that for as long as I've known you. If they're that hostile towards you and you're one of them, how do you think that they are going to treat us?"

It was a good point, a very good point, in fact; one Lyra hadn't really thought about. She'd been so sure that her family wouldn't turn on the poor, almost defenseless man-made weres that she hadn't considered the fact that the born weres might think otherwise. The made weres wouldn't be able to defend themselves against most of the born weres should a fight occur. She also understood where Jack was coming from; he knew none of these people and for all he knew they were dangerous. He was taking her and Graham's and Taylor's word for it, and at this point she wasn't the most trustworthy of people in his eyes.

"I don't really have an answer for you. Mainly, I just need you to believe me. People are usually on their best behavior at family meetings. They're supposed to be a diplomatic kind of thing so fights are extremely rare. That being said, if it does pass and a fight does occur, a made weres at a disadvantage. Ultimately though, Jack, I don't see a better way to do this. I mean, we could continue to go at this alone, but we have very limited resources and connections. I honestly believe our best bet is to get the family to take us on. Even if it's just the seven packs that have endangered weres. Just know that if you think otherwise, while the family will respect your wishes, they're going to close in and protect their own and will be ruthless in the way they do it. That is the last thing that I want."

Jack was not looking at her again; instead he stared at the far wall with his hands clasped in his lap. Though his face was blank, he was tapping one index finger on his opposite hand; other than that there was no movement. She knew better than to interrupt his thought process, but she really wanted him to understand where she and her cousin were coming from. She thought this was all moving quite fast; she couldn't imagine what it would be like for Jack.

One thing she did know was that Jack was pissed. Everything about his body was stiff as a board. Not that Lyra blamed him for his anger; if roles were reversed, odds were she wouldn't have been able to keep her temper down the way he was.

He was certainly trying the best he could, that Lyra knew for sure, to set aside the anger he felt and concentrate on the problem at hand. The fact that Lyra could visibly see this inner struggle told her flat out how strong his reaction to her news was. She knew better than to speak and instead sat in silence watching him out of the corner of her eye so as to not seem like she was staring; it needed to be him who spoke first.

Several minutes went by before Jack's voice, rather quietly, wafted over to her on the bed. "We will see how this meeting of yours pans out because honestly I cannot see any other option available to us right now. But I want you to know that I don't forgive you for keeping this big of a secret from me. Yes, I understand why you would've kept it from me in the beginning. I never would've believed you unless you changed in front of me, but once the accident happened, once we were put into this problem together, you should have told me. You should've let me know that you were faster, stronger, that you could change only a part of your body at once. There is so much of this that you kept a secret that you should've told me. We are still friends, we will always be littermates, but I find it very hard to like you right now."

That last sentence slithered from his mouth; as. As it reached Lyra's ears it felt covered in some toxic oil that sank into the pit of her stomach. "Now, I'm going to go downstairs and explain all of this to our pack, as I'm fairly certain most, if not all, of them, are down there right now. While I do that, you and Taylor can set up this little rendezvous or whatever you want to call it or you can come down and listen to me explain this to the pack, but you're not going to interrupt. You're going to let me explain to them the secrets you kept. On second thought, I think it's better if perhaps the two of you stayed up here." With that he didn't even look at her; he stood up, hands still clenched into fists, walked to the door, only unclenched long enough to open it, and slammed it behind him on the way out.

Lyra wasn't sure what the best move would be next. So she ended up just sitting there on the bed, recovering from the initial shock of Jack's outburst, her eyes stinging. She knew she shouldn't have been surprised. It was warranted and in character, but for whatever reason, it caught her off guard anyway. After she wasn't sure how long, but it couldn't have been more than a few minutes, Taylor came up to join her in the room. He plopped into the chair Jack had vacated, phone in hand, and blew a deep breath, watching her.

"Man, Lyra, I don't know how you managed to phrase that, but your alpha is pissed. Beyond pissed, really. He came downstairs like a thunderstorm and looked me dead in the eyes, telling me that I best be getting upstairs while he updated his people. Don't get me wrong, I waited a beat or two before walking up here—can't have him thinking he's in charge—but I certainly didn't want to be down there for this conversation. Also, right before Jack came down I got a text message from your uncle. It's clearly a mass text message to the entire family from the wording, letting everyone know that there will be a family meeting at seven o'clock two days from now and that attendance is mandatory. Looks like we've got ourselves a date with destiny. I don't want to leave you alone here, my lady, but I really should go see, if not call, Bishop and let him know exactly what's happening."

Lyra looked at her cousin's childhood friend. "I had a hunch that you'd already told him about us. From the way he gave me a formal greeting at the pack A meet and greet."

Taylor looked down at his phone and didn't respond, but then he didn't really need to. There was no other way Bishop would have known to do a formal bow to someone of Lyra's stature when in wolf form.

Before anything else could be said, the door to the bedroom began to open; both Taylor and Lyra exchanged glances before looking at the door. Neither of them had been paying enough attention to notice who had been walking down the hall. The door opened wider and revealed Hazel standing in the doorway with watery eyes.

The other woman didn't say anything; instead she closed the door behind her and crawled up on the foot of the bed, sitting cross-legged on the opposite corner from where Taylor sat. "I didn't want to listen to the anger in his voice and since I already know most of the information he's telling everybody I figured I was more needed up here. How are you two holding up?"

Lyra's heart ached a little as she looked at her good friend; Hazel had such a tender spirit that she couldn't even stand to hear Jack upset with Lyra. That was just who Hazel was; she was the most caring person Lyra had ever met in her entire life. She gave her friend the only thing she could think to give, a reassuring smile even if it was a little sad around the edges.

"We're hanging in there; even though it's not pleasant to have that much angry frustration pointed at me, I can see where he's coming from and even understand, kind of. He feels betrayed and I know if the roles were reversed I probably would've reacted stronger than he did, but then he probably wouldn't have kept it a secret because you know how terrible Jack is with secrets."

Just as she'd hoped, that last sentence brought a watery smile to Hazel's face.

Taylor sighed loud enough to get both women's attention. "Hazel, will you stay with our girl awhile? At least until I get back. I really should call Bishop and let him know what's happening as soon as possible. I can't in good conscience leave Lyra here to tell Bishop in person, but I can go into the backyard and make a phone call. Will you be all right staying up here till I'm done?"

As Hazel nodded in response they all heard heavy footsteps walking down the hall. Lyra knew it was Ryan from the sound of his gait. She had not remembered seeing him downstairs, but she was somehow not surprised he arrived between then and now. The footsteps didn't sound upset; they would've been clipped if that was the case. Taylor stood and was almost at the door when Ryan entered the room. Ryan inclined his head to the other man before walking to the opposite corner of the bedroom and sitting down on the floor with his back against the wall.

After several seconds of everybody watching him, he held his hands up in the air. "I don't want to talk about it. I will also be more than happy to stick around Lyra until you get back from your phone call, and although I know you won't be uncomfortable with it, I can certainly stay with her if you feel the need to actually leave."

Lyra shifted her attention back to Taylor in time to see his inquisitive expression as he inclined his head in response to Ryan. "Thank you, that's much appreciated, but a phone call should be fine." Then he turned to Lyra with a forced smile. "I'll be back within ten or fifteen minutes." Then he left.

The three of them sat in a slightly uncomfortable silence for Lyra didn't know how long. She didn't know what to say or how she should act in this situation. She was so used to keeping her life compartmentalized that to have the two major sections collide never occurred to her outside of the occasional whimsical thought. Now that reality was upon them and forced her and the others like her into the light, Lyra felt as if there was no correct response, nothing that would get her relationships back to as strong as they had been before.

It ended up being Hazel who broke the silence. "At what point did you leave? How far had Jack gotten?" She looked over her shoulder to their pack mate.

Shrugging his shoulders, Ryan let out a loud breath. "He made it through werewolves in the magical sense, I guess you'd say, and the seven weres that pack L are after were born into it, not made like the rest of us. He got about part way through the plan to ask for help from Lyra's family by the time I just got sick of it and walked out. Sure,

I should probably be down there, as second, listening to the plan but honestly, he is not taking this well, probably because of stress, and I really don't want to be there in case he says anything that he'll live to regret or that'll make me want to punch him in the face."

"Yeah, me too," Hazel agreed, before they fell back into a less awkward silence.

Lyra wasn't sure what to make of Ryan's reaction. He did not seem upset or frightened or surprised. In fact he seemed relatively calm about the whole thing, the way Ryan used to respond to things.

"Are you upset?" she ventured.

Ryan closed his eyes and laid his head back against the wall. "Honestly, no. I am too busy being grateful that you are still alive—even better, awake—to be mad about this. Sure, you kept a secret from all of us but I understand why you did it. It makes perfect sense. And if there are werewolves out there that have been doing this longer than us, they are the perfect people to train us, back us, and help us improve our odds in this situation. I just don't think anger really has a place right now. I'm too tired and we have too much road in front of us, in my opinion. As for the whole born werewolves thing, I guess, sure, it can come across as quite the surprise, but it makes perfect sense to me. Berman had to get the idea from somewhere. I don't know, I guess I just can't work up enough energy to be surprised. Maybe at some point later I will be."

Lyra was taken aback by Ryan's statement. She expected some anger or frustration; granted, not as strong of a response as Jack's. For Ryan to have a perfectly calm response was a relief but also curious and made her want to poke at it to find out exactly why it didn't bother him. Sure, he said there was enough going on right now and he understood why she did it, but that didn't seem like enough to her. Closing her eyes, Lyra sighed. She was honestly just too tired and too wiped from her revelation to drum up the energy to probe Ryan. She could always do it later.

"Please don't be offended but I think this whole waiting and then confessing to Jack has wiped me out. I'm just gonna sleep if that's all right with you," Lyra said, as she laid back on the bed, not before patting Hazel's leg. She felt completely drained and now that the adrenaline was wearing off, her level of pain was rising. She preferred the pain over being stuck in an induced sleep.

For a few moments, Ryan simply smiled and nodded before finally speaking, "Absolutely. Do what your body needs to do to get your energy back. But know that I'll be here just in case you need someone, and Hazel will be reading one of the magazines she left in the nightstand."

She wasn't sure how to take that; it. It was both comforting and unnerving. She knew a lot of her pack mates had been rotating in and out since she'd been unconscious, but somehow knowing this peaceful Ryan was watching her sleep made her not really want to go to sleep.

It was as if he read her mind because a second later she heard a chuckle. "Don't get too weirded out. I actually brought a book with me that

I'm halfway through, so I'm going to be reading, not just staring at you as you sleep."

Lyra exhaled a nervous laugh but didn't respond, as she knew it would only continue the conversation longer than her body needed it to. Instead, she rolled facing away from him and concentrated on falling asleep.

Chapter 5

Jack knew intellectually that it wasn't as warm outside on Justin's front porch as it felt. Jack was unsure of how long he and Seth had been standing there in silence. He appreciated his good friend's sense to let him be without having to hold a conversation. Though the blood had stopped roaring through his veins, it was still at a low simmer from the news Lyra sprung on him earlier.

He'd gone from being relieved she was finally awake, that there was finally hope, to having his world almost decimated in a matter of minutes. She had been born a werewolf, raised one her entire life. Nothing about their circumstance was really new to her. Sure, there were little things here and there, but the shock of suddenly being a different person Jack thought they all experienced together didn't happen for Lyra, and for whatever reason she didn't feel it necessary to tell him.

Sure, he understood why she wouldn't want to explain the transition to him. For all they had known at the time, there could've been vast differences. But they had been dealing with this for years. She had years to come clean and it wasn't until there was a problem that he was deemed okay to be brought into the loop.

It was the secret part that bothered him the most, not so much the secret itself. He had long since given up on the idea that the world was black and white. Once he got past the initial shock that werewolves were real, his brain was able to accept it with relative ease. It seemed like a logical jump that if a man could create werewolves, surely nature would've already done it.

He felt a new spike of anger at the thought that it could be these born werewolves that piqued Berman's interest to begin with and caused him to run his life-altering experiments. Lyra and her family could be the reason his pack was the way they were. He immediately dismissed that thought process; playing. Playing the blame game in this particular case was not going to get him anywhere and it certainly wasn't going to help him process any of this new information, let alone deal with the problems they already had.

Giving a bone weary sigh, Jack moved to sit on the steps of Justin's front porch. Seth immediately followed suit. "I can't believe this has been going on behind our backs. That this whole problem is much bigger than we initially thought."

Seth waited a beat as if he wanted to chew on his words before saying them. "I'm still stuck on the fact that there are more like us. While not exactly like us, pretty dang close. I mean, there could be thousands of werewolves, not just four hundred. There are whole communities that we don't have to hide from, we don't have to pretend to be normal with; that, to me, somehow makes our world a little less alienated. I take some comfort because that means odds are some of the stuff we struggle with—granted, not all—has already been dealt with before and now we can reach out to people that have been through everything before or know those that have our answers. That is too much of a relief for me and it overshadows everything else."

Jack looked over at his friend. He understood what Seth was thinking and even, to a small extent, agreed with it. But Jack couldn't get over Lyra's hiding of something so big that it could've helped them early on when they were transitioning into life as werewolves.

"You need to get over this, Jack. Seriously, I understand you're upset, but think of it this way: if they had come forward to help us in those early stages, especially in that first year, they would've been opening themselves up to scrutiny by those running the project. And considering they've kept themselves a secret this long, it certainly wouldn't be in their best interest to pop out of the woodwork now. I can't imagine most of them would be okay with a few of them outing themselves just to help us. Sure, maybe they could have helped us too once the project left us alone, but thinking like that doesn't help us any, and it doesn't change anything, but it does give us an opportunity to work with them now. So, if this meeting really is in two days then you have two days to wrap your head around all this and accept it for the good of your pack because working with these people will most definitely be in our best interest."

It wasn't often that Jack heard Seth give a bucking-up type of speech. Usually Seth was more laid-back than that and gave occasional advice or sarcastic opinions and in the end he was very much a "to each their own" kind of guy, so the fact that he was not chastising, but encouraging Jack to move on, made Jack wonder if he really was overreacting a bit. After all, it wasn't the shock the werewolves were real that was getting to him; it was everything else.

"Not saying that I agree with you right now, but maybe you're right. Honestly, I don't know; I think just getting this information is making it harder for me to absorb. Once I've thought about it and had some time to reflect on it myself, maybe I'll be okay or maybe I'll be more ticked off. But there is one thing I for sure agree with: working with this family of Lyra's is probably our best bet so regardless of how I actually feel at the time, I will be sure to be calm and collected for this meeting." It was the best Jack could do. He'd fake it for the good of his pack but part of him didn't want to trust Lyra or her cousin.

Seth nodded. "I suppose that is the best I can ask for under the circumstances."

Neither said anything after that; both. Both of them just continued to sit on the front porch steps and stare off down Justin's driveway. Jack wouldn't have even been able to tell anyone what his thoughts were in those moments. It was just a black tangled mass of emotions.

Jack lay with his left foot off the couch when his phone rang. He was lying on his back, staring up at the ceiling, weeding through the events of the past few months when all of a sudden Death Cab for Cutie pierced through the air. Taking a moment to get his breathing back in check, Jack snatched the phone from his coffee table and looked at the screen, which read Bishop. Jack knew this conversation would be about the meeting in two days or about the news Taylor had just broken to him; Bishop was reaching out to someone else who would still be in shock. Part of Jack didn't want to answer, simply because he didn't want to talk to anybody else today, but more of him felt guilty because he knew the shock Bishop was feeling.

Sighing, Jack tapped the screen before setting it on speakerphone and laying the phone on his chest. "Hey, Bishop."

"Jack, this is... an interesting situation we seem to find ourselves in."

A snort was the only response Jack had in him.

"Yes, well, I wanted to get your thoughts on meeting these people on their home turf. Part of me keeps balking that this is a set up, but I know Taylor would do nothing to endanger the pack. Still, I can't help but think this family will not be getting anything out of us joining them so what incentive is there beyond appeasing those that belong to their family who were in the experiment and anyone who feels sorry for us? It makes me wonder whether they're hurting for numbers because, as I'm sure you've noticed with Lyra, sometimes Taylor appears to be knocked around a bit and if they do that to their own, what are they going to do to us?"

Jack took a second to take stock of the fact that Bishop wasn't in shock about werewolves being real or that it had taken so long for them to come to light; he was going straight to the welfare of his pack. He shifted his thought process in the same direction. "I honestly don't know, but I brought that up to Lyra and it appeared that had not occurred to her, which honestly worried me more. Can't imagine they'll let us bring weapons with us, not that many of us have any, but I think that we are honestly going on just a good faith gesture and relying on the ones that belong to our packs to not be setting us up for surprises. Who knows what these born werewolves are capable of since, unlike us, they were born into this nonsense."

The silence on the other end made Jack wary. It wasn't the silence in itself because Bishop wasn't one to speak before thinking, but the timing of the silence tugged at Jack's curiosity. "Bishop?"

There was a hesitant pause on the other side of the phone. "Yes, Jack?"

"Why are you not more surprised? Maybe I'm reaching, but this sounds like you have had more time than a couple of hours to come to terms with the fact that there are natural werewolves in the world. My pack was pretty shocked, I'm pretty shocked, but you, you're looking for the strategy in it. So you processed it very fast or are in denial about it or you have had more time than I have had."

The pause on the other side of the phone told Jack everything he needed to know.

He let a string of curses. "Seriously? How long have you known?"

"Two or three weeks, maybe." There was nothing else: no justification, no scrambling, just that statement and nothing more.

"And you didn't think to tell any of us?"

"It was certainly not my secret to tell and it was made very clear to me that I was one of maybe three made werewolves that knew the truth. And I understand their rationale for keeping it secret so I certainly wasn't going to be the one to share it."

Fury spiked through Jack, but he knew better than to cause an argument with another alpha, especially one that was his ally and friend. "Good night, Bishop." Then he hung up the phone.

He might not be able to yell at Bishop and question his keeping the secret, but he certainly didn't have to keep talking to him. Jack was half surprised when his phone didn't ring again but then there wasn't really much more to say.

Jack let his phone drop onto the floor, closed his eyes, and concentrated on his breathing in order to slow his heart beat down. He couldn't help but feel he had lost control of his pack, not that he had a lot of control to begin with. But their fate seemed to basically be in the hands of this unknown new type of werewolf and that simply did not sit well with Jack. It was one thing for scientists with unknown resources to be trying to hunt them down. While that was horrible and they had no game plan against it, they were now introducing a new variable into the equation and they had no idea what sort of complications were going to come along with it. Deep down Jack agreed that the extra muscle and knowledge were what they needed right now. He just couldn't help the feeling that this meeting was them making a deal with the devil.

Chapter 6

Enclosed spaces had never been something that bothered him; not when he was young, not when he was a teenager, and not when he was in the military. Not any time in his entire life had Parker Holmes cared about enclosed spaces. Crowds, on the other hand, had bothered him, but now that he was only known as 071, enclosed spaces were one of the worst things in the world. He had no idea how long it'd been since he didn't live in a cage. Hell, he couldn't even remember the last time someone spoke his name.

He used to spend his days since coming home from overseas as a cop; nothing fancy. He liked devoting his life to helping others; to protect and serve his community. When he was young he wanted to serve his country, as his father, his grandfathers, and the majority of his cousins had. It was a family tradition he was proud to uphold; even his girlfriend at the time understood.

She had been fine waiting a few years for him; that was the plan, anyway. Then two years in, she broke up with him. No real reason, and she refused to communicate with him when he asked what changed. So, in a rash decision he made his four years eight.

When the eight years were up, Parker applied for the force in Bellevue, then the weirdest thing happened. He saw an ad looking for newly returned veterans to help test equipment that could save the lives of soldiers overseas. They wanted people who'd returned within the last five years and Parker knew he had to do it. He owed it to his brothers and sisters who died overseas to help any way he could to protect those that were still there and those that would go. He volunteered; his boss even worked his shifts so he could go, once he explained how important it was. At first it seemed fairly normal; there was equipment that seemed to him to be like anything else. Then they brought in other soldiers, soldiers that had been in the program a few months longer than him. They were faster and stronger; —it was amazing. Parker almost couldn't believe his own eyes, yet he was happy to see they were making something of value. He didn't know what it was since the armor they were using looked identical to him. He just chalked it up to not being the smartest guy and probably not noticing they were handing them different equipment.

A couple weeks in they told them they needed booster shots. He couldn't remember the rationale they used, but it seemed simple and logical at the time so he took the shots, two a week for a month. That was when things turned bad. That was when he learned what was really going on. At first there was pain, lots of it. He just assumed it was his body reacting to whatever was in the boosters that had helped the other soldiers get stronger, but by the end of the last round, he knew something was wrong. This was not how a healthy body felt. He and two others were comparing notes when they came in for a checkup. A few days after the shots, they had them running on the treadmills, just a row of treadmills hooked up, monitoring them. Then the room filled with this gas and although the five of them were in there screaming and yelling, demanding those watching turn it off and trying to leave, the door was locked from the outside so they couldn't get out. Parker could feel the panic bursting through him as he and one other tried to break the door down, while the others tried to break the two-way glass, through which people were observing them. It didn't last long as the gas filled their lungs. It hurt to breathe and they began to cough, not getting enough air before they all blacked out.

That was when he woke up in his cage. The cage that would be almost all of his existence. He didn't know how long he'd been in there. He knew it was longer than days because he watched the shifts of the doctors or techs or scientists or whoever they were. There were enough shifts to make Parker believe it was at least weeks, if not months. They only let the people in cages out to test. To test their blood and urine, hair and skin. They never let more than one of them out of a cage at a time and there were always at least four security guards with Tasers if they ever set foot out of the cage. They tested his speed, stamina, and strength.

A few days after he first arrived, Parker saw one of the soldiers who had been there longer than him. Parker knew he hadn't been there long because he was still sick to his stomach and weak, but this guy next to him was strong. The man tried to fight off the guards with their Tasers. He managed to get through two of them before they brought him down. Then they dragged him off. It was a long time before they came back in. The man was weak, bruised, and no one within the row of cells Parker could see tried to fight off the guard again.

They'd stopped calling them by name once they had put them in the cage. Before that it had been polite. It'd been "Mr. Holmes," and he always told them to call him Parker, trying to be humble and personable to these people he thought were there to help. But he knew, now, these people were not trying to help soldiers. No, they were recruiting able-bodied men and women so their specimens were in the best physical condition. Some days were worse than others to get through. Parker was not delusional; he didn't hold out hope that this would all be a bad dream or that these people would get arrested and it would end. But he knew the moment he stopped holding onto hope of leaving this place was the moment he was guaranteed to shrivel up and die there. So he clung to his name, to the memory of the woman he left behind to serve his country, and he clung to the memory of his family, wondering what they thought happened to him. Were they worried? Surely they noticed. Were they praying for him? Was he a missing person yet? There were days when it was almost impossible to think about the pain, that he'd survived years of war to return home only to die in the dark underground cage a few miles from his family, just because he wanted to help. Just because he wanted to help.

Chapter 7

"I'm sorry, you're planning to do what now?" Boone asked Graham, scrubbing at his face. "Look, I may not have been born into this family like you all were, but this seems like a bad idea to me. It wouldn't have ever occurred to me to introduce the made werewolves to the family. The family can eat them all alive. Even if they don't, the local betas certainly will think about it. Those little upstarts are already trying to prove themselves against your father's family. They practically have visitors' passes to the compound with how often they're jumping the walls, attacking people, or just attacking people outside the walls. Do you really think it's a good idea to introduce people from the experiment into all that?"

Graham knew that Boone wasn't questioning him to be rude or insolent, but the dominant wolf in him automatically snarled at the other man. "I don't really think that there is a better plan right now. I think that it is the lesser of two evils to introduce the made wolves into our world and give them extra connections and extra protection from whatever the scientists are trying to do than to leave them in the dark by themselves. And let's not forget that it's us the scientists are after, not the other made weres at this point. Really we need to make the family see this as their problem as much as it is ours. The only way to do that is to get some of the made weres into the family."

Boone dropped his head, shaking it. Graham looked at the other two wolves. Reed was a very submissive wolf, so even if he disagreed with the decision, he wasn't going to say anything against it; he'd always been that way, so Graham hadn't been worried when he asked the other six to meet him at Green Lake about causing an uproar. Boone and Kipling were really the only wildcard factors in this discussion. Graham knew Lyra, Taylor, and Dylan were all fine with the plan of taking the main wolves into the family because ultimately they wanted to protect their packs and this was the best, if not the only, way to do it.

When they first got there, Kipling had been flirting with his cousin and Graham hadn't liked that too much, but once the other wolf noticed how serious Lyra was, it soon stopped and he hadn't said a word since. Graham had started to explain the plan to them, but now he was shuffling his feet.

"Look, where I come from in Alaska there really is no defined family, but instead there are lots of smaller beta families that have divvied up the land into their own territories. This whole system that the lower forty-eight, and apparently everywhere else, uses is really foreign to me. The fact that these, I don't know if you would call them lone wolves or not, band together to form beta packs in order to take territory from the family that controls the area doesn't make sense to me. It all seems so structured; regardless, let's say the family decides to bring them in on a temporary basis. What's to say that when all is said and done and the scientists aren't a problem anymore that the family won't kick out the made wolves or force them to make their own beta pack? Because we all know that if the made wolves have to look out for themselves in our world, it's going to be a problem.

Especially when you consider other families outside our territory are not gonna look too kindly on us bringing in outsiders."

Kipling brought up a good point and Graham knew it. There was no guarantee that the packs would be safe in the born werewolf world, but there just didn't seem to be another way. Before he could answer, Lyra replied for him.

"Ultimately, what this all comes down to is working with the trouble you know versus the trouble you don't. We don't know anything about the scientists, but we know, within reason, all of the variables in this world we grew up in. I would rather take comfort in knowing the dangers we might face than being stuck out here with an enemy we can't even track down."

There was mumbling of agreement then silence again. After a second, Boone started walking away from the group, but before Graham could say anything the other man held up his hand over his shoulder then spoke loud enough for the group to hear.

"I may not like this plan, but you bring up some good points. I'm calling Charlie now and getting all this out in the open before we potentially send all the sheep to slaughter." With that he walked farther away, pulling out his phone

"Well, isn't he just a little ray of sunshine," Kipling quipped before pulling out his phone and moving in the opposite direction.

Reed quickly followed suit, which left the rest of them standing amongst the trees. No one said anything at first, but then they really didn't need to because Graham was pretty sure none of the alphas had taken this news well. Except Bishop, because apparently that man had already known, which Graham was not too thrilled with. None of them said anything until one by one, the other three men wandered back over, each with an unpleasant expression. They all at least made sure the alphas would be walking into this situation with their eyes open. As far as Graham could think, that was really the best thing they could do for them. Once the last man had returned, and they each confirmed they had spoken to their respective alphas and explained that the world was much bigger than they'd initially thought, there was not a lot more for them to say. They said their goodbyes and each headed their own way home except for Lyra and Taylor who were heading to the compound to get Lyra's dogs before heading back to her apartment.

Graham was mostly sure that the family would at least temporarily welcome the made werewolves into the family. As soon as they did he would get the resources for tracking down the scientists and what exactly they wanted from the made werewolves, not to mention who was pulling the strings. There was no way the lab assistants were doing this on their own. They needed to find those connections and snuff them out. Then, and only then, would things maybe have a chance at getting back to normal. Graham snorted at that thought as he started his car. Who was he kidding; life had never been normal.

Chapter 8

Seth lay on the middle of his floor, staring up at his ceiling. He really needed to get a new pullout couch but just hadn't managed to find the time to replace the old one he had gone to college with. He debated turning on his TV; the small coffee table where the remote sat was only about half a roll away. His studio apartment wasn't really big enough to warrant anything more than minimal furniture, so it would be an uninterrupted roll to the table.

He knew when he heard his cell phone ring from next to the remote that he was not going to like whatever the call was about. For a moment, he considered not answering it, pretending he was asleep or had put the phone on silent, but he was too responsible to follow through with it. The pack had been through a lot lately and he couldn't bring himself to simply unplug. Sighing, he rolled himself over onto his stomach, extended his arm, groped across the table until his hand circled his phone, then he put it to his ear.

"Yeah?"

"Seth, I've got an idea to run by you."

Jack was using his authoritative voice, which meant Seth was not going to like whatever this idea was.

"And that idea would be?"

There was a pause, almost as if Jack was hesitating or trying to find the right words. "A couple of the other alphas and I got together and there has been some developing information about these pack assistants that we want to look into."

Seth propped himself up on his elbows, curiosity piqued. "Don't beat around the bush, Jack. Just tell me what's going on."

There was a heavy sigh through the phone. "I'd really like for you swing by the pack office so I can show you, but we have basic information about where some of these lab assistants work and live and the thought is that we could have a couple people follow some of these guys after work for a day or two just to see what they're up to. Whether they go to a different lab, where they might be doing some kind of related experiments, or if there's some kind of home base. Or if there's somebody else they're working with."

Swinging himself up, Seth scrubbed his face with his free hand. "Let me guess, I'm your choice to be one of these… trackers." He wasn't sure why bitterness threaded through his voice, but he wasn't sure he could have stopped it.

"Yes, if you're okay with doing that, it would be much appreciated. I have more information here at the office,e and if you agree to it, Mathew is meeting with a group of them in about an hour to walk everybody through their assignments. If you don't want to do it, that's fine too."

He knew it wasn't fine. Jack wasn't sure he could trust Ryan to do this kind of thing, which made Seth the most reliable choice. As much as he didn't like the idea of sneaking around and following someone, Seth could see the merits of the idea. "Okay, Jack. I'm home now, but I'll head over to the office." He hung up without any further comment.

As he got up, Seth grabbed his keys and wallet from the kitchen counter on his way out the door thinking, not for the first time, about how one stupid film appreciation class had gotten Jack and him into this huge mess in the first place. If they hadn't been taking that class, they wouldn't have been getting a movie from the library and none of this would've been their problem. As always happened when his mind went down this rabbit hole, he immediately felt bad. That would leave Justin, Lyra, and Hazel out on a limb. He was sure Lyra had enough can-do attitude to push through just about anything, something he admired in his friend, but he wasn't sure that she had the strength to carry the other two if Jack and Seth hadn't been there. He was pretty sure if she had to be the rock for all three of them, she probably would've withdrawn from the other two and might've collapsed. He knew that it was best for them that he and Jack had been in that library, but that didn't stop him from wishing he had never let Jack convince him to sign up for a film studies course.

The entire drive to the pack office, Seth mentally went through his schedule to see exactly what days he was available to go traipsing around after some lab assistant. He did have to work, and sure he was lucky, as where he worked it wasn't a huge deal if the engineers set their own hours. But he still had a strong enough work ethic, and he didn't necessarily want to go missing in the middle of the workday to go do pack business. He was pretty sure he could rearrange things the rest of this week, but if it was next week they were looking at, there would be a problem. Not only did they have the family meeting coming up, which was going to cause its own set of problems that Seth really didn't want to spend too much time thinking about, but they didn't know how the dynamics were going to change if the family decided to take them in. This whole thing could be obsolete by then. Or they could be shut out of the investigation entirely.

At that frustrating thought, Seth yanked on the doors to the main lobby a little harder than necessary and made his way up to the pack office. He noticed, not for the first time, that the sign, banner really, above the pack office hadn't changed since before this whole incident started. It was almost as if Syrus didn't have it in him or didn't think it was appropriate to display a sense of humor at the moment. Seth appreciated the other man's assessment of the situation but was also saddened that the pack prankster wasn't even in a mood to make jokes. When he headed into the office, he was surprised to see nobody there, but the light in Jack's back office was on, so Seth just headed to the back corner.

When he got there he could see Jack standing in front of one of the billboards in his office, staring at it through squinted eyes and frowning. Seth went to stand next to his best friend and looked up at what appeared to be simplified org charts. On the left at the top was a picture of Berman. There was a string hanging down from him with a question mark. Then on the right half, at the bottom, were lab assistants with strings attached to each and to the name of a lab company Seth didn't know, as well as to a picture of Dr. Paul, one of the scientists from part of the program in the early days.

Above her were several more question marks and next to her was a scientist he didn't recognize right away. The face seemed vaguely familiar but not familiar enough for Seth to have a name to put with the face. Below the poster, on the shelf, were stacks of documents that looked to hold brief bits of information about various people. A decent search had clearly been done on as many people as possible. Seth was a little impressed that while all of this nonsense was going on, Mathew had been able to use the resources in a more useful manner.

Jack shifted his attention to Seth but motioned at the board. "As you can see, they figured out that the lab assistants aren't in any way connected to Berman, but instead they seem to be connected to Dr. Paul, as well as a Dr. Minkin. The initial intel that's been gathered, as early as today, on Dr. Minkin is that he originally put in to be on the project but seems to have, for one reason or another, been declined. Our current theory is that Dr. Paul and Dr. Minkin want to gather up the most powerful among us, which we now know are the born werewolves, to study. We don't know if they're trying to replicate what was done to us or whether they want to build upon it. Either way, no one is terribly thrilled with the idea of them getting a hold of anything to do with any of us. That is why we want to have them tailed. If we can find enough information about what exactly they're doing, we might have some leverage to accomplish something instead of always being on the receiving end of surprise attacks."

Seth took in the board. More so he took in where the strings were placed. "So these three strings directly under Dr. Paul—I'm guessing that means they work for her?"

Nodding, Jack tapped the pictures of the three lab assistants in question. "Yes, they work in her lab and several more work for the same company. It's just too big of a coincidence for us to ignore."

Something about this chart gave Seth a sense of foreboding. He wasn't sure whether it was finally knowing, at least at the lower levels, who they were dealing with that was causing it, or whether it was the fact that none of it could be traced back to Berman. That meant they still didn't know what he was up to or where he was. Ultimately, what it came down to was currently he was not a threat to them. Dr. Paul and the lab assistants were, as well as whoever was funding their little experiment.

"Has anyone looked up the company they work for to see if maybe it's a corporation that's behind this whole thing?" Seth asked

Jack shook his head. "No, they looked into the company and it was some kind of plant-based chemistry. I'm not entirely sure. I didn't understand a lot of the mission statement from the company that we have in the files. We're pretty sure that all of this comes from somewhere else, that there must be some other place they're meeting."

"Yeah, I get it. You said the meeting with Mathew is in an hour?"

Jack nodded. "Yes, thank you, Seth. I really appreciate you doing this. I know you're much better at being inconspicuous than I am."

Seth looked back at the board. There were just too many question marks, and he doubted trailing some of the lab assistants for a few days was going to eliminate many of them. "Honestly, Jack, do you really think us trailing a couple of the lab assistants is going to make a huge difference?"

He watched as Jack puffed up a little bit in agitation. Clearly he wasn't as sure as he would like to portray that he was. "It's better than doing nothing. And if they keep coming after our own then yeah, doing anything, even if it ends up being futile, is better than doing nothing. You never know, maybe you'll stumble upon something, find a location, or we'll hear something that'll give us another lead. Right now, I have to believe this is our best bet because I don't think we can rely on the family to really be looking out for us on this front. They might be more equipped to fight, but I don't think they have the same information that we do."

Seth really wanted to mention how defensive Jack sounded, but he knew better than to say anything when Jack was on the defense. It would only cause a fight neither of them was really in the mood to have. So instead he started skimming through the documents that were in front of them, gathering bits and pieces of information. Mainly it was just a lot of background work on each of the individual lab assistants as well as Dr. Paul and Dr. Minkin but not a lot beyond on that.

When it was time for the meeting, Seth didn't say anything; instead he just headed over to Mathew's pack office. He wasn't sure what he would've said since Jack seemed to be concentrating all of his attention on that paperwork in hopes of finding something. As Seth got in the elevator, he saw that there were already two men that he knew vaguely in passing; he'd seen them a couple times but never actually met them. They nodded to each other and when Seth went to press the button, he could see they were all headed to the same floor. They all rode the elevator in silence, continuing not to say a word, even when Seth knocked on Pack M's door and Mathew swung it open, ushering them in. When he stepped inside, Seth scanned the room; other than Mathew and Mason there was only one person in the room he recognized: Boone. The man was standing away from everyone else, though it wasn't clear if that was his doing or if the others were giving him a wide berth now that word was out about what he really was.

Seth was not given much time to think about it, because Mathew quickly walked passed them and waved the six of them to stand on the backside of a rolling cork board. Once Seth reached it he could see that it was simply a larger version of the map Jack had shown him.

"Alright, I assume your alphas informed you of the plan, as it stands right now, but I am going to run through it just in case. You will each be assigned a lab assistant to tail. We want them followed, starting when they leave work and finishing when they settle in at home for the night. We are looking for anything out of the ordinary, preferably a lab other than the one we have listed as their place of employment. I have a tracking device for each of you. If you can get a chance to put it on the underside of their cars that would be ideal. I know it is not exactly legal, but I am open to suggestions if you have any."

They all exchanged glances but no one spoke. Seth didn't particularly like the idea of using a tracking device. It felt wrong, but then he reminded himself that these were the people who, on multiple occasions, tried to abduct Lyra. If this was what it took to guarantee her safety he would do it.

Mathew seemed to take the silence for acceptance because he simply nodded before handing each of them an envelope. Once they each had one, he addressed the group, "Okay, each of you now have all the current information we have on the person you will be following. At the bottom of the envelope is the tracking device. Please start tomorrow evening. The faster we can figure out what these people are hiding, the better. I ask that you follow for two days. After that I am pretty sure we will have our hands full with these born werewolves. Hopefully one of you will luck out and we can rid ourselves of this threat and move on to the next, whatever it may be."

There was a feeling of resignation in the air, as if no one was very pleased with the idea of what they were about to do. At the same time, none of them argued or questioned; the five of them that did not belong there merely shuffled out of the office.

Seth didn't bother to go back to Pack F's office. He had no interest in talking to Jack; all he wanted was to be alone. He would read the file, and familiarize himself with the tracking device from the comfort of the floor of his studio apartment.

The first night of surveillance was a blur of boredom for Seth. The lab assistant he was assigned to trailing, Grayson Dark, was rather boring. In the file, Seth had read Grayson drove a white CRV; armed with that information, Seth headed to the parking lot of the company Grayson, as well as Dr. Paul and several other lab assistants, worked at. It took him a few moments but he saw two of the others also waiting in the parking lot when he got there. He mused to himself that they would have to hide better than that if he could already see them, but then he knew what he was looking for. Once a man who looked like the picture of Grayson walked out of the building with one of the other lab assistants and headed to the white CRV, Seth turned on his own car but left the lights off so as not to be too obvious. He then followed the other man to the apartment complex that was registered on his driver's license as his home. Seth waited outside the building for two and a half hours before deciding that Grayson was in for the night and going home himself.

He wasn't sure if tonight would be any more interesting. The downside was the apartment complex Grayson lived in had a secured parking lot, which would make a tracking device a little difficult to put on and there was just enough traffic in the company parking lot that someone would notice him puttering around underneath a vehicle. Unless Grayson went somewhere interesting tonight, Seth would not have a chance to put a tracking device on the car.

He couldn't help but feel that this was almost an exercise in futility. So far there had been no reason for him to follow Grayson; he got nothing out of it, no information at all. It was basically a waste of time. And he was willing to bet that had anybody else gotten anything, he would have heard via text or call from Mathew or Jack. He understood that this was covering their bases and in theory it sounded like a good idea, but in the moment it simply felt like a waste of time.

When Grayson exited the building, Seth once again turned on his car without turning on his headlights, ready to follow the other man to the Tukwila apartment complex. About ten minutes after leaving the parking lot, Seth felt his curiosity spike when they got on the freeway going north instead of south. He was careful to be at least three cars behind Grayson at any time, so as not to arouse suspicion. That was a little bit easier said than done, since at seven-thirty at night the freeway was not as full as it would've been during rush hour. Eventually, they pulled into a development of row houses or connected townhomes just outside Kenmore. Grayson turned off into a cul-de-sac and Seth continued a few houses down and parked across the street from the cul-de-sac and watched as Grayson knocked on the third house of the left.

Seth was debating whether to trace around the house to see if he could see or hear anything inside when there was a rapping on the window of his passenger-side. His adrenaline spiked as he scrambled to come up with an excuse for why he was sitting in his car in an otherwise clearly quiet neighborhood. When he looked at his window, Boone's face shone in the street lights.

Instead of rolling down his window Seth took out his keys and got out of his car; clearly Grayson had gone into the house of the lab assistant that Boone was following, or they were meeting someone else entirely. Either way this might just be the tidbit they needed. If nothing else this would be the perfect time for him to tag the car.

When Seth was standing directly in front of him, Boone finally spoke, "I wonder what makes your guy come visit my guy after work hours? What do you say to a little close surveillance? To be fair, they might just be a couple. But I'm willing to bet it's something of more interest to us."

"Sure, take the lead; you're better at this kind of thing than I am," Seth answered.

There was a flicker across Boone's face; Seth was sure it was something close to gratitude. Clearly Boone expected Seth to give some kind of fight or balk at the fact that he'd be working with one of the born werewolves. That thought saddened Seth, that some of them would side against their own simply because of the birth circumstances. Sure, he didn't like the lies or the secrets, but he understood why and he probably would've done the same thing if roles were reversed. He just didn't have it in him to hate people for trying to protect their own.

The emotion left Boone's face quickly as he gave a curt nod and began walking towards the cul-de-sac, assuming Seth would follow. At first, the two of them walked side-by-side nonchalantly as if they were headed to a friend's house. Once they were past the first house in the cul-de-sac, Seth could see that there was a small path almost dead center in the back of the cul-de-sac that led to a small park. It looked to be only big enough for swings and a little bit more playground equipment, nothing large.

When they had passed the house in question, Boone whispered only loud enough for Seth to hear.

"It looks like all the backyards are connected, as well as being postage stamp yards. That is certainly not going to work in our favor. They're both werewolves so they'll hear us open the gate and it looks like we might have to jump two or three fences just to get to his unless there is some kind of valley between the yards of this cul-de-sac and the next. Let's walk to the park and see if there's some kind of pathway." Boone's tone conveyed that he was clearly frustrated with the lack of an easy opportunity for them to spy on the two lab assistants inside.

When they got to the park it became clear that, while not the easiest way to do things, they might've gotten lucky. The park had five walkways leading to separate cul-de-sacs; each of them had identical fence lines and the way the fences were built gave a small alleyway, maybe four feet wide, between the back fences of one cul-de-sac and the next. It seemed Boone had the same idea Seth did, as they both scanned around the park in unison to see if there would be anyone seeing them walking down that pathway. The fences were about six feet tall so if they both hunched a little no one would be able to see them unless they were on the second floor. Even then, with how dark it was, they would have to be really looking.

As they passed the first set of fences Boone whispered again, "We're in luck. It appears the gates to the fences are all on the backside. I can't imagine the people we're looking for don't have a lock on their fence, but at least it's something."

Seth simply grunted as a reply.

When they got to the lab assistant's backyard, they both took a small step back so they could look into the house. Seth could see a light on in what appeared to be the kitchen and as he saw some movement, he dove back next to the fence. The last thing they needed was to be spotted. Boone appeared to have done the same thing, because the other man crouched beside him.

"There goes that idea; if they're in the kitchen they'll see us do anything, whether that be open the fence or hop over it," Seth complained.

Boone narrowed his eyes and scanned the fence line in both directions. "These houses look fairly new. I would say five years, ten maximum. I have done a little work in construction and I've noticed that some of these new non-wood fences tend to have gaps at the gate, whether on the ground or between the gate door and the rest of the fence. If we are lucky, the gap will be big enough for us to see through."

Boone then got down on all fours and proceeded to crawl slowly along the fence; it turned out the door was simply on the other side of Seth because when Boone got there he laid himself flat on the ground and peered into the backyard. He then scooted over away from Seth, creating room for

Seth to lie down next to him. "There isn't a lot of space, but I can see the kitchen table. If I inched my head sideways, I would probably be able to see more but then I run the risk of them seeing my face."

Seth lay flat and army crawled until he was side by side with Boone. The kitchen was well lit and both men were sitting on opposite sides of the table with stacks of paper in between them. Grayson was pointing at the page in front of him and making a slashing motion while the other lab assistant frowned.

"My hearing is not quite good enough to make out what they're saying with the walls and windows between us. But something tells me we want to see what's on those papers. It's too bad I don't have my camera on me because it has a night vision mode and I don't want to risk taking out my phone and taking a picture because the light will definitely alert them somebody's here. I wish I thought to do this last night when he came home from his girlfriend's house. I could've ding dong ditched him, hopped the fence, and gotten a closer look." The last was a growl as if he was more chastising himself than informing Seth.

Seth let out a sigh; there was no way they were going to be able to see anything useful other than the two of them collaborating. But he hadn't seen Grayson bring any bag big enough with him that night to warrant all that paperwork. "Did the guy you're tailing bring that paperwork home with him tonight?" Seth asked.

Boone looked at Seth for the first time since they had started walking past the fences, his expression curious. "No, he didn't. That means it's in the house. Which means we can give ourselves access to it when he's not home."

He couldn't help but get excited even though the idea of breaking and entering bothered Seth's inner moral compass. He wasn't sure where the line was between doing what was necessary and doing wrong. Sure, these lab assistants wanted to kidnap people and test them and force them to train instead of living their own lives. But they were willing to break into homes. Kidnapping was worse, but where was the line where they came farther into the gray area, closer to the lab assistants and less like the victims?

He was saved from that train of thought when Boone pushed himself back from the fence and declared, "We'll not get anything else tonight. I assume you're going to follow your boy home but now would be the perfect time to put the tracking device on his car, if you haven't already."

Seth nodded and followed suit. The other man was right; this was the perfect opportunity since this neighborhood seemed relatively quiet. He had to go back to his car to get the tracking device out of the backseat. It was dark enough that he was pretty sure he could do it and still be undetected. Both remained silent on the walk back to his vehicle and while he put the tracking device on Grayson's car.

Once they were back at Seth's car, Boone leaned on the hood with his hands in his pockets, scanning the neighborhood around them. "It looks like my guy's in for the night. You want me to keep you company until your guy leaves?"

Taking a moment to give it some serious thought, Seth pulled out his phone to check the time. It was already almost nine-thirty at night. He had no idea how more than an hour had flown by since he first arrived.

"It's up to you. I'm going to give it another forty-five minutes or so then I'm heading out myself even if he's still here. The tracking device is live on his car so it's not like we will not be able to find him if we need to."

Nodding, Boone settled more onto the hood of the car, clearly deciding to wait it out with Seth. The two of them leaned on the car in silence for at least ten minutes before Boone's voice filled the void. "So, don't feel obligated to answer but how are things going on your end? While I know Lyra, I don't know her well enough to know if she's agitated because of the situation or because of something that's happening with the pack. Normally I'm not one to be nosy but disharmony anywhere, especially with her or her cousin, could cause us problems."

There was no definite answer to give. Part of Seth didn't want to answer because he felt it was his pack's own private business, but he understood the other man's concern, even agreed with it. If Lyra and her cousin were the main bridges between the family and the packs then having one of them be rocky wouldn't do well for any of them. He could understand the concern Boone would feel. The seven born werewolves that were in packs were sticking their necks out in hopes of gaining protection for their made werewolf brethren. If the roles were reversed, Seth wouldn't want anything jeopardizing that either.

"She isn't necessarily an easy thing to explain," Seth began. "Let's just say there are members of our pack that aren't necessarily taking the revelation that Lyra was born a werewolf well. I have faith that eventually things will work themselves out because the alternative is that they never speak to each other again or rip each other apart emotionally. Truthfully, both scenarios are equally likely at this point, but I am hoping that the dire situation we find ourselves in forces them into peace long enough for them to mend fences on their own."

Boone just nodded and for several minutes Seth thought he wasn't going to speak again. "I could see that. Here's hoping things work out for the best. Because in the few years that I've been part of a pack, I've come to realize just how important interpersonal connections are. When you're lone-wolfing it by yourself, it doesn't matter who you do and don't get along with, as long as the local family who runs the territory doesn't have a problem with you. Even being in a family of werewolves you don't have to get along with everyone. Heck, unless there's a full family meeting called, you don't even really have to see anyone. Pack is different, though. We are all up in each other's business in a way that I can't say I'm entirely comfortable with."

The snort came out before Seth could stop it. "On that, you and I agree."

They were silent longer this time than before. In Seth's mind and before he knew it he was saying it out loud, "So what exactly can we expect from this family meeting tomorrow?"

When an answer didn't come right away, he looked at the other man; Boone's expression said that he was clearly thinking out the answer before responding.

"Since he called all of the family one of two things will happen. Either each household will have a representative there or the majority of the wolves will be there. If it's only a representative then there could be as little as thirty people. Considering what a big deal is being made of this, I am willing to bet there will be more than one hundred people in attendance. The meeting will be in the atrium of the main building and they will pull some very werewolf-y tactics to be intimidating. They'll hide in the shadows, since we're meeting at night. The center of the atrium will be the only section of the space with a semblance of light, it will depend on wither they light the torches scattered throughout the space.to create nervousness for us, because we won't exactly see them all and won't know how many there are. They will also all arrive before us; it'll be a kind of power play to show they have the upper hand and make us feel like we're almost late. But as long as no one shows too much fear we'll be fine. As soon as someone starts acting like they're afraid or nervous we might lose the vote."

That did nothing to ease his concern. Knowing that the born werewolves were going to be pulling out power plays when the made werewolves were already on unsure footing only fueled the fire of his unease. When he got home tonight he would have to text or call Jack and let him know that this was happening so that word could get out that they were going to have to go out of their way to show no signs of weakness if they hoped for this deal not to fall through. For the first time Seth was starting to wonder if the born werewolves were looking for a reason not to take the made werewolves on. He had figured it'd taken some convincing on Lyra's and the others' parts to get this meeting in the first place, but if there were things in place to actively put them on edge, their chances might be slimmer than they originally thought.

He found himself asking, "What is the general consensus? Are people really against helping us?"

"Yes and no. I'm not in the thick of it like some of the others are, but I've heard snippets here and there. There are those that don't want to get involved and think that ignoring the problem will make it go away because it doesn't affect us. The other school of thought is that should the scientists get a hold of one of us seven made werewolves that are actually born werewolves, it could open a whole can of worms that affect the worldwide werewolf community. And if we're the cause for the world knowing we exist, our family will be hunted into extinction. Ultimately it's self-preservation that got the meeting pushed through. Sure, there are a couple people that genuinely just want to help us, but they're the minority. I know that Lyra is going to want to appeal to people's sense of community and their good nature, but I'm not entirely sold that that's the best way to get this done. But we'll see." He shrugged.

It hadn't occurred to Seth that the werewolf community at large would be affected by the things the scientists were doing. Now that Boone said it, it made perfect sense. If they found out that the born werewolves' DNA was different, it would only be a matter of time before they figured the rest of it out. And if the community was as harsh as Boone was making it sound, then helping the made werewolves was definitely the lesser of two evils if the other option was the entire family being wiped out.

The sound of a car starting pricked Seth's ears and he turned to his left to see that Grayson had started his car and was backing out of the other lab assistant's driveway. Boone pushed off the car and in one step was back on the sidewalk.

"You better get after him then." As Grayson's vehicle drove by them, they both turned the other way in case he recognized their faces. "I'll see you tomorrow evening." With that the other man started walking the opposite direction toward what Seth could only assume was his car.

Seth jumped in his own vehicle, started it, and drove after Grayson. Luckily the development wasn't that confusing, but was fairly straightforward and he remembered how to get out. When he turned onto the road he could see Grayson's car up ahead of him and stayed back and one lane over since now the roadway was only sparsely populated. Seth tried not to get lost in thought as he followed Grayson back to the other man's house. Once it became clear that was where Grayson was headed Seth turned off and headed home.

From the floor of his apartment he texted the number Mathew had put in the envelope, letting whoever was on the other end know that he had planted the tracking device. Knowing he was probably in bed, Seth opted to text Jack instead of calling him. He made it brief, only stating that perhaps the born werewolves might be putting on some power plays and that he should call him in the morning for more information. Once he'd done that, Seth lay there staring at the ceiling again. He knew he should head to bed, but with his thoughts swirling around he knew it would be a while before his mind would let him sleep. So he continued to stare at the ceiling, letting his thoughts whorl until he drifted off, still on the floor.

Chapter 9

Lyra had been a bundle of nerves for two days, even though she had been grateful to finally be back in her own home, with her dogs and Taylor since he refused to leave. It was a relief and a comfort to be able to get back to her normal routine of teaching classes, reading, and exercising the dogs. She hadn't heard a word from Jack, or anyone else from her pack minus a few well-meaning text messages from Hazel since she had told her family's biggest secret. So she had no idea how they were taking things or what they thought of her or the other natural born werewolves. So, in a way, having Taylor there was a comfort because she wasn't alone. But, on the other hand, he was a reminder that everything in life changed, again. This was on top of the fact that the family meeting loomed over their heads. The entire pack would be there; hopefully that played to the family's sympathies about this plight they were going through. If not, they would have no chance of getting everyone in. Not to mention this meant that her worlds were colliding and she had no idea how they would interact with each other. She was worried about how the made wolves would handle being introduced to a more violent world than they were used to. She was also worried about her family because introducing the made wolves would increase their number drastically enough that other families might take notice and cause problems for them. There was no guarantee either way how the other families would react to their world being introduced to strangers. It had been forbidden for so long Lyra doubted anyone would respond well.

She coped the only way she knew how: sticking to her routine, which was somewhat hindered by Taylor being there and the fact that every three days she had to meet with her aunt for a checkup and to get a shot of the suppressant. Apparently, if she didn't take the suppressant every three days she would be worse off than she was and it would be harder for her to be brought back. That was something she tried desperately not to think about. There were enough problems going on right now and her aunt assured her that as long as she got those shots once every three days there would be nothing to worry about. So she tried to take her aunt at her word and pushed it to the back burner, trying not to think about what it would be like to need a shot every three days for the rest of her life.

When Wednesday finally arrived, Lyra felt like she hadn't slept in weeks. Her nerves were shot and every little thing seemed to send her into tailspin, but she knew for the sake of her pack, as well as her family, she would have to maintain as much composure as she could manage. She expected the day to go by incredibly slowly, but in actuality it seemed to end almost as soon as it had begun.

Since she and Hazel were going to carpool to this meeting, Taylor agreed that he would drive to Hazel's and then follow in a vehicle behind them; that way they would at least have the illusion of privacy and he could still keep tabs on her. Lyra was grateful that Taylor didn't insist on riding with them, but at the same time she was sure he wanted the excuse for privacy as much as she did.

Instead of rapping at Hazel's door, she just texted her friend, letting her know they were there and telling her to come on down when she was ready. Surprisingly, they didn't have to wait long before Hazel came bounding down her steps. Lyra gave a brief smile to Taylor before getting out of his car and heading over to Hazel's. Unsurprisingly, when Lyra joined her, Hazel enveloped her in a bear hug and whispered in her ear.

"I know this is hard for you and I'm so sorry. I wish there were something I could do to make this all better, but I can't tell you how grateful I am that you're not still in that stupid coma. I don't think I could've handled our littermates on my own too much longer." With that last statement she gave one more hard squeeze before letting go and giving a sad smile to Lyra.

As they got into the car and Hazel started the engine, she began making small talk, which Lyra surprisingly appreciated because it made things feel almost normal again.

"How are you feeling? Your aunt mentioned that you would probably still be in pain."

Lyra answered, "The pain is not unbearable. Sometimes it's a little hard to push aside, but I think the fact that we are in a stressful situation helps make it easier to ignore. It isn't overwhelming, thankfully." She added the last when she saw Hazel's shoulders stiffen.

"As far as I know, we haven't heard anything from Pack L in over a week; considering how hard they were pushing you and the guys, you would think they would do something. I can't help but wonder if they're laying low because of those two buildings we searched. But considering they didn't find anything, it makes me wonder what would make those buildings important enough to warrant them no longer going after you guys. It also makes me wonder whether this was all a test to see if we would rise to the occasion and search those two buildings or if we would rollover, so to speak, and do nothing. It just seems weird to me that now that they know you have that drug or whatever it is in your system, they back off. Maybe I'm thinking too much on this."

It seemed as if Hazel had been thinking about this for a while but simply had no one to talk to, and now that Lyra was awake and in her car, she wanted to get all of it out before she lost the opportunity.

Lyra tried to think of something reassuring to say but nothing came to her. "All I can think of is that they want to see what we'll do now that the drug is in my system. Or they're moving to the next phase of their plan. Or they're trying to plan accordingly now they know we're willing to search their buildings in order to find information."

They both sat there thinking as Hazel drove toward the compound. It did seem strange to Lyra that they hadn't heard anything from the scientists since she was out and now that Hazel was bringing it up she was curious as to why that was. Was it possible that they knew she was out of commission? She didn't like the thought. If they knew she was out of commission, or if they had planned on her death, they were playing on a more dangerous playing field than she initially thought. It actually hadn't occurred to her that maybe the drugs were meant to kill her, but then again maybe they weren't; maybe it was simply a test to see how her system would react to them. It wouldn't be the first time they were used as human guinea pigs.

"Do you really think this is going to work? That having the family take us in will actually help our chances? I know that they have a lot of money and crazy connections but aren't you worried about exposure? Yes, the family can hold their own, but if these scientists happen to grab a born werewolf on its own and bring it in to test the differences, that opens up a whole new realm of possibility and danger."

Luckily, Lyra had already thought about this. "We just have to be careful. As long as we give them no reason to think that born werewolves exist, then we shouldn't be in danger of them discovering us. Born werewolves try to be pretty careful anyway, so I don't think much will change."

Hazel seemed to be marginally comforted by that but did not say anything else. Which was fine with Lyra; she wasn't entirely sure she could have kept up a full conversation with how nervous she was. When she, Graham, Taylor, and Dylan talked about it, they weren't entirely sure there was a backup plan if the family turned down the made wolves. While she was out, there had not been much headway in discovering any new information regarding the lab assistants or the scientists behind them. The alphas had people chasing down several leads, but so far they had only tracked down the places of work of the nine lab assistants. Graham's alpha told him four worked at the same laboratory and they were looking into that lab as the most promising lead. Lyra was pretty sure Hazel did not know any of that but she wasn't about to tell her. Lyra did not think it would help her friend any to know that not much progress had been made.

"I think I can safely say that I'm more nervous this time to be here than I was the other two times I have been on the compound combined," Hazel commented, as the huge gates to the property came into view.

Lyra could admit, at least to herself, the property looked intimidating, but then it was supposed to. The great iron gate had all sorts of sensors on and around it to prevent people from breaking in. Not to mention the wall was covered with ivy and other vines, giving it not only a neglected and more posing image, but making it harder for someone to scale the wall, as the vines were so thick it wasn't a simple matter of reaching through them to get to something solid. It also didn't help that the compound was huge; there was a wooded area in the back so that people could run in wolf form freely without worrying about passing hunters. She remembered someone saying once that the property was more than one hundred acres, but she didn't know if that was true or not. There were also individual houses, varying in size depending on the importance of the inhabitants, where individual families lived. Or in some cases just one person and in others groups of single people. All in all there were about seventy people that lived on the compound full-time and room for more should that be needed. Lyra heard stories when she was younger that when the property was bought generations ago, the idea was that the entire pack could live in one community, making it harder for outsiders to catch them. Modern amenities made the wall necessary and it also made it necessary for the pack to begin living on the other side of that wall in the community at large.

As they reached the gate, Lyra knew there were half a dozen cameras trained on not only their car but the vehicle behind them that she knew held Jack, Seth, and Justin. She had no doubt that the majority, if not the rest of her pack, followed behind in some order. Taylor had either taken up the rear position or taken a back way around the main roads and beat them there. Lyra hadn't wanted to chance any of the family's wrath so she hadn't taken Hazel on the shortcut when giving directions. She waved at the cameras before rolling down her window, knowing that there were speakers on either side of the car so that the people at the gate would be able to see and hear anyone in the car.

"I am vouching for my vehicle as well as the one behind me, not that you should need it because as part of this meeting, security had me send photos of everyone in my pack this morning." Once she finished speaking she watched the gate. A moment later they heard a clicking noise as all the locks disengaged and it began to open. Her heart raced faster as the gate opened wider and wider.

This could either end in their favor or they'd crash and burn. All Lyra could do was hope that she wasn't just getting them into deeper trouble than they already were in.

Chapter 10

Jack didn't know what to think as he, Seth, and Justin rolled up to a huge gated property in Jack's SUV. Up until that point there had been a general discussion about what they thought they should expect from the so-called family meeting that Lyra and her cousin were making them go to. As soon as they followed Hazel's Prius onto a private drive conversation stopped. It wasn't as much the fact that the house was on a private drive. Jack had half expected such a thing based on how secretive Lyra's family was and based on what secret it was they had to keep. Intellectually, he knew they couldn't be headed to a cookie-cutter home in an overpriced development, but the sheer magnitude of the property was still intimidating.

The drive was lined with old trees. Jack had never been one to be able to identify one tree from the other. From how large these trees were they had clearly been here a while. They weren't spread out either; each tree seemed as close as it could get without disrupting the root system of the trees on either side of it. It gave a sense of an intimidating privacy to the property beyond, almost as if the trees themselves were in on something that the property owners were trying to hide, which Jack supposed was true. The drive up was at least a quarter of a mile, though Jack hadn't been paying that close attention. Then the roadway opened slightly to reveal smaller, less driven on dirt paths circling on both the left and right side of a well-trimmed hedge that had to be at least seven feet tall. Directly in front of them were huge iron gates that appeared to be something you would see from Victorian era movies, though they had to be newer than that since they were big enough for two cars to drive through side-by-side. Just beyond the fence Jack could see a hill and on it was a huge manor house. The monstrous building would have been more at home in Europe than the West Coast of the United States. It looked as if it stood there more than a few decades. It clearly stretched on beyond what they could see from the car. The only noise was Seth cursing as he looked out the front windshield from the seat beside Jack.

Their cars stopped behind Hazel's and as they watched, Lyra's hand reached out and poked some button on the tiny box to the right of the gates. Whatever she said must've been acceptable because the large metal gates creaked slowly open, allowing the train of pack F's cars to drive through.

"Does anyone else feel a sense of foreboding like you would find in a horror movie? Something about those gates reminds me of teeth," Justin asked warily from the backseat.

Seth grunted an agreement but beyond that there wasn't much of a response. Jack was too busy watching the manor house that was getting bigger the closer they got to it. Once they were through the gate, Jack could see that the roadway they were coming in on was finally paved and split in two directions in a large circle leading up to the front door. As they headed up the slight incline, Jack glanced in his rearview mirror to see that the two other cars holding his pack mates were still behind them.

When he looked forward he could see that there were already rows of cars almost using the circle as double lanes of parking. But he was surprised when Hazel pulled off to the side at least six car links from the next car forward. Not questioning it, but knowing he could ask once they were all out of the cars, Jack pulled behind her and the rest of the pack vehicles followed suit.

By the time he got out of the car, Lyra was already standing next to his car's engine, and Hazel was walking towards them. There was a minute or two of silence as the rest of the pack came to stand at the front end of Jack's car. Jack had wanted to ask why they were parked so far away, but when he saw the solemn and tense way Lyra was carrying herself he felt he didn't really need to know that badly. He couldn't remember the last time he'd seen her this solemn and serious. Part of him worried being brought back from the dead might've affected what was fundamentally Lyra. Jack pushed the thought aside, knowing that right now it wouldn't be helpful. In fact, it would deter him from thinking about and experiencing everything in the present and that was what he and his pack needed him to be doing.

When the entire pack was standing there Syrus let out a sigh. "I assume there's a reason we're parked so far away from the front door?"

Lyra didn't look at him, didn't even turn her head. She just stared beyond the nearest car in front of Hazel. "Because wolves have good hearing. Not to mention you never know who might be skulking about."

It was said with such deadpan that Jack felt his attention tugged to where Lyra was staring and sure enough in the bushes to the right of the car he could see two sets of glowing eyes. Clearly the family wasn't so sure about the made werewolves after all, because they had scouts hiding out even before the made wolves reached the building. Jack felt himself frown. This was not how he wanted this partnership to begin. If the family was already suspicious that probably was not a good sign.

Two giant wolves burst forward from the bushes where the scts of eyes had been and ran straight for Lyra. Jack felt several of the nearby pack mates tense with the movement but Jack could see the wolves' expressions and knew they meant her no harm. Within a second or two they were standing in front of her, waggling like her dogs would upon seeing her. Both were jumping up so their forepaws were in the air and they stood like they would in human form. Before she even spoke, Jack knew who the two identical wolves were in front of them simply by Lyra's reaction. She gave a sad smile and knelt down so she could rest both of their heads on each of her shoulders and pulled her arms around to circle them, giving them each a hug.

"I've missed you two as well."

There was a curse from Seth over Jack's shoulder. "Are you telling me those two mammoths are her brothers?"

"Looks like," Jack replied.

After a second Lyra stood back up, putting her hands on her hips as she looked sternly at the two wolves. "The two of you need to get going. If Mom or Dad or one of our uncles catches you out here you are going to be in for a world of hurt. You know you're both too young to be attending family meetings like this, so go on back to the house." When they didn't move immediately, Lyra made a shooing motion with her hands. "Get," she ordered, louder.

There was a beat when both of them looked at her before turning and bolting in the opposite direction beyond the manor. Jack could see Lyra's shoulders relax marginally; seeing her little brothers seemed to dissuade some of her stress. He watched as she took a deep breath and squared her shoulders.

"All right, everybody. Let's get this over with," she said, without even looking over her shoulder. She waited a beat before starting up the driveway.

Jack looked over his shoulder and exchanged glances with Seth, who simply shrugged. Part of him was relieved to know that no one else knew exactly what to expect from the next couple hours. When they reached the door Jack found it interesting that Lyra's initial response was to go straight for the handle to open it. Then she hesitated and stopped herself before moving her arm farther up so that she could grab the knocker at eye level and rap against the door three times. Jack itched to look at Seth again but refrained just in case someone was watching; the last thing he wanted was people thinking he was relying on the other man. He needed them to see him as a strong alpha. As soon as that thought crossed his mind he felt bad that it was Seth he was looking to for help and not Ryan. Though the man was a strong second, Jack had simply gotten used to looking to Seth instead of Ryan over the last month or so. Since Lyra had been out Ryan hadn't been the same second he had been before. Now that Lyra was up and about again Ryan was closer to being his former self, but he wasn't quite there yet. All those thoughts were cleared from his mind as the giant wood doors in front of them began to open. At first Jack thought both of the double doors would open but after a second only one was clearly moving. There must've been some sort of formality in place Jack wasn't aware of because as the door opened, Jack got a quick glimpse of a hallway lit with candles before a man who was about six and a half feet tall blocked the doorway and looked solemnly down at them.

"I, Lyra, from the house of the Beta along with Pack F of the Pacific Northwest University packs, whom I vouch for, are seeking an audience with the leader of the family at this meeting."

Her words were so formal and seemed so practiced Jack wondered if the other six wolves bringing packs with them tonight said the exact same thing to the doorman. Clearly it was not the first time he heard it because the doorman gave one single nod before opening the door wider and moving out of the way so they could all walk by. Jack chanced a look over his shoulder and could see Mathew and his pack a minute or so behind them and he found himself wondering whether the doorman would leave the door open for them or shut it and make Dylan go through the same routine Lyra had.

As he stepped inside Jack saw a grand entry. Despite the fact there was clearly modern electricity, it was lit solely with candles. This made it hard to make out many of the fixtures in the room, not that there were many. There was a grand chandelier above their heads that held what had to have been more than five dozen candles. There were also two six-foot candelabras, one on each side of the door as well as one on each side of the double doors that stood about ten feet in front of them. These inner double doors looked almost identical to the front doors, but there wasn't enough light for Jack to know for sure. There was also a hallway on each side of the double doors, most likely leading to the back of the manor. The doorman shut the door behind them, the old wood creaking as it slid into place. Then he moved to the front of the group before grabbing the handle to the left of the two doors in front of them and opening it, making a sweeping gesture with his hand to infer that they should walk inside.

Though Jack wasn't sure inside was the right word; the door led out to a huge courtyard, the likes of which Jack had never seen before. It was as if the whole middle of the house didn't exist and instead was simply a façade around this outdoor space. As they walked through the doors Jack looked up and saw there was a rim that circled ten feet out from the wall, all the way around, creating an overhang. Jack looked in front of them from where he had taken up his position, half a step behind Lyra. In front of them was a dais with three chairs. The right one was perhaps half a step off the ground, the left a full step and the one in the middle a step higher than that.

Each of the giant chairs was occupied by men who bore enough similarities that Jack guessed they were Lyra's father and uncles. Sure enough, as they stepped closer, he recognized the man on the left as Lyra's father. Behind each of the men stood two others, clearly guards; they stood in a basic bodyguard pose, with their arms clasped behind their backs, scanning the room at large. There was no other furniture in the room, at least not that Jack could see. There were no lights, no electricity, and no fire. The only light coming in was from the moon, which meant Jack could not see a great deal of what was under the overhang. They were only lucky it was a cloudless night so there was enough light that Jack could get an okay look at the faces closest to them. He tried to be less than obvious as he scanned the crowd of people that almost circled around them as they moved to the very middle of the space. He couldn't count, but Jack was pretty sure there were at least fifty people standing, sitting, or in wolf form watching them. He was somewhat relieved that when they stopped walking, he found himself almost standing shoulder to shoulder with Bishop. He hadn't been paying enough attention to the center of the room to have seen Bishop's pack. Jack chastised himself a little for not noticing and for being so awestruck at the space they were in. Then he reminded himself that was probably the point of the space anyway.

When he glanced over Bishop gave Jack a brief half nod and Jack returned the gesture before looking past him. Beyond the other man's entire pack he could see Graham and Rachel in front of their pack on the other side. Part of him wanted to confer with the other alphas, to check in to see what they thought of the predicament they found themselves in, but he knew better. Anything he said in that courtyard would be heard by at least half of the werewolves in it and for all he knew their hearing was better than the man-made werewolves and all of them in the room would hear it. Though there were people around them talking, they were doing it quietly enough that all Jack was hearing were snippets of murmurs, not actual words. It made him uncomfortable to be in the center of the room, knowing that everyone in that room was talking about him, looking at him and the other alphas and their packs. He knew he needed to stand his ground, to show he was a strong enough alpha, and that no one should mess with his pack. It was easier said than done, but Jack knew he had to do it.

He had no idea how much time passed but eventually all seven packs stood in the middle of the room, surrounded by werewolves they had not known existed a week earlier. Part of him found the whole thing to be rather melodramatic. Under normal circumstances he may have tried to crack a joke or laugh to himself, but when he considered just how dire the situation actually was, suddenly the fact that it was melodramatic didn't really seem as important or funny. The man on the middle dais sat quietly, contemplating the seven groups in front of him for several minutes. The people around them didn't seem antsy or confused by this action so Jack assumed this sort of thing happened regularly. To him it seemed like a bit of a power trip, but he wasn't really in a place to make a comment as they were, after all, here to ask for help. Patience wasn't necessarily Jack's strong suit, though, and after a few more minutes he found himself relieved when the other man finally spoke.

"Thank you, everyone, for coming today. I know this was indeed short notice and several of you have not had the chance to update yourselves with the current situation," Lyra's uncle started, as he looked out around him at all the people in the room, pointedly not looking at the seven packs in front of him. It was an interesting move and Jack assumed it was a way of letting everybody know which group he cared more about. Which Jack could understand. After all, as the head of the family, Lyra's uncle needed to appear as if the family's safety was his priority and not some young dumb kids who happened to be standing in front of him, even if among them was his son and his niece and some of their childhood friends.

When no one responded in any way he nodded his head and turned his attention towards the people directly in front of him. "Now, I am going to give up the floor to my niece and my youngest son, as I believe they have something that should be brought to the attention of this family." He made a gesture with his hand, sweeping it out before him as if providing his family the opportunity to step forward.

Clearly this was a normal gesture because both Graham and Lyra stepped forward almost in unison; they took three distinct steps towards the dais and towards each other, as if trying to draw the attention away from their own packs.

Both of them bowed slightly to Graham's father before Graham spoke.

"Thank you, Father, head of this family. I appreciate you, as well as everyone else here." He pivoted in a semi-circle so that he could encompass the whole room. "For your time and patience in this matter. As many of you know, a scientist snuck on to some college campuses and made himself some scientific werewolves. He made with science something very close to what nature made eons before now. We don't know if he encountered several of us and that is where this idea came from or whether it is pure dumb luck. Regardless, the made wolves are here now; that is who we are bringing before you. The government set up a program to help all of us, however, it fell apart. Recently the old scientist's lab assistants, as well as some scientists who we have yet to meet, have been paying extra attention to my cousin, five others who are born werewolves, and myself. We do not know whether they realize what we actually are or if it is just coincidence and they think we simply are stronger than the others. Either way, they have been putting a close eye on us and have tried to abduct my cousin, the little Luna, on several occasions."

At first, it seemed like a dramatic pause but then Jack's ears picked up the murmuring in the room at large; clearly not all of the werewolves, the born werewolves, had been privy to the whole story about what was happening outside of the compound.

"They have, as I'm sure many of you have heard, drugged our little Luna and our Luna has been able to decipher a type of suppressant to help stop the symptoms of the drug itself. This is a drug she had never seen before and the suppressant that she was able to come up with must be administered once every third day if Lyra is to stay relatively healthy until we can find the antidote for what was given to her. This type of advancement is not something that the made werewolves and their groups can handle. It is simply too big and too vast and too devious and too out-funded for what we are capable of doing. Because of this we are coming to all of you, asking for sanctuary for the made wolves."

There was more murmuring, except this time it was louder and there were more voices. Jack couldn't quite make out the words; the family clearly was not fond of that idea.

"We wish the manmade wolves to become members of the family, as they are for all intents and purposes the same as we are. If they had been born werewolves and had these capabilities they would already be part of our family, so it seems unfair of us to turn them away now. If that is not possible, we at least wish them to have sanctuary here, and to be able to use our resources to help solve the problem that is before us. We need the family's help and the best way to do that is for the family and the packs to collaborate together. Keep in mind that should you turn down this request, any blood shed from here on out is innocent blood and it is on your hands." He looked directly at his father and uncles when he said the last. Several of the science-made werewolves shifted their feet back and forth, clearly nervous about the situation at large and Graham's last words.

A woman Jack couldn't really see stepped out of the dark on his left side almost parallel with the dais. "Daughter dearest, I raised you to be more convincing than this. To face those among us who are affected by these attacks your cousin speaks of."

Once she had started speaking Jack recognized her as Lyra's mother. It'd been a while since he'd seen the woman, so he wasn't surprised it took him so long to recognize her. At the same time, part of him felt bad for not picking it up sooner. Her arms were folded across her chest and her eyes poured directly into her daughter's.

Lyra inclined her head and turned slightly, so that her body language opened to the packs, but in doing so she was turning her back to the section of the family in the shadows to her left; it was a very calculated move. Jack watched as Graham squared his shoulders, facing head-on so that he could see the directions his cousin couldn't.

"Will the five of you please step forward?"

Before she had even finished speaking, the five other wolves the scientists had been interested in began to weave their way from different parts of their tightknit man-made werewolf group and fanned out on either side of Graham and Lyra. There was more murmuring as people began to recognize which of their young were being affected by this situation.

When they had all lined up, Lyra pivoted again to face her uncles and father; when she spoke her voice was as even as a knife blade. "If you cannot bring yourselves to welcome the manmade wolves into the fold for whatever reason, look at it this way. These scientists have discovered us. They've discovered the natural born weres. They might not have figured out exactly what we are yet, but it's only a matter of time if they keep coming after us like this because they do know that we are stronger and faster and all-around better than most of the manmade wolves and they are going to want to know why. They have already made it known that they will take whatever means necessary, whether that means abduction or trickery, to get us to come in so that they can perform tests on us. If you will not do this thing for the manmade wolves, who so desperately need your help, do it for us, for the family, and for yourselves. With the way they're going it is only a matter of time before they discover the rest of us, and I'm pretty sure that I can speak for the entire room when I say the last thing we want is scientists getting into family business and discovering exactly what we are and what we can do. Now I know that the go-to is to destroy any threat to us, but frankly we don't know who the head of the serpent is yet, which is why we're asking for your protection. Because whether you, the family, like it or not, if these scientists use our pack mates against us we will come running to help them even though we know they are bait."

There was silence in the large space. Jack was surprised. For whatever reason he expected murmuring to break out or someone to at least be snippy. A man who was maybe between five to ten years older than most of the manmade weres stepped forward from where he stood to the left of the dais before them.

The man had sandy-blond hair cut close to his head, he was tall, maybe somewhere just over six foot three and had a sneer on his face. "I, for one, am not allowing useless humans into our family, especially when they come bearing problems with them. I see no need to borrow problems when we already have our own. We can easily pluck our own from amongst this group and keep them away from the others and let the scientists do whatever it is they're looking for. It may sound harsh but what do you think the other families will say when they hear we've taken on humans?"

This time there was a buzz and Jack couldn't tell whether it was because people agreed with what the man had said or not. Neither Graham nor Lyra spoke that time, which surprised Jack. He actually expected them to jump in and say something. There was clearly some dynamic he wasn't aware of at play.

Then a man with similar hair and face but taller with a larger build snorted and folded his arms from where he stood just a step away from the middle chair that held Graham's father. "That is quite enough, Franklin. You have to look at this in the big picture sense, which is not your strong suit." The man looked at Franklin with a bit of disdain. "If they have gotten so advanced that they can create their own werewolves, clearly they are not that far from discovering us. It is in our best interest to nip this in the bud and the best way to do that is by helping these manmade wolves with the scientists that are out to discover what makes them tick. The last thing we need is the scientists perfecting this madness and creating an army of werewolves. We all need someone to put a stop to that and I think this is the best way to do it. Not to mention that this is some of our own asking for our help. I, for one, back my brother and my cousin in their request."

There was more murmuring, only louder now, before the woman who spoke earlier and two other women, one of which Jack recognized as Luna, stepped forward. The woman Jack didn't know seemed to speak for the whole group. "My sisters and I fully back our niece's decision and commend her loyalty to these people in need."

The buzzing went up in volume before another man around their parents' age and a woman holding his hand stepped forward from the opposite end of the dais. "We back our son in his decision and we also wish to help these young people who are clearly without guidance."

The bulkier of the two men standing behind Lyra's uncle's chair took a step forward. "I, as well, agree with Dylan and Lyra's families and support my son in this endeavor. I also agree with Shane that helping these young people might just be in our best interest." He then went back toward where he was standing before, arms behind his back.

It sort of avalanched from there, bits and pieces of the group came forward from the dark, spouting some kind of connection to the seven weres that brought them all there and after a while the connections grew thinner, but people still backed the idea. It was becoming clear that the idea Graham's father was hoping for worked. People wanted to help the helpless whether they were humans or werewolves.

When things finally died down the bodyguard standing behind Lyra's younger uncle stepped to the side, which seemed to be enough to get the room's attention. "My nephew and I wish to support this decision, especially on behalf of his older brother who is in the group before us. We are both aware that in order to take such a large group into our family they will require sponsorship and I'm sure I not only speak for my nephew but for all of us who voiced today that we are more than willing to take on the sponsorship role in the accountability needed to bring these young people into the family." As he stepped back there was more murmuring.

The man known as Franklin hadn't said much since the crowd seemed to be against him, but he took this opportunity to sneer again. "Oh really, Donovan? Which one of these humans do you claim is your nephew?"

The bigger man glared down at Franklin. There was clearly some sort of power struggle there, as instead of outright challenging him he simply gave a dismissive look at the younger man before looking back to the packs in front of him. "My older nephew is Ryan of Pack F. Due to his father's human nature my nephew was born a halfling and not a full werewolf and though a bit of a curse, this science experiment was somewhat of a blessing in disguise in that it made him into the werewolf nature didn't seem to let him be."

Jack felt his body run cold. His brain stopped processing for a second and clearly he was not the only one because he watched in slow motion as Lyra turned around to look at them, since Ryan was standing right next to Jack. Her eyes were round as saucers, and her mouth was slightly parted. None of the family would've seen her expression; it was fairly obvious that this caught her by surprise. When Jack could finally bring himself to look at his second, the other man was giving the stoic expression he was known for. Jack knew this was not the time or the place to bring it up, but he so desperately wanted to shake the other man and ask why he was keeping such secrets, especially since everything was now out in the open. Jack struggled to keep his face blank. He wasn't sure how well he succeeded, only that he had to be doing a better job than Lyra. She finally blinked multiple times before shaking her head and turning back around. As she turned back, Graham spoke.

"As you can see, Father and councilmembers, the will of the family is to help us, the victims of Berman's experiment, so I plead with you on our behalf to call a vote and decide whether you will indeed help us or turn us out towards the enemy that hunts us."

That statement seemed a little dramatic to Jack, but this wasn't his world. For all he knew, dramatics were a regular part of these meetings. Part of him wanted to speak his piece and try to convince these men and women that helping them was in everybody's best interest, but most of him realized it was not going to be in anyone's best interest for him to speak. His opinion was not going to hold water with this audience, as he was basically an outsider and not somebody who held any authority.

"I call for a vote," declared the dark blond next to Graham's father, whom Jack was pretty sure was Graham's oldest brother from the way he'd chastised Franklin when no one else did. Jack vaguely remembered somebody mentioning Franklin was the name of one of Graham's brothers.

"I vote in favor of helping these packs, for giving them asylum and a joint partnership. To alleviate worry some might have, I suggest a probationary period. We will give them six months as part of our family and if it doesn't work we can always walk away then. All in favor say 'aye'."

Lyra's father and younger uncle both voiced their agreement, as did a number of other voices in the crowd, but not as many as Jack would have hoped. Once there was a pause, Graham's father spoke, "All opposed?"

Jack was not the least bit surprised when Franklin jumped in with his opposition. He was then followed by several voices, though not as many as before.

Graham's father waited, as if making sure the silence was final before speaking.

"I am in favor of helping these people, as it seems is most of the council, therefore the ayes have it. These seven groups will be on a six-month probationary period and hopefully we will solve this little problem in that amount of time. That way if this doesn't work out we will at least not have to worry about their safety."

"Now, if you will all be so kind, we have further family business to attend to and probationary members are not privy to all of the family business." The last was said with a little bit of a bite, though Jack didn't know why. The seven weres in front of him seemed to breathe a sigh of relief in unison before they all turned and began walking out of the hall, ushering the rest of the manmade weres as they went.

No one in their large groups spoke as they headed out the main doors and took their separate ways on the driveway towards the various cars. It was as if there was a weight in the air around them that none of them were sure how to handle. No one, Jack was positive, knew exactly how they were going to be able to handle this new situation or what it was going to entail and what it would mean to them. He couldn't help the worry that crept into his mind: had they really done what was best for them? Or was this just giving them a more dangerous world to live in? Jack's thought process was interrupted when they reached their section of cars and Lyra turned towards the rest of the pack before shoving Ryan hard enough for him to take a step back.

The hurt and anger was obvious on her face. "You were family, Ryan. *Family*. You never told us! All this time your brother was one of the young chosen ones and you never said anything. We would have taken you in is one as our own. You didn't need to live in solitude."

Jack wasn't entirely sure he understood what Lyra just said, but it was clear Ryan did from the bitterness on the other man's face.

"Halfling, Lyra. I'm well aware what your kind thinks of halflings." It was said with so much disgust Jack was actually surprised. He'd never heard anything like that from Ryan before.

Lyra shoved him again, more angrily this time, but Ryan was ready for it and braced so his body didn't do much more than sway.

"You were still family and after all this Berman nonsense we would've taken you in. We would've taken you as you were before, but you had no excuse after and you knew. You knew all about us and didn't say a thing. Why? Why would you choose to be so alone?"

Ryan scoffed before looking her straight in the eyes. "Because we're matched, Lyra, so what good would it do?"

Jack had no idea what Ryan just said but clearly it was some kind of bombshell from his angry expression and Lyra's complete and utter shock. A shock that was mirrored in Hazel's face behind Lyra.

Lyra sputtered for several seconds, as if trying to start a sentence but was unable to, before finally she glared at Ryan and spun on her heels and bee-lined straight for Hazel's car, ripping the door open and slamming it shut behind her. Hazel, on the other hand, gave Ryan a sad look before moving in a much more sedated pace. Then Ryan skulked his way to Syrus' SUV and tugged the door open, a little harder than necessary. Syrus and Sadie exchanged glances before following up to the car and soon both vehicles had left.

The rest of the pack all exchanged confused looks before the other car's occupants made their way to Kelly's vehicle. Soon it was simply Justin, Seth, and Jack standing next to Jack's SUV.

"Did that make any sense to anyone?" Seth asked from where he stood on Jack's right.

"I have no idea," responded Justin, "but I do know that whatever it was just made life a little more difficult and is probably going to cause some drama. You know, the things we really need right now."

Seth snorted but didn't say anything else.

The three of them turned towards the car and headed out in silence. Jack agreed with Justin; this sort of complication, whatever it was, was not what they needed right now. The only thing Jack was sure of was Justin was right—it was going to cause drama.

Chapter 11

Hazel could not remember the last time she had seen Lyra this drunk. It was no small feat considering the werewolf metabolism went through alcohol pretty quickly. But here they sat in Lyra's living room with three decent-sized whiskey bottles, two of which were empty, sitting in front of them. The dogs lay across the room, each on their own dog bed. It was as if even the dogs knew to give Lyra a wide birth. Hazel was buzzed, she was pretty sure she would end up spending the night. Lyra was a full on angry drunk. Not that Hazel could blame her; Ryan dropped a bombshell on all of them. Not only was he born with a werewolf parent he hadn't told anybody about, on top of that he said, in front of everyone, that he and Lyra were matched.

Hazel wasn't sure at first what that meant. Then somewhere around the start of the second bottle of whiskey Lyra spurted out what the words meant. Apparently in the families of natural born werewolves a male knew when he found his mate because her scent would make him feel at home. It would make him feel subdued and give him a level of contentment he would never have known before.

Apparently it was so obvious a reaction there was never any doubt it was happening. Those two individuals were called 'matched' and Ryan just admitted in front of all of their pack that he and Lyra were meant to be together. All this time they had known each other, he had known the truth of the situation and he kept it from Lyra. Hazel could totally understand why her best friend would be livid. At first she thought the level of agitation was going to reach a point where she would have to step in before Lyra did something stupid but eventually Lyra seemed to calm herself down, to a certain extent. Now she was still agitated but it was a more benign anger.

Taylor had been with them in the beginning and even taken two shots with them. But then he heard the word 'matched' and it looked as if he would become physically ill. He had then turned to Hazel and excused himself. Saying that he would sit in his car and he would be there until she left so that they could have time to talk, and she would either need to just let him know when she was leaving or one of them could call him on Lyra's phone if they were going to bed. That had been Hazel's first inkling that matched was a bigger deal than they needed right now.

Lyra poured what would've been the equivalent of three shots for normal person into her glass before downing it. She then eyed what was left of the last bottle warily, as if estimating whether they even had enough. When they were in college Hazel would've thought this was absurd, but now she knew better.

"This just complicates everything," Lyra exclaimed, reaching out to the now empty bag of chips, growling in frustration, before getting up to grab more. "He didn't seem remotely interested, just another nice guy. Then I get Kipling's number, text back and forth some, I mean we were all set to go on a date before I knocked myself out of commission. Ridiculous. Now he just ruins everything with that proclamation."

Gretchen S. B.

Hazel knew about the texting Kipling, Lyra mentioned it to her as something she was more than passively interested in. Considering he was the first born were Lyra had ever been interested in Hazel figured it was going to be something serious. She could see Lyra's frustration because it would be weird to date someone else if she and Ryan were truly meant to be. It would be a struggle to date someone else, no matter the level of interest, knowing that information.

"You can't just un-hear that. It's not like I could be like, 'oh, I misunderstood you'. This pretty much changes my whole life." Lyra's voice was a tad bit louder this time and her gestures larger before grabbing the bottle and pouring more whiskey into her glass.

Hazel pushed her glass away; she really did not feel like consuming any more alcohol today and considering this was the last bottle of whiskey Lyra had, she wasn't too concerned about getting sick, although she would probably have a hefty hangover in the morning.

"You could try dating Ryan?" Hazel commented hesitantly; she knew odds were Lyra was going to have a strong reaction to that.

She wasn't disappointed when Lyra scrunched up her face. "What?! No! First off, he's shown no finesse or interest and then he goes and does that word vomit in front of everyone. Not telling me he's a halfling, I mean, really okay, yes to be honest, halflings are not always treated well in the werewolf world. It's really kind of crummy and terrible and I could kinda get that. But I am not the type of person that's going to treat halflings badly.

He could've told me at any point. There was no worry about divulging family secrets because I already know. Then he just blurts out in front of everyone that we're matched. Let's be honest, even if not everyone knows what that word means you pretty much figure it out; it's a pretty obvious word." She downed the contents of her glass again.

Hazel sighed. "On the bright side, you got all of us into the family, at least on probation. So that is something."

Instead of filling her glass another time Lyra swirled the whiskey bottle and watched liquid splash against the sides of the container. "Yeah, hopefully that was doing the right thing. I am relieved. Bare minimum, it at least gives us extra eyes and ears on this whole thing. You have to wonder if Ryan doesn't know any better. Maybe it is a complication because of the whole science-made werewolf thing. What if he's mistaken about us being matched?"

It sounded like Lyra was reaching to Hazel; she couldn't imagine Ryan, who was fairly levelheaded, jumping to a conclusion like that but at the same time it could've been a side effect of the experiment. She dismissed that thought; Ryan was smart, he would know the difference. Ultimately, it just seemed like Lyra was trying to think her way out of a situation that made her uncomfortable.

Before she could say anything, Lyra's phone started ringing. Lyra let out a groan before swinging herself around towards where the noise was coming from, and then she reached up, since they were sitting on the floor, onto the couch where she had set down her phone at some point. When she looked at the screen, she cursed.

"It's Ryan's uncle, apparently. I only have his number for emergencies. I wasn't aware he had mine." Then she tapped the screen and put it to her ear. "Hello, this is Lyra."

She didn't make a sound after that, so apparently Ryan's uncle had a lot to say. The quiet lasted several minutes before Lyra took a breather and began nodding. "Sure, let me give you Jack's number. You should probably start with him." There was a long pause before she continued, "I get that but this is just the way things are run. Do you want the number or not?" There was enough bite in Lyra's voice to make Hazel curious before she finally rattled off Jack's number and hung up.

"Dare I ask?"

Though Lyra was a bit miffed she wasn't truly angry, so Hazel wasn't too worried.

"Someone brought it up to the council that if we are to be involved in family politics then you should all be tested and trained. We can't afford other families or betas thinking we are weak or that you are easy targets. So the guard wants to set up trainings with each pack."

Hazel nodded, now she knew why Lyra was irritated. "So you sent him along to Jack because as alpha it would be his job to handle it."

Her friend gritted her teeth. "Yes."

Knowing it was best to keep her mouth shut, Hazel bit back her smile. Lyra didn't like deferring to anyone when it came to something that would affect her own life, especially Jack. But both Hazel and her best friend knew it was best to maintain appearances that the pack had a hierarchy until they knew exactly where they stood with the family. From all the stories she'd heard over the years, Hazel knew that there were people in Lyra's family that would take advantage and be on the lookout for any holes in the pack social structure. She knew her friend well enough to know just because Lyra thought it necessary didn't mean she was going to like any bit of having to kowtow to Jack, even if it was only for appearances.

"We should get to sleep," stated the now surly Lyra. "If we're going to be training and such, on top of our regular jobs then we need as much sleep as we can afford to get. I am definitely not looking forward to any of this."

Hazel pushed herself to her feet and held out her arms to help Lyra do the same. "Would you rather still be in that coma?"

Lyra grunted as she got up, "No, but that's because mainly it seems nothing got done while I was out."

Hazel shook her head as she followed her friend down the hallway; at least they had backup now, even if that backup was just shy of openly hostile and suspicious of them. Hazel knew eventually things would work out okay, they had to, she couldn't accept that life would continue to be this never-ending trial and she wasn't sure she could stand being so close to losing Lyra again.

Chapter 12

Jack was at a loss; all these new politics and new information and the new world that had opened up in front of him were giving him a migraine. He still wasn't one hundred percent sold that Lyra and Graham's family could help them. To him it just seemed like they were getting into bed with a group that was more dangerous than the situation they were already in. Even though he was mad at her, he trusted Lyra to have the pack's best interest at heart. Despite her many faults and the trouble she got into regularly, at least he knew at heart she was doing her best to look out for their pack.

Scrubbing at his face, Jack let out a heavy sigh before turning and looking at Seth, who sat across from him on his couch, sipping a beer. "So, what are your thoughts? Not including whatever the hell happened with Ryan after the meeting. I have no idea what that was but I get the feeling it's going to be something that is just going to complicate the situation more than we need."

His friend snorted, taking a long swig of his beer before putting the bottle down on Jack's coffee table. "Yeah, that was weird. From Lyra's reaction it's definitely a big deal, whatever it is. I have a sneaking suspicion it has something to do with their love life. Which I will not spend too much time thinking about because it's only gonna want to make me punch him in the face. I'll just skip past putting further thought into that situation. As for these born werewolves, I have no idea what to think. They are clearly more dangerous, ruthless, and more suspicious than we are. Which could be good or bad. I don't like the idea of us trusting these people we don't know with our safety in the current situation we're in but I have to agree that we don't really have much choice in the matter. With all due respect, your council doesn't really have the know-how to get anything done."

Jack nodded; part of him wanted to disagree, to say that the idea of an alliance was good for them and helpful but Seth was right. While it was nice to have a consensus and have people make decisions together for the greater good, they were on the same boat when it came to knowing about being a werewolf. Though Mathew had connections, they didn't come in as handy as all of them would like.

Before he could say anything else Jack's phone started to ring from where it laid next to his water glass on the table. Jack and Seth exchanged looks; usually no one would be calling this late unless it was an emergency. Jack picked up his phone and saw a number he didn't recognize; spikes of worry-laced adrenaline raced through his system as all sorts of ideas ran through his head on who was going to be on the other side of the phone.

Sliding his hand across the screen, Jack answered, "Hello, this is Jack."

There was a split second of silence before a deep rumbling voice answered him.

"My name is Tucker, I am the captain of the guard for the Gamma family, though more colloquially I'm Ryan's uncle, one of them that is. I'm calling on behalf of the council; I received your number from Lyra, as she told me I would need to go through you for matters such as these. The council decided they do not wish the addition of you made wolves to be a weakness for the family. It has been decided that we will test all of you and if we find you lacking, we will train you on how to fight in our world, that way should another family or some beta wolves decide to attack, you will not be our weakest link. The last thing we need is having adding you to cause us more problems than we already have. So I'm calling you to schedule a testing session with you and your pack and to get contact information for the other alphas so that I may schedule with them as well."

Jack didn't answer right away, as he let the information swim around his head. He wanted to balk at being considered the weakest link but then he considered watching Hazel or Bryce, or half his pack fighting weres who have been fighting their entire lives. Even he himself would probably not be a match for anyone that came after him. But he didn't like being called a weak link so he tried to weigh his words as carefully as possible; at least he could use this opportunity to get a little more information.

"I understand where you're coming from when you say we are the weakest links and I can even accept that is most likely true, however, I want to know why us being weak links would be a problem? Are you currently in some kind of war we should know about since we're hooking our wagons together? And what exactly are beta wolves?"

There was a heavy sigh on the other side of the phone. Jack wasn't sure if it was in frustration with not getting the information he wanted right away or if Tucker was worried about not being able to fully explain a complicated situation. Since he didn't know the other man, he dismissed that thought process. There was no way he'd be able to figure it out on his own, so it wasn't worth spending too much time thinking about.

"No, we are not at war, there are some tensions between us and a northern California family. As a sort of peace offering, one of our councilmembers and one of their councilmembers have switched places for the next few months, a gesture of goodwill that is fairly common practice amongst the families."

"This means we have very little time, if word hasn't gotten out already, before people realize we might have a weakness in you made wolves. Families are very territorial; they work politely with one another. If a family thinks they see an opening, or weakness in another family, they won't necessarily hesitate, if they have the resources, to pounce and take territory from that family. Beta wolves are wolves that live either in a family's territory or just outside it, around the perimeter but are not part of the family. There are a plethora of reasons, of which I will not get into, why beta wolves would not want to be part of a family. It is fairly common for beta wolves to band together and attack a family at their compound or base of operations in an effort to dethrone them and take that territory from the family and then become the prevailing family of that territory. An overthrow like this usually happens once or twice a year worldwide. I'm sure there have been times where you've seen Lyra with bruises or cuts, this is usually because some betas have attacked our compound or there has been some kind of match or disagreement within our or with another family. It is not a peaceful world we live in and it is best for all involved if we prepare you as best we can for that."

Clearly the family was not as stable as Jack initially thought if these attacks happened with some regularity but by the same token they had never taken over, as far as he knew. Regardless, it was still not pleasant news, even so it would be in his pack's best interest to get as much training as possible, especially if this new world they were going to be a part of was as violent as Tucker was making it sound.

"Very well, let me know what days you were thinking and I will run them by my pack and get back to you. In the meantime, I'll give you the numbers of the other alphas in our group."

Jack was surprised to hear a sigh of relief from the other end of the phone; had he really thought that Jack was going to put up some sort of fight? It made him wonder whether there had been some sort of rumors about what it was like or whether Tucker and the others were just as confused about the pack hierarchy as Jack was about the family's. Tucker rattled off several days and Jack made a mental note before going into his phone and giving the other numbers to the captain. Much to Jack's surprise before they hung up, Tucker thanked him. Something about that gave Jack a little bit of hope and comfort, a small part of him wondered if maybe, just maybe, this transition wouldn't be as unforgiving and hard as he'd initially thought. Maybe they would get lucky and the shock of the existence of born werewolves would be the worst in this whole mess. But somehow Jack couldn't bring himself to fully believe that.

Once Jack was off the phone, Seth arched an eyebrow at him. "So they're worried that we are the weakest link? Does this mean they want to meet with us? I'm assuming that's not going to be enough and there's going to be some sort of test of our training from the program?"

Jack shook his head. "Not quite; they are going to tcst us to see how well we fight and train where we are lacking. Apparently this world that Lyra grew up in has, unsurprisingly, a lot of fighting. I guess families don't really intermingle well so they're concerned that the addition of us weaker wolves might encourage a hostile takeover of sorts. And apparently there are werewolves in the area that are not part of the family that would also see us as a weak link and use that as a chance to try and revolt against the family and take their territory."

For a moment Seth simply blinked at Jack as he processed the information. "Really?!" It was more of an exclamation than a question so Jack just looked at his friend instead of answering. Seth cursed before running his hand through his hair. "Great, just what we need." The other man picked up his beer and downed the rest of the contents before getting off the couch. "I need another beer."

Jack's phone rang just as he was drifting off to sleep; groaning he rolled over to see who would be calling him this late, expecting it to be some kind of emergency. Much to his surprise it was Mathew's name that appeared on the screen.

"What, Mathew?" Jack's voice came out a little gruffer than he had expected it to but he didn't try and curtail it with an apology, it was relatively late for a phone call.

There was a pause as if his curtness had thrown Mathew off but it only lasted a second or two. "We had a bit of a breakthrough tracking the lab assistants. Tonight two of the tracking units on lab assistants' cars went to the same third-party location. It was a new location for both of them and they were each there for almost three hours. A quick search told us this wasn't a business or restaurant of some kind, that it was just a run-of-the-mill office building. So we sent Boone and one other wolf from the same pack down there to check the place out after we did the initial search. Sure enough, when I got there it looked like some kind of warehouse or office space just outside Issaquah. It looked surprisingly vacant until they did a closer loop around the building to find that all of the windows had been blacked out, which is not necessarily something you would do if the building was for lease or indeed empty. There is clearly something they want to hide. The two of them have already reported back to us and since there doesn't appear to be anybody there this late at night, several of us are going to head down there to check the place out. Since one of your wolves is the prime one they're after I wanted to give you the choice of coming along. I know that it is late at night so feel free to decline but the option is available to you should you wish to take it."

Jack felt a jump of hope, just a small one. This could be the lab they were looking for. He pulled his phone away from his head to see that it was already 11:15; chances were it would be close to midnight by the time they made it to Issaquah. It would be worth it if they got any information and Jack needed to be a part of it; he couldn't sit out and let these people trying to get at Lyra slide by. The others were fully capable of handling it, of searching a building, but Jack felt responsible. He felt he needed to be there.

His pause must've been too long because he heard Mathew over the phone again, "Jack? It's slightly time sensitive so I do kind of need some indication of your answer."

"Yes, text me the address and I'll head straight there; once I'm there I'll delete it off my phone."

There was a snort. "Get a pen and some paper and write it down, that way there isn't necessarily too much of a digital trail, even though I'm guessing you're going to program it into your GPS. Just to be safe we're going to park a few buildings down and walk up."

Jack scrambled out of bed and moved into his kitchen to grab the first pen and paper he could find. Once he was ready Mathew rattled off and address, which Jack repeated back to make sure he had it right, then the two of them hung up.

He was fully awake now with the prospect of finally getting information on what it was these doctors and lab assistants wanted. He had a sneaking suspicion that the two buildings they had found earlier were more a plant and didn't necessarily have the most information. With any hope these new buildings that they had to work to find might reward them with actual information they needed. With new sense of hope Jack raced into his bedroom to change before heading out of his apartment.

When Jack arrived to the designated location he was surprised to see Mathew, Rachel, and Bishop standing in a small circle towards the back of the parking lot. With them stood Charlie, Boone, and another wolf Jack didn't know. It was an interesting group Mathew had chosen, but then maybe he had just alerted the alphas and they were all coming themselves instead of sending others. Either way, it would tell Jack a little something about how everyone was thinking about this location.

As he walked up to the group, Bishop spoke to him first, when he was about two yards away from them, "Hello, Jack, I see you didn't trust anyone else in your pack to do this little B & E as well."

It honestly hadn't occurred to Jack to call anybody else. He supposed he could've called Ryan or Seth to come with him, but the thought never crossed his mind until Bishop brought it up. Now that he was thinking about it, if they were really going to break in to a building, which he was assuming they were, he really didn't want to incriminate any of his pack mates. Plus, the fewer the better he felt, as last time they were in this kind

Berman's Chosen

of situation there were so many of them in both buildings and it had gone wrong.

He didn't really have a response for Bishop so all he did was shrug.

This seemed to be enough of an answer because Mathew chimed in, "Well, now that we are all here let's make our way across the back of the property to this other office building; Boone, Eddie, would you two please lead the way."

Boone and the wolf Jack didn't know both nodded and proceeded to walk towards the building. There seemed to be a grassy property line between the small strip mall they had parked in, which was currently closed, and the backend of an office building. One of the two clearly had a large property, as the two buildings were not as close as Jack would've expected them to be. It was a decent location for them to set up shop, as there was enough anonymity on the larger property for the other companies to not necessarily see what they were doing.

Seven of them walked in silence until they reached the back of the building. Once they reached the back doors they all stood in a small circle.

"I know what several of you are thinking, but our friend Eddie here works for AAA and his father is a locksmith so he has already let me know that he is fairly confident he can get through this lock with minimal effort. We just need to stand here and block the general view of what he's doing, even if it is late at night."

Eddie nodded and started removing something Jack couldn't quite make out from his jacket pocket then moved towards the doors. He

155

could hear the sound of metal scratching metal but didn't turn to look and see what exactly the other man was doing. After several minutes of silence Eddie whispered, "Got it."

Mathew motioned for them all to head towards the back door.

As they followed, Jack found himself wondering why breaking and entering into a building didn't seem to bother him in the slightest. He never would've imagined himself as someone who would have no problem breaking the law. At the same time, here he was with several others breaking into a building they were pretty sure was occupied, in the middle of the night with not a care in the world, other than hoping they didn't get caught. It was not exactly where he imagined himself when he'd thought about his future as a college student. Life had really changed in a short time.

Once they were inside and the door shut behind them, Mathew stage whispered, "Let's fan out and look around on this floor. It doesn't appear to be a very large building so between the seven of us will be able to tackle each floor fairly quickly. From what Boone and Eddie could figure out this looks like a two-story building. There's the floor we are on and upstairs so we should be in and out of here within an hour, two tops."

With that they spread out, each with their own flashlight. Mathew had had a handful of them that he had given out as they walked over; Jack made sure to keep his flashlight low because even though the windows had been blacked out he wouldn't take the chance of a passerby seeing his flashlight as he headed towards the farthest right corner near the windows.

After about five minutes it became clear to him that this was probably a staged office space. At first he thought it was a legitimate office space with an open floor concept but then he started glancing at the paperwork on the second desk he passed, then frowned as he realized they were invoices for what appeared to be office supplies as well as memos on the company dress codes. This was not the kind of thing he would expect to find in a secret lab of some kind.

"Does anybody else find the paperwork on these desks to be a little strange considering who we think the inhabitants of this building are?" Bishop asked from about a third of the room away.

Jack grunted before answering, "Yeah, I've got something about a dress code. And something that looks like an office supplies order for office supplies I haven't really seen yet."

"Jack, what's on the office supply list?" came Mathew's voice from farther away.

Jack put his flashlight closer to the paper so he could get a better look at the itemized list. "We have the usual: pens, pencils, and that kind of thing, then halfway down there are four color copy machines as well as two vending machines. This building is too small to warrant four copy machines even if the second floor is set up exactly like this. Not to mention, unless they're on the second floor, there are no vending machines down here; we would see the lights."

A flashlight at about hip height slowly passed through the room, it was high enough to see that it was Boone scanning the room with his flashlight but still keeping it low enough to be under the windows. With that scan they could all see that the entire room was filled with maybe two dozen desks, a large conference table, a break room with no door, and a seating area where someone could wait towards the opposite end they had come in. But there were no copy machines or anything remotely like a vending machine in sight.

"Either these are all decoys, or the invoices are encoded. I bet you anything that all this paperwork means something as long as you know how to read it."

Mathew held his flashlight up to his chest. "In that case, everyone take pictures of all the paperwork you come across, it's going to be tedious but you never know what some of this might mean."

Jack took pictures of everything on the desk in front of him; since there were no drawers of any kind that didn't take him long. He then went to the first desk and took pictures of it. After about twenty minutes they all met up at the front of the room next to the couches that were set up like an impromptu waiting room.

"All right, everyone, I saw the stairs that go to the second floor towards the front of the left-hand wall. Shall we head up?" Rachel asked.

There was nothing more than grunts of agreement so she took the lead, motioning her flashlight to where they were headed. The stairs were wide enough for only two of them to walk side-by-side and even then it was a little cramped. Once they made it to the second floor, they reached an entryway with another door. This one with a large, more sturdy lock on it. Something about it made Jack think this would be where they had something to hide.

"From the looks of it I should be able to get that open but I'm going to need two or three people standing directly behind me flashing light on the lock since I am going to need both my hands," Eddie said, as he crouched down in front of the door.

Both Charlie and Boone walked to stand directly behind him, flashing their lights at the lock. When they flashed the lights on it Jack could see that there were in fact two separate locks on the door.

After a few minutes Jack heard the telltale click that said Eddie had effectively unlocked the door. The door slid open before them to an almost oppressive darkness. It somehow seemed darker than the first floor. A second later either Boone or Charlie's flashlight scanned inside the room.

"There are no windows. There are none in the entire room. It's as if the room is smaller as well, like they built an extra set of walls inside the main walls. I believe we can safely turn on a light switch without warranting attention from the outside world," Boone said, a moment before light flashed on in the room.

Clearly the switch he had seen was right next to the door, but soon after the initial flash of light, what was in the room itself got everyone's attention and not in a pleasant way. Jack unknowingly stepped closer, almost into the room, as did everybody else. Along the right wall, as well as part of the back were seven holding cells. They were clearly not meant to hold someone for long, as there was no toilet or bed. It seemed almost like an intermediary place. On the right-hand side was medical equipment. Jack had no idea what most of it was but he did get a foreboding feeling about the refrigerator he saw with a glass front. There were vials, three of them, with a slightly green tinted liquid. He had a sneaking suspicion that might just be what they injected Lyra with.

Without anyone saying a word they fanned out across the room, and began to look for any sort of paperwork that may explain exactly what they were planning to do with this room. They were all taking pictures as they went.

Both Jack and Rachel moved to the two tables bumped up against one another in the corner of the room next to the door that formed an L shape. He headed to one end and she the other, each of them scouring through the paperwork that sat in piles that were clearly organized in some form, though Jack didn't know quite what. He scanned each page; not wanting to take the time to read everything, he made sure to take pictures, three pages at a time, of everything just in case it could come in handy later. After a few minutes he found a sheet with scrambled notes that listed three different doctors' names. The sheet seemed to be from some kind of notepad because there was a logo at the top for Garrison LLC, a company Jack had never heard of. The idea that they might have somewhere else to leap to gave Jack a little bit of hope.

"It looks like they just started whatever it was they were planning to do here. There doesn't seem to be a lot of information at this particular site anyway, as to what exactly the overall plan is. It's clearly a makeshift site so there must be a bigger compound somewhere," Rachel muttered from a few feet away.

Jack wasn't sure whether she was saying it more to herself or whether she was intentionally saying it loud enough so that he could hear her.

Less than a minute later he heard her gasp. "Jack you're going to want to see this." The severity of her tone had Jack dropping the papers he had in front of him and bee lining over to her.

He wasn't the only one that picked up on it, as when he looked up the others were headed towards her as well. Rachel was looking slightly wide-eyed at a piece of paper she held out in front of her. As Jack began to read he felt his temper rising; the page started out talking about the drug in Lyra's system. He only knew that because it referenced the vials in the refrigerator to his right as well as the intention of injecting it in whom they called the 'female subject'. The report talked about how they had notes at a different location from the scientist. One of the doctors whose name Jack found on the paperwork had figured out a way to suppress the drug's effects but it was not a long-term solution and eventually a cure of some kind would need to be found. But that the suppressant would help keep the female werewolf complacent because her choice would either be to stay with the scientists and receive the suppressant or to die a painful death.

Jack couldn't believe it, these people clearly showed no sense of morality that he had seen, but he couldn't believe that they would just inject someone with a drug that they had no idea how to cure. The fact that they had intentionally given Lyra something without knowing the exact reaction she would have or how to fix it boiled his blood. She wouldn't stay so the only thing they could think of was to give her no choice, to trap her there in one of the cold cells across the room.

There was cursing over Jack's shoulder. "These people are sicker than I gave them credit for," Boone growled.

There were several mumbles of agreement. Then they stood there for a moment as if no one was quite sure where to go from there.

Mathew cleared his throat from where he stood on the other side of Rachel. "While this is extremely upsetting, I do believe our best bet is to get a picture of everything and then clear out of here as quickly as possible, then decide what we're going to do with this information."

"I'd like to burn the place down," Boone responded.

Jack couldn't help but agree with Boone, anything that was built or housed equipment that was going to be used to trap his littermate needed to be destroyed.

"While I agree with your sentiment, I believe that this building could be of more use to us intact than if we destroy it. Think about it, not only could we set up the camera to watch the comings and goings of the inhabitants of this building but having it exist and having them not know that we know of its existence gives us a kind of security should we ever need to play that card. If we destroy yet another building they're going to grow more cautious and it will be harder for us to find the next one." Mathew's voice was more calm and steady than Jack's would've been.

"He has a good point," Rachel agreed. "Let's get all the information and get out of here just in case there's some kind of security that we don't know about."

Knowing it was a good point and that the building's continued existence could come in handy didn't make Jack want to destroy it any less. The part of him that wanted to take care of his pack wanted to destroy the immediate threat and wasn't too concerned about future ones. He fought his instincts and walked back to the other table and continued taking pictures from where he'd left off.

No one said anything while they continued to document everything in that room. Once they were done they gathered near the door, making sure there wasn't any evidence that could necessarily be traced back to them. They left the building and headed back to their cars.

Mathew turned to all of them just before they started to go their separate ways. "I know everyone is tired and frustrated but I do believe we should make one last trip back to the pack offices, making sure we're not followed back, and print out everything we have on everybody's phones. We can print multiple copies so that everyone has one. That way all of us, equally, have every piece of information and we don't have to worry about different puzzle pieces."

There was some mumbling of agreement before they headed back to their cars. Jack drove to the pack offices in silence; he even turned off his radio, not wanting to hear any noise. He wanted to be completely alone and that included the voices of strangers over the airways.

Jack didn't pay much attention to Mathew's words as the group all handed over their cell phones and he hooked them up one by one to a printer, downloading every file they had from the office building and printing out copies. It seemed like a very expensive piece of equipment to Jack, but he wasn't one to delve into ordering office supplies too often. He got the gist of what Mathew was saying, he would print out copies of everything for everyone and save a copy on a USB drive; he was also saying he would give a copy to the IT specialist he had hacking into the various systems to see if it would help them along any. With any luck they would have more information on the company whose logo they had found on several sheets of paper.

As the individual files were printing, Boone's alpha, whose name Jack couldn't remember, mentioned he was pretty sure he could supply and set up security cameras outside the office building they just left with no visibility from the occupants of the building. He wouldn't be able to do it until tomorrow evening, or night as he didn't want to seem suspicious while there could be people still milling around. Mathew seemed to agree that was a good idea and since Jack didn't have anything to add he kept himself quiet.

He didn't have the urge to interact with anybody else in the room; it was as if the situation they were in had completely drained him. He felt exhausted and the overwhelming need to be alone so instead of tuning into the conversation the others were holding, he made his way over to the board Mathew still had the web of lab assistants on. They were bits and pieces filled in that weren't on his version but Jack couldn't muster enough energy to be frustrated with that. He was sure Mathew would send information along once they'd connected all the dots. At least now, hopefully they would know all of the doctors involved, as it appeared the lab assistants had noted which doctor they were working with each time they filled out a memo, or notes.

Mathew walked over and handed Jack his packet of information, a stack of papers much thicker than Jack had initially anticipated. He inclined his head to Mathew and the other alphas and left. He was pretty sure they were not discussing anything he needed to stay for, and if they were Rachel or Mathew would let him know later. He had no intention of bringing this packet of information down to his pack office; the last thing he wanted was to panic his littermates by leaving this kind of information laying about. True, that giant web was in his office but that wasn't incriminating. This file of information could contain all sorts of things and really Jack felt it was his job to go through it and screen it before letting his pack mates see it, since he had no idea what sort of information was in these pages. So he headed straight home but once he was there, even though he was exhausted, he couldn't bring himself to sleep so he lay in bed with the file open next to him and began going through everything, sheet by sheet.

He knew there were people who were more equipped or better trained to go through this paperwork, who would pick up more than he ever could but Jack would feel like an incompetent alpha if he didn't at least look through every single shred of evidence that involved their current dilemma, though he planned to eventually memorize at least the general idea if not all of it.

Eventually sleep overtook him, he knew it was coming on because the words on the page stopped making sense and he had read the same paragraph comparing stats of different werewolves four times. The documents, heavy laden with data, slowly slid to the floor as Jack dropped his hand. Even as his body swung into sleep he knew that slumber was going to bring him nothing but nightmares for the almost three hours he had until his alarm went off.

Chapter 13

071, they just kept calling him 071, it was as if they hoped he would forget his own name. The sad part was he was beginning to answer to it. He had been pacing his cell in the hopes of keeping insanity at bay; he knew better than to try to talk to the others, he had been shocked with a Taser on a long stick the first time he tried. There were not a lot of things to keep a person occupied in these tiny cells. Each of them was allowed to leave for three to four hours in an estimated day and those usually were not in one stint. If they were lucky the people in lab coats would bring them to the treadmill room, where they had been gassed, that was the only exercise allowed. He would take that opportunity to run as fast as he could for as long as he could. Although that seemed to be exactly what the people in the lab coats wanted. He hated feeding into what they wanted from him, all hooked up to the monitors that beeped and gave readouts he didn't understand but the need to exercise, to stretch his muscles farther, was stronger than it had ever been in his life. He can only assume it was a side effect from whatever experiment had been done to them. He wasn't sure if the others were having the same changes but something in him found it hard to believe that they were not.

The young blonde in a lab coat, flanked by four security guards, came walking down the corridor towards his row of cages. She was the youngest of the scientists; she'd clearly been doing this for a shorter amount of time as well because sometimes when she thought people weren't looking he could see the twinge of upset in her eyes at what was being done to them, though he'd never seen her raise a complaint. His heart thumped faster with both excitement and dismay as she stopped in front of his cage and motioned towards the door for one of the guards to unlock it. While he was excited to finally get out of his tiny cell after who knew how long, he dreaded what would be done once he left. He maintained the protocol by lacing his hands along the back of his skull and standing up straight as two guards flanked behind him, hurling him into the corridor.

The guards were not friendly people, not that Parker would've expected them to be; they had ever-present scowls on their faces and seemed to look right through those being experimented on. He wasn't sure where they were taking him as the two other security guards moved to walk in front of him, between him and the blonde in the lab coat. If they had gone to the left, odds were they would've been going to the room full of treadmills, the most benign of outings. Since they headed up the hallway straight from his cage he knew it was going to be something along the line of tests.

They had walked for no more than a minute or two before the blonde spoke over her shoulder.

"We're going to be doing something new today," she announced in an almost chipper voice. "We're going to fit you for some new equipment." There was nothing after that, leaving him to wonder what could possibly be waiting ahead of him.

They wound their way out of the room with all the cages; he tried to count them once. Though not all of the cages were occupied he knew there were at least two dozen men and women down there. They hung a left after the last of the cells, which made him a little nervous; he had never gone this direction before. That was when the blonde in the lab coat started chattering on excitedly, almost absently.

"You really do have some very impressive stats. You were already in fantastic shape but your new numbers since the changes are extraordinary. You really are a perfect specimen for this next section of the experiment and this next process. Unfortunately the first batch only had a sixty percent success rate but we've made some tweaks and I really do think you are a prime candidate for this second wave."

His blood ran cold at the same time he felt his breathing speed up. Nothing good was going to come from what they were about to do to him. Not that anything good had happened thus far. Still if it only had a sixty percent success rate the first time it didn't bode well that the second generation of whatever technology or drug they were using would be much better. He must've slowed his pace because he felt one security guard's stick jab in his back.

"Keep up the pace, 071," the voice barked gruffly.

The growl that bubbled up from his chest couldn't be helped and earned him another jab, harder this time. He had to fight the urge to lunge at the guard; whatever they had done to them made him feel more aggressive. He had never been an overly aggressive guy but ever since they had gassed them on the treadmills he found his temper to be stronger and quicker than it ever had been.

Surprisingly, the woman in the lab coat looked over her shoulder at them, making a clicking noise with her tongue. "Now, now; you know as well as I do that our volunteers in this experiment have strong gut reactions to anything they interpret as mistreatment. No need to punish them for only doing what is becoming natural to them." She turned her head back around to face forward.

The idea that they were volunteers at this point was almost laughable. They had volunteered to help test some kind of equipment, not to be experimented on and certainly not to be held hostage in cages. The fact they wanted to maintain that their victims had volunteered for this was insane. It had to be some sort of convincing their own conscience that they were not the monsters in this situation.

Nothing else happened on their walk to an unmarked door with no windows on either side. Something about there not being windows made him nervous, even though he knew the odds of someone complaining about what was being done in this facility were slim. Something about the lack of windows made him think that he was about to walk into a scenario even more unpleasant. One of the thugs hired as security stepped in front of the blonde woman and opened the door wide; she nodded as she stepped through and disappeared to the left. As much as he didn't want to walk into that room he knew he didn't have a choice, especially with four armed guards surrounding him. Adrenaline pinged up and down his system. Something unpleasant was about to happen and there wasn't a single thing he could do to stop it; he felt so helpless. There was something about this situation; this room that made him want to walk through the doorway even less than any building they stormed overseas.

As they walked to the doorway he scanned the room. It looked like a regular, unassuming, doctor's office that could've been anywhere in the country. There was a box of sterile gloves on the counter with the sink and a table with paper on it with a roll at the foot. The walls were a cream color as if to encourage a calm sense of normalcy. It was eerie in the cold sterile mess of the rest of the building; it made him more uneasy instead of less.

The blonde woman was reaching into one of the lower drawers under the sink; when she turned back around she was smiling and holding what looked like a very sophisticated dog's collar, tags and all. It was a pale, ugly green with a metal plate on one side that read 071. His heart sped up with those numbers. She meant to put that on him. As if he was some sort of pet and not a human.

He started to back up involuntarily, away from the woman. All he succeeded in doing was bumping into the two security thugs standing behind him. Without warning one of the sticks was shoved up against his back and he heard the button a split second before the shock was delivered to his body, bringing him down to all fours as he snarled at the pain and electrical current shooting through his body. They were stronger than normal Tasers. He had seen others lose the contents of their stomach, what little contents they were given. He struggled to maintain his dignity as he fought through the pain. He was hit again from another angle but not quite as long. This one was clearly meant to simply startle or distract him.

He heard himself cry out in pain, unable to concentrate on anything as the fear and panic and anger coursed through his veins, chasing after the electrical current. He concentrated on his breathing and curled his fingers into his hands, digging the nails into his palms to give himself something to concentrate on. He knew better than to attack the guards, it would only lead into more: more shocks, more bruises, more pain.

When he finally had control of his breathing he felt it, the cool metal across the back section of his neck, slightly off to the right side. The woman in the lab coat had used his pain as a distraction to put the collar around his neck. This time he was aware of the growl bubbling up from his chest. It got louder and louder as he felt his hands uncurled from his now bloodied palms and dig into the floor.

The need to change was almost overwhelming; it was like an itch throughout his entire body. All that did was bring pain, pain in every muscle yearning to change shape, begging to follow the impulse as if the muscles were telling him that changing would end the pain but he knew it wouldn't. Changing was painful and in the other form he had less control, which would do nothing to help him in his current predicament. The itching became stronger. It was as if it was moving in deeper and deeper like bug bites on every inch of his body, inside and out. Only a bug bite could be ignored. This itch was so strong it was the only thing he could do to fight it. He felt several of his nails snap from his hand digging too hard into the linoleum and the concrete below it. Normally that level of pain would've stopped him but there was too much else going on, his senses overwhelmed, he fought it as long as he could but then he felt his body start to change. It started first with his hands; he felt the bones and muscles realigning, stretching, preparing themselves to accommodate his other form. It weaved its way up his arm like a vine, the itching being replaced by the pain of everything relocating. The noise coming from his throat now was more in pain and frustration, a yell instead of the aggressive growl. It became impossible to concentrate on the world around him. Once the change hit his chest the pain was almost blinding, overwhelming; the itching lingered still in several parts of his body. There was nothing else; the world centered around the change. There was no one else in the room with him. He wasn't even in the room, his entire world narrowed down to the morphing of his muscles.

The change seemed to take forever even though he knew it was no more than two to three minutes. He felt the change finish and knew where he had once stood now others would see a snow white wolf, larger than a normal wolf, his head reached just shy of four feet. He let out a howl, as he did every time he completed the change. It was a release for all that extra energy bouncing around him. He looked up from the ground slowly to see the blonde woman looking at him with shocked awe with a small remote in her hand. He growled at her, everything in him wanting to attack her, to rip apart her flesh in angry frustration of what was done to him.

Gretchen S. B.

The Taser striking his hindquarters made him jump and snap in the direction of the security guard who poked at him. Which only succeeded in him getting poked by two other guards. He felt his hind legs give out behind him. Even though the Tasers were for some reason less painful as a wolf than a human didn't mean it still didn't hurt. The anger-laced adrenaline shooting through his body almost succeeded in making it ignorable. Then he felt a jolt through the metal piece of the collar around his neck and he heard himself yelp. A split second later, the rest of his legs collapsed out from under him. He couldn't, no matter how much he concentrated, get them to do more than twitch.

Before he could think too much on it to figure out some way to get himself out of that predicament he heard the clicking of the low heels the blonde woman wore moving towards him. "There now, now you'll be much more amenable. This collar we've put on you is something of a prototype, a beta test really, it sends a signal to your brain, making you stay in your wolf form once it's on. It also makes you easier to handle, so to speak, thanks to my tiny remote here. These remotes, when in range, can send commands to your brain, other than the command to change form, that is. If you choose to attack someone you shouldn't or not follow directions, this tiny little remote can make your legs stop working quite easily. Now the effects are temporary so don't worry too much. In about five minutes or so you should regain power over your limbs; we fixed that particular problem after several of the first group never regained their legs."

"There is also a speaker, of sorts, in the collar that will emit a loud high-pitched dog whistle, which will be used in cases of training, mostly. The battery life isn't great; it needs to be swapped out every eighteen to forty-eight hours depending on how much it's used. You really don't need to worry yourself about that. We're currently working on a newer model that will have a speaker so that someone can give you commands. You may be wondering how we're managing all this and the answer is quite simple really: we took advantage of you being unconscious after gassing you on the treadmill and implanted a transmitter into your upper back/shoulder region. This gives us a little more leeway and wiggle room should we find something else the collar needs to be able to do. This way it will be easier to control you in your wolf form and therefore we can take you outside the facility."

His body battled between angry, frightened, and the glimmer of hope that came with the idea that he would be able to leave the facility. If he could leave he had a chance to escape. If only he could find a way out of this stupid collar once he was gone. All he needed to do was pretend to comply then wait until this battery came out or ran out and then make a break for it. That semblance of a plan gave him hope. Maybe, just maybe, he could get his life back or even better, report what these people were doing here and get them shut down. He was grateful that his wolf face didn't show his emotions like his human one would. The last thing he needed was them knowing his thoughts.

"Now, since we know that the collar seems to be working fine we're going to take you, well, the guards are going to take you, back to the cell to get used to the collar and used to being in this alternative form full time. You will also be removed from your cell more often so that we can train you to get used to the collar. We're very excited about this collar breakthrough because we can't wait to see what kind of affects you staying in this form will have." The smile she was giving him was the same kind of indulgent smile an adult would give a child when they told them there would be a surprise visit to the ice cream shop. As if he should be excited about what she was telling him.

He was able to hold down his growl, thankfully; he didn't want to experience that high-pitched noise she was talking about on top of being stuck with his legs immobile and helpless.

The blonde woman made her way to the door, now holding a clipboard she must've gotten off the counter, making notes on it as she walked. "I have to get going, there are a lot of you guys to check up on, but once your legs are working again, security here will escort you back to your cell." With that she left the room.

Parker expected the security to start prodding at him, trying to get him up faster. They didn't strike him as the smartest of men, so they would think prodding him would get him up faster. He was surprised when they just stood around and talked over his head. It wasn't anything important, small talk about some football game that must've happened within the last day or two. He took the opportunity to concentrate on his body. On what exactly everything felt like, to see if there was some way around the immobility. Much to his dismay there wasn't; several minutes later he started to feel the numbness in his legs be replaced by that tingling sensation that happens when your legs fall asleep. He immediately started moving which garnered security's attention and they stood back in formation around him.

"Now that you've got your legs back we're on our way back to the cage," one said unnecessarily.

Another of them opened the door and he didn't try anything on the way out or on the way back to his cell. He needed them to think he was on good behavior. His only chance of getting out of there would be if they took him outside the facility thinking the collar would work. All he needed to do was find out where the battery was and either bust it or wait it out. He didn't know how long it would take before his chance would come but simply knowing that it glimmered just out of reach gave him the first sense of hope he'd felt since he had woken up in the cage.

Chapter 14

"They're awfully chatty," Ryan grumbled under his breath.

The snort came from his left. "Easy there, little brother. If you had mentioned to them that you were family you would be over there as well," Ryan's older brother, Griffin chastised.

Ryan gave his brother a droll stare. "Thanks, because this isn't annoying enough."

His brother snorted again and slapped Ryan on the back a few times as their uncle walked into the room, signaling that the tests were probably about to start. "It will be fine, Ryan," Griffin said before walking to stand beside their uncle.

Ryan knew he could more than hold his own against the other science made werewolves. It was the born werewolves that would present a challenge. It wasn't that they were that much stronger or faster than he was, but they had been training most of their lives. He had only had his uncle training him in the last few years since the experiment. It made him feel woefully unequipped in this world.

Though he was relieved they were working with the family because it meant those secrets were out in the open and it also meant that there would be less concern about him and Lyra possibly seeing each other because now they would have the family standing between them and the scientists. The problem was that Lyra was destined to be the family's next Luna, the family healer. A Luna was always somewhat outside general family law, which meant their mate needed to be able to hold their own in this world, because there would be times where it was the Luna against the family council. Ryan was terrified that even though he would bet his life on Lyra and he being matched, he knew he wasn't strong enough to be the mate she needed. But he wasn't sure that training with the rest of the made wolves was going to help him get there, help him protect her where he had been unable to weeks prior. Ryan needed to be deadly, like the Scotsman. But he wasn't sure the family would help him get to that point, in fact he wouldn't be surprised if they tried to prevent him and Lyra from being together.

"All right, Pack F, my name is Tucker. I am captain of the guard for the gamma family; we're all here today so that I can see exactly what it is that were dealing with when it comes to your... werewolf abilities. My nephew here, Griffin..." Their uncle waved to Ryan's brother. "As well as these seven over here, who I'm sure you recognize." He pointed to the seven including Lyra standing off to his left. "Will all be observing you as you run through the tests; at least one of them will be doing the tests with you to show you where the average born werewolf skillset is. The level that you need to become."

The last was said very solemnly; if Ryan didn't know better he would've thought it sounded almost like a threat. Before Ryan could puzzle out his uncle's tone, Griffin was informing everyone that they would be running a lap around the property along the fence line to see how fast they could all run. The group of them was already at one side of the yard so all that was needed was for them to line up into two lines. They were instructed to put people that seemed to be faster runners in the back;

this included Lyra who came to stand next to Syrus before smiling and winking at the other man.

"Oh, it's on," challenged Syrus as he smiled back at Lyra.

Not a moment later Griffin blew the whistle and the group of them began to sprint. It wasn't very long before Lyra and Syrus were in the lead. While Ryan was by no means slow, he certainly wasn't fast so he ended up towards the high middle of the group. He watched as Lyra slowly broke away from Syrus; it was as if she felt free to run at a natural speed that she had been hiding all this time. It made Ryan growl and forced himself to move faster until only Syrus, Lyra, and Kelly were in front of him. Ryan hadn't been to the property since he was a preteen and even then it had only been a handful of times; he was pretty sure that the run around the outside of the property would be about three miles. He forced himself to work on keeping up, he couldn't fail at this, he couldn't be seen as less than. Being a halfling meant that he was less in the eyes of the born were society; he had to prove that being a made were made him someone to contend with.

As he reached the finish line he could see both Syrus and Kelly in front of him bent over and panting. Both men had clearly put in more effort than they thought they were going to need initially once they saw how fast Lyra was. Ryan came to stand beside Syrus and Kelly, fighting himself not to bend over and catch his breath. He was not about to show any sign of weakness in front of the other weres. Instead he made eye contact with Taylor and Graham, who stood a few feet away, frowning at him. He wasn't sure whether word got out to them about him and Lyra being matched. Part of him hoped that it was simply out in the open and over with but a larger part of him, the more realistic part hoped it hadn't. Knowing Lyra, she'd probably kept quiet, because he wasn't ready to face them should they decide to challenge him in a show of aggression. He needed to be ready to face that kind of challenge head on and right now Ryan wasn't sure he could hold his own for more than a few minutes.

The rest of the tests were what he would've expected if they had gone back into the program; there was lifting and agility along with it; they tested how fast everyone could change and how much clothing they could leave on when they changed back. As he would've expected, the people in the pack who did the best of each exam varied depending on the skill. Ryan himself fought to be in the high middle, if not the top three for everything.

When they had gotten to testing different skills such as smell, sight, and hearing, Ryan was not able to help but puff himself up when Lyra opened with the comment, "No, you're going to have to be farther away and quieter for Ryan. He can hear things through the phone, across a crowded room; he has really good hearing, even for a born wolf so make it a challenge for him."

His uncle looked at him appraisingly at that and smiled with a sense of pride before almost doubling his distance from Ryan before talking, facing away. Ryan struggled ever so slightly but luck was with him and he was able to get the words right. It'd been at that point that Ryan solidified himself on Taylor and Graham's radar because the last test was combat in both human and wolf form, to which Graham sparred with the men and Lyra with the women.

When Graham got to Ryan his eyes narrowed slightly. Ryan wasn't sure why but he got the distinct feeling the other man saw him as a threat, not in the traditional sense, but a threat nonetheless. It was in that moment Ryan knew that should he ever try to fulfill their match and start something with Lyra, Graham and probably others would do their best to put a stop to it. Lyra might say that he would've been accepted as a halfling, and maybe he would have as a friend or little brother. But there was no way they would be okay with a halfling being matched with their Luna in training. In that moment Ryan felt himself swell with anger, anger at Lyra being injured, anger with the secrets, anger with everything, and he let that anger flow through him as Graham squared off and lunged.

Ryan dodged but wasn't as fast as Graham, as he didn't practice. But he got most of his body out of a way. So it was simply the side of his arm that Graham took, tugging him down to the ground as Graham rolled, pulling Ryan back so he ended up falling flat on his back. The wind was knocked out of him but Ryan knew better than to let himself get stunned; he immediately rolled over onto all fours and watched as Graham stood in front of him. The other man began to smile but it wasn't a nice smile or even a teasing one, then he lunged. Ryan was still on all fours, which gave him very little maneuverability. All he could do was roll himself out of the way next and there was no way, even with all the anger running through him that he was going to be getting the upper hand on Graham. All he could do was defend himself as Graham advanced, getting faster and faster. Even though there were two times when Ryan was able to get a punch in, he simply was not used to training at such a fast speed. He was used to being faster than most but not when his opponent had been training at this speed his whole life. With Graham crouching beside him, claws at his throat, even though his inner wolf roared with the anger and frustration and need to subdue the other man, Ryan yielded because intellectually, he knew he couldn't win. There was almost a full minute before his uncle Tucker's voice, slightly laced with a growl, pierced the silence, "Ever so kindly remove your claws from his throat, Graham. This isn't a place to show off."

Graham stood up and moved back, watching warily. Ryan took his time getting up because he wanted to appear as if Graham's show of aggression meant nothing to him. It wasn't really training they were doing, but testing the waters of what the made weres could do. After the grapple between Graham and Ryan, Ryan noticed Lyra was standing further away from her cousin than she had before, not exactly standing with their pack at but making it clear that her allegiances were not so black and white. It was good to know, even if that wouldn't help him any.

Once they had been dismissed and everyone was packed, Ryan and his brother were standing off to the side together. Their uncle strode over, looking him up and down before snorting. "There is only one thing that would cause that kind of aggression and that, my dear sweet nephew, is a girl. As far as I know, Graham is in fact not matched. Which means that our poor Ryan is most likely matched with Lyra and that kerfuffle shows us Graham is aware of it. Does that sound about right?"

Ryan knew he shouldn't be surprised that his uncle figured all that out. As captain of the guard for six years he heard almost everything.

"Seriously? Is he kidding?" Griffin asked, wide-eyed.

. "No, I'm not kidding. Because there is no way for our dear Ryan to make a move on the little Luna otherwise."

"I think I'm offended by that."

His uncle snorted again. "I don't care about you being offended. I'm pretty sure I don't have to mention how bad it would be. Nor all of the family politics that go with courting a Luna. A little irritation is kinda low on the radar. So, what are you going to do about it?"

"So far, I haven't done anything. I haven't made a move on Lyra. Then there's the outburst I had in front of our pack. That is how the whole thing actually came up. I didn't mean to but I told her we were matched in front of the whole pack."

Griffin hissed in sympathy.

His uncle rubbed the bridge of his nose, which he only did when he became irritated. "Stay away from her, that is your safest bet, but with that outburst you have put yourself in a corner. Or you can choose to go after your match. It is going to be an uphill climb and you need more ammo in your arsenal than you currently have. "

That very thought had been percolating the last few days and he knew what his best bet would be. "Stay with Uncle Leo a while."

His brother waved his arms to get their attention. "I repeat, are you serious? You matched to the little Luna I've grown up with? That's a little unnerving and now you're talking about staying with that crazy lone wolf with the hope he can jump-start your fighting skills? Have you lost your mind?"

Tucker didn't say anything but narrowed his eyes, clearly weighing the possibility.

Ryan used the silence to push on, "It is a kind of training, living out there by himself. Packs of wild actual wolves cross his territory, or what he deems his territory; would be nice to get away from all of this. Now that I know Lyra is about as safe she's going to get, time with the hermit might actually be a good idea."

His brother turned to their uncle. "And what do you think about this? Please tell me you don't think this is a good idea?"

Both brothers' full attention went to their uncle. The older man did not seem phased by their stares but instead took his time answering. "I can understand why you feel this would be your best option. Training away from those who are not your biggest fans would give you a leg up. I don't know if this is the best time for you to be disappearing, politically, but since you have the summer off… I don't think it is a bad idea. If you feel it's best then I say do it."

Ryan's brother sputtered.

"Thank you, Uncle," Ryan responded and turned away before his brother could interject. He then pulled out his phone and called Uncle Leo.

Leo did not have a cell phone, he claimed they were a burden of modern society so the only way to get a hold of him, other than going out to his house, which he didn't appreciate unannounced guests, was his house phone. And that wasn't something he necessarily answered regularly. If you didn't catch him in the house he would usually respond three to four days later. If he responded at all. It really depended on what his temperament was at the time and who was calling. After the fifth ring Ryan was worried this was going to be one of those cases and prepared himself on exactly what he was going to say when he heard a click on the other side of the line.

"Yeah." Clearly Leo had just come back into the house from his aggressive tone.

Ryan didn't let that phase him and rushed into an explanation before his uncle could hang up, "Hey, Uncle Leo, it's Ryan. I know you prefer things short and sweet so I'll to make this as quick as possible. I know you know about this whole science experiment thing that made me into a werewolf like Mom's side versus a human like Dad's side. There've been some changes and we're kind of throwing our lot in with the family in hopes it will help us defend ourselves from some people that are after us. The downside of this is that now they're testing us and want us to be able to fight as well as them. But I don't think they intend for us to truly be able to fight as well as them, me in particular. So I'm hoping I could go stay with you for two or three weeks before I have to get back to work for the school year, and learn from you the sort of thing that I wouldn't be learning from the family."

The snort that came over the other side of the phone sounded exactly like his uncle Tucker, though Ryan didn't have a death wish, so he didn't mention it.

"Yeah, the family will always have the family's best interest at heart. Sure, boy, come on out in the next day or so and I'll give you a crash course in being a werewolf. Make it harder for them to take you by the scruff of your neck and put you where they want." Then the line went dead.

That was Uncle Leo's way, he didn't believe in exchanging pleasantries, just say your piece and move on to the next thing. Letting out a sigh of relief, Ryan slid his phone back into his bag and hustled out the front doors, hoping he could catch up with Jack and let him know his plan. Because the last thing he needed was for Jack to get huffy with him now that they seemed to be on okay terms again. Plus, Seth would be more than capable of taking on, temporarily, the place as Jack's second. All he had to worry about was how he was going to word it because telling Jack he was leaving because of Lyra wouldn't go over so well, especially considering Jack was already pissed at their pack mate.

Chapter 15

They had gotten through the initial testing of all seven packs in a little more than two days. Though there weren't a lot of surprises, Graham wasn't thrilled with the prospect of going with Tucker and Lyra to report to their fathers and their uncle about just how big the gap was between the born werewolves and made ones. Though they had hoped to be mistaken, Graham and Taylor had known they wouldn't be. That there wouldn't be any surprises in the skillset of the made wolves.

He followed behind Tucker and Lyra as they walked into his father's study with the three brothers already waiting for them. Graham looked around at the study that had not changed for as far back as he could remember. It had been his grandfather's study before it was his father's. Book cases lined the walls, filled with a smattering of different items and old hardbound books, about half of which were filled with historical lineages or pack rosters, births and deaths of all members going back hundreds of years. Others would be used by the Luna; in their particular family the Luna did not have her own study. It was something to do with three or four Lunas ago and a bit of an uprising. Since then it was decreed that any of the Lunas after that would share a study with the head of the family so that he would be able to keep an eye on her. Though there was no longer a need for that, the tradition continued. Graham was very interested to see if his oldest brother and Lyra would have the same agreement or if she would demand her own space. There were no computers of any sort in the study. The study was more for show than an actual usable space. All of the technology would be in their individual offices, in each of their individual homes so as not to have everything in one place. The study itself was more like a parlor for visitors or a place where the three brothers could talk without worry of being overheard.

"What is the verdict, Tucker? How concerned should we be with the strength of these new wolves?" asked his father.

Tucker stood at attention, as he usually did when addressing or being addressed by one of the three men in front of them. None of the captains before him did that to Graham's memory, so he could never figure out why Tucker did it. The closest he could come up with was the other man had spent six years in the military when he got out of high school.

"Sir, it is about what we expected. Though they are not bad, all things considered. None of them seems to be much better than what we would consider somebody to be in their late teens. They are roughly an average of five to ten years behind where they should be for their age. They are not going to be an asset, I believe, in a fight. Some of them I truly believe are at their limit as far as skill is concerned; they simply do not have the range of capability that someone in the family would have. That may be a problem," Tucker reported.

His father frowned before looking at both Lyra and Graham. When neither of them gave any kind of denial his frown deepened. "Really? This is not good news. I had hoped that there would at least be room for improvement should they fair what we expected but you're saying that there probably is not room for improvement?"

Tucker simply nodded.

Graham's youngest uncle shifted in his seat to sit up a little straighter before looking at both of his brothers. "This doesn't bode well after Councilman Richard's outburst and the ultimatum of sorts from his head of the family."

That last part made Graham worry, Councilman Richards was the councilman on loan from another family they had a tenuous relationship with; the last thing they needed was for him to be stirring the pot not in their favor. "What exactly has happened?"

His father gave a heavy sigh before answering, "Councilman Richards told his home council of our addition of about seventy-five, by his count, new wolves that are on probation in our family. To say that his leader was displeased is an understatement. We believe Richards also made it clear that these new wolves were almost sheer numbers only and would most likely either be incredibly weak or they are being used as ringers to bolster our numbers for an attack. Which, as you know, is the last thing we need. We have a sneaking suspicion Richards might be cutting his visit short and heading home to bolster things there. On the plus side, this means we get Donovan back, on the downside it means all of our work trying to improve our relations with them goes down the drain. I also have a sneaking suspicion that now that word is out, prematurely, about these extra wolves we might be under attack from local betas if not neighboring families. You can understand why we'll be asking the seven of you to be staying on pack grounds for the next few days just to be safe."

"Exactly how long are you wanting us to stay here?" asked Lyra, her voice weaved with disgust and worry.

His uncle ignored her tone and simply answered, "Until at least Tuesday. We are meeting with several other family heads at the investment office, which by the way you and Graham shall be attending that meeting as representatives of these made werewolves. That is not a request so clear your schedule. It is my hope that will clear things up a bit and stabilize this some but it may also create a more volatile situation than the one we already have. I want to be prepared for both so I'll say tentatively Tuesday but don't be surprised if it ends up being longer. Until word gets out where all the made werewolves live, I believe they are relatively safe in their own domiciles, though I do believe the alphas should be keeping track of the members of their packs. It is my understanding that they have a good reign on the whereabouts of their pack mates as it is, so all we can ask is they maintain that."

Graham could feel the need to argue coming off of Lyra but she managed to keep her mouth shut. It was something she learned to excel at since they were young; instead of openly rebelling, she could give off the energy that truly expressed how she felt while keeping her face, language, and voice relatively neutral. It would give no one a reason to pick a fight with her while still signaling her disapproval of the situation.

Graham, on the other hand, wasn't thrilled. "While I have no problem staying on the compound because we may be attacked, I am not happy about the fact that we may have dragged the made werewolves into a situation where born wolves could be attacking them in their homes." He gave his father direct eye contact.

His father's lips twitched but not in a happy or friendly manner. "Son, we have purposefully not taken residential information from any of these made wolves so there is nothing on the books about them yet. Simply let them know to make sure they're not being followed and everything should be fine. If it turns out that Tuesday doesn't go well we will deal with that then."

Graham knew there was no argument to be made against his father. As the head of the family when he decreed something that was the end of it. Unless someone was to challenge him but to challenge him in anything was to challenge his position as alpha. If he decided he took some kind of offense to the challenge, the challenger would find themselves in a physical fight to submission or death with the current alpha. So while Graham wanted to argue that the made wolves should at least have some sort of protection, he knew it wouldn't get him anywhere so he just nodded briskly and looked to Lyra.

She made eye contact with him before turning slowly back to his father. "We will, of course, pack our domiciles and be here later tonight. But we do ask for the rest of the day to get word out to the made wolves to be on the lookout for people following them and let them know that we will be indisposed for an indeterminate amount of time."

His father nodded graciously. "That is acceptable."

Lyra inclined her head slightly before turning to Graham and nudging her head pointing out, indicating that they should leave now and not wait through the rest of this meeting. Without a word Graham followed her out, not only of the office but the main building, neither of them stopping until they were in the circle driveway.

Then Lyra turned to him, worry plain on her face. "I don't like this, any of it. I thought for sure that having the packs working with the family would help us but now I'm starting to wonder whether we just added more trouble on. I know that we didn't have much of a choice because the family has more connections and power backing them than the packs will ever have but at the same time I feel like I'm endangering my pack."

His cousin had always been more attached to her pack than Graham had to his own. While he didn't fully understand it, he accepted that was how she felt but in this particular circumstance part of him agreed with her; he didn't want to be endangering his pack.

"I get that but we really didn't have a choice. Think about it, we're basically playing into the scientists' hands. I know that you probably haven't heard everything that went on at the warehouse as yet but they wanted us to find those locations. Those locations were set up for us to find, maybe not initially, but it was definitely a test and we did better at it than they expected so I sincerely think that bought us some time but eventually they're going to come back. They are going to come back stronger and harder, and we couldn't handle that alone, we just don't have the resources and the family does."

Her arms wrapped around her as if she were hugging herself in an attempt at comfort. "I know, but I feel so trapped. Most of my pack is mad at me. Ryan, well, that's a completely different thing. And the fact that we might've caused more interfamily problems… What if we introduced the packs to this world only to cause more problems for the family, so much so that your brother wins and we are kicked out? What do we do then? You know as well as I do that'll be good enough excuse for beta packs and the like to attack some of the made wolves; they will not be safe either in their own world or in ours."

The thought of the made werewolves being kicked out hadn't occurred to Graham but now that Lyra had brought it up it terrified him. One or two groups of beta wolves could make a decent dent in the made wolf population. They had the sheer numbers and could overpower them but a beta wolf group would not go down without a fight.

"We call the alphas. You call Jack and I'll call Rachel; we'll let them know exactly what's going on and tell them to let the other alphas know, that way we were all at least prepared for what's to come."

Lyra nodded before leaning in and giving him a fierce, tight hug. Before he could wrap his arms around her and hug her back, she let go and was walking towards her car, pulling out her phone as she went. Graham didn't follow her, he knew his cousin well enough to know she would want her space. He pulled out his phone and called Rachel. His alpha was relatively levelheaded, but he knew she wasn't going to like this. She was going to be pissed that her pack might be endangered. Not wanting to be overheard, as soon as he heard his alpha's voice, he began walking towards his car. This was going to be a long conversation, one probably best done in person. "Rachel, I'll meet you in the pack office and a half an hour. I'll explain what it's about then. That work for you?"

There was silence on the phone; for a second he could almost hear her weighing her anger and frustration at being dictated to. "Make it an hour, I have to finish up something first." Then she hung up, not waiting for him to say whether he agreed or not, trying to assert dominance where he had already been asserting it.

Not that he could blame her; he had thrown down the gauntlet first. The tango between them went back and forth like this because Graham was not allowed to take an alpha position in the packs. His father made it very clear to the seven of them when this whole experiment first happened that they were not to take a leadership role in any of these groups. That they should keep their heads down and blend in; they couldn't do that as a team leader. That being said it wasn't in Graham's nature to be a submissive wolf so he had risked his father's frustration and anger by becoming a second. His father hadn't been thrilled but since Graham wasn't the team lead he didn't punish his son.

Rachel knew Graham was a more dominant wolf but she didn't understand, until after Graham informed her that wolves could be born and not just made, why he had not just volunteered to be alpha. She hadn't been thrilled to know the truth but she accepted it, which Graham appreciated. There was one quality Rachel had that made her a good alpha: she very rarely exploded or let things fluster her. She would set it aside and worry at it later when she could process it properly, but she had a very level head, even when Graham's more aggressive personality showed.

Starting his car, Graham drove off the property and headed towards the downtown offices.

Rachel was waiting for him when Graham arrived at the pack the office. She was sitting in the office chair at one of the three computers they had against the far wall with individual desk setups so that pack members could work from the pack office if they needed. She had also pulled out another chair from its desk so that she and presumably Graham could sit facing each other. She didn't say anything, just looked at him then glanced down at the chair before sliding her phone onto the desk an arm's reach away. Graham took the cue for what it was and plopped down in the chair across from her. She waited patiently for him to settle in with her arms folded across her stomach with her elbows on the armrest; her face was just on the unpleasant side of neutral. He didn't know what he had taken her away from or if it was simply the news that put that look on her face; either way Graham was sure that it would not go pleasantly.

"My father had Lyra and I, as well as Tucker, the captain of the guard, report on how everyone was doing and where we stood and the report went about what you would've expected. But while reporting my father told us that several of the other families are unhappy with us, even under probation, letting in several dozen new adult werewolves and that they haven't decided whether they see it as a threat or not. Because of that they're going to have a multifamily meeting on Tuesday at my father's office downtown. Until then, they want me, Lyra, and the others to stay on the compound in case someone decides that this is an act of war or sign of weakness and attacks. We're unsure if that means some of the beta groups will attack the made werewolves. Because of this Lyra and I have decided to tell you and Jack, and through you the other alphas, that everyone should be watching their back and making sure they're not followed home from wherever they go during the day because the last thing we need is a group of betas attacking a lone made wolf in their house or work." Graham leaned back in the chair and gauged Rachel's reaction.

Rachel took a deep breath and closed her eyes. "You're telling me this move to protect ourselves might put us into a different harm's way."

It wasn't really a question so Graham didn't respond.

"Okay, explain to me what a beta is and then I'll call Jack and come up with some sort of strategy for how to deal with this." She sighed with her eyes still closed.

It was hard to describe the world he'd grown up and it had been pounded into them through childhood and adolescence that one did not talk about the werewolf world. That there were those that would hurt or kill them if given the chance, that the world at large couldn't know about them and to have almost free reign to do so now didn't do anything to stop that crippling need to keep his mouth shut.

"Each territory, I guess you would say, has one family that runs it. You can choose to join the family or you can decide to be a lone wolf or join a beta family. Beta families generally are single individuals that live either on the outskirts of a territory or in a territory under the radar and they, most the time, actively try to dislodge the family and take over the territory themselves. It doesn't always happen, maybe once or twice a year worldwide, because families tend to be so much bigger than the beta groups, but they are known for attacking compounds or family residences or a single household where family wolves are known to live."

There was silence for a moment as she processed that. "So, you're telling me that there are basically groups of playground bullies wandering around trying to take territory and that if we get on their radar and they decide they wanted to chase some of us down they'll try and pick us off one by one?"

All he could do was shrug; Graham had always been a part of a family so he didn't have a working knowledge of how betas reacted to anything. He'd only ever met two betas in his lifetime, one really, because Boone had been more of a lone wolf before moving to Seattle than a beta. Lyra's uncle, the Scotsman, had been a beta wolf in Boston for years when he met their aunt when she was traveling to meet other Lunas. He had met her and she had become his driving force instead of territory, much to the chagrin of his compatriots. Even knowing that, he had never held many conversations with the Scotsman, especially about his time as a beta.

"I honestly don't know how they operate but Lyra and I want us to be prepared for the worst case scenario. That worst-case scenario is if they decide to pick off made werewolves one by one it will be very similar to the way Pack L operates, only there will not be bribery. They'll just try to take them out when they are alone or in pairs but if everyone is aware, or if they're being followed then it should be relatively okay."

There were several curses before Rachel finally opened her eyes and reached over and swiped her phone off of the desk. "Do you think Lyra has talked to Jack yet?"

Graham shook his head. "I have no way of knowing. I assume she's going to try and talk to him today, however I'm not entirely sure whether she'll succeed because I don't know their schedules. I won't know for sure until we're both back at the compound tonight."

"Okay, I'll just text Jack and tell him to call me later tonight; hopefully that gives your cousin time to talk to him. I'll hold off on calling the other alphas until I've spoken to him. Am I going to be able to get a hold of you over the next few days, should something happen?"

"Yes, definitely. I'll have my phone on me and I'm still going to go about work and my routine; it will just be where I am in the evenings that's different." He was almost relieved to give her that much good news, or at least not bad news.

She nodded slowly. "Okay then, unless there's anything else that you need to discuss with me I have to get back to running errands that seem relatively unimportant now."

Instead of a verbal response Graham shook his head, stood up and headed into the office waving over his shoulder, relieved that the conversation had been relatively painless. He worried for his cousin because unlike Rachel, Jack could be rather explosive and her conversation would go by no means as smoothly. At least there was some comfort in the fact that they would see each other tonight and whatever hurt Jack may cause Graham, Taylor, and especially Dylan might be able to mitigate some.

Chapter 16

Mathew called Jack a few hours ago to let them know he would be holding a multipack meeting in his office. It was time to get everyone up to speed as a group so no one would have less puzzle pieces than anyone else. He also made some vague comments about them needing to decide how they were going to move forward. Jack had been downtown at work; he decided to swing by the pack office and work from there until the meeting, or at least read through part of the paperwork they had found one more time.

Weirdly, there was no one else in the pack office; it used to be that you couldn't come in without having at least one other person there, whether they be hanging out or meeting as a group. Since Lyra's kidnapping no one ever seemed to be there unless they had to be. What had once been a warm, inviting place with a sense of home for his pack mates now was a shell of its former self, only reminding them that the safety they felt was a mere illusion. Which meant there was no one there to ask him what he was working on or pester him as he read.

About ten minutes before he was going to head up to Mathew's office his phone went off; looking at it he saw Lyra's name and the picture she had snapped of one of her dogs appear on the screen. The small wisp of happiness he usually felt when one of his pack mates called was overwhelmingly stamped down by the dread and frustration that her call would probably not be heralding good news. He also still wasn't exactly thrilled with her about all the secrets she had been keeping. For a split-second he was tempted not to answer it but then guilt and a sense of duty made him slide his finger across the screen.

"Yes, Lyra."

There was a second of silence on the phone; her breathing didn't even come through the speaker. "Jack, I'm not going to be staying at Justin's for a few days."

Jack felt his body stiffen and anger set in but before he could jump in she started to speak even faster.

"It's okay, I'll be fine, I'm just kind of stuck needing to stay on the family compound. You see, my uncle had Graham and me, as well as the guy testing us, report to him on how... advanced the made werewolves were with their strength and agility. Those results combined with the councilman we have on swap with another family has my uncle worried that some of the beta wolves might take this opportunity to attack the family compound. And before you ask, beta wolves are werewolves without a pack who spend a lot of their time trying to take over family territories. Because of that my uncle wants as many of us staying on the compound as possible, that way if something happens there are more of us there to defend. If anything's going to happen it will happen in the next few days because my uncle is meeting with several heads of neighboring families on Tuesday. When word got out that we were gaining a large number of pack members, even on probation, it started to make other families nervous so a meeting was scheduled at the family's company's office to sort of explain why he was doing such a thing. That means, as long as that meeting goes well anyone who's going to attack has a very small window to do it."

Even though he could hear his heartbeat in his ears Jack took a second before answering to make sure she finished her explanation. "Are you telling me that you will not be under the pack's protection for a minimum of several days because there is a new threat that may attack your family? Am I right in assuming that these beta wolf attacks are why you would sometimes appear with minor injuries?"

Her response was so quiet he almost didn't hear it.

"Yes."

Taking a deep breath to give himself a second before responding, Jack clenched and unclenched his fists. "So these beta wolves are, I'm assuming, likely to attack your family compound or else your uncle wouldn't want to have you all there. So that puts all of you in danger because of us but I have to ask, how likely are all of us made werewolves in danger because of our association with your family?" He kept his voice as even as he could while he spoke.

"Honestly? I don't know. And that's not me avoiding the question. I genuinely don't know the answer. Could they attack the made werewolves? Yes, but it will take some time for them to figure out who you are. The betas will have to get on the family compound, in order to even figure out who the made werewolves are. That is only because you visit the compound. They would have to get close enough for cameras to pick them up. At that point, if they figure out who some of you are, they might attack but they are about as likely to attack you as they are family members right now because they don't know how strong or how weak you are and they won't necessarily risk the family's wrath just for that. If this multifamily meeting goes poorly and we're left out on our own then the made werewolves might be sitting ducks because it'll be family and betas alike coming after not only our family, but the made werewolves as well."

Fury burned through him so bright he got a tunnel vision of white for a split second. He waited several breaths before responding through clenched teeth, "Are you telling me that the packs are now in more danger because of the association with your family than they were before?"

"I... I don't know. If the scientists running the experiment had truly planned on kidnapping all of us and testing all of us, then maybe the threat level is the same. But if they had just meant to test the seven, to see if they could replicate what was different in us than in the lab assistants then yes, the made werewolves are in more danger now than they were before."

Lyra's voice sounded so sad that if Jack hadn't been so angry with her he would've felt pangs of compassion. "And you don't think that this was something we should have heard about before signing up for all of this?" He hit speakerphone so that he could pace the room unhindered to prevent himself from punching the wall or the desk.

"I wasn't thinking about beta wolves, Jack. I honestly was thinking it wouldn't be this big of a problem to take in the made werewolves. I didn't think about how the other families would see it. I didn't think beta wolves would think to challenge us. All I was thinking about was the best way to save all of us from the threat at hand." Her voice gained momentum and volume as anger threaded into it. "If it'd just been us seven that I thought were in trouble, then we would've gone to the family and not bothered you with it at all. We would've simply vanished without a trace. But we wouldn't let the family steal us away in safety when we didn't know what the outcome for you all would be. It's not in my nature to run from a problem, Jack, especially if that problem means danger for those I care about. You should know this better than anyone because you are the exact same way. So yeah, maybe we're all in a different brand of hot water now and maybe I screwed up by trying to help everyone but the way I see it, at least now we're all in it together. There are no secrets, no pretending to be something we're not. We're all in the trenches having to deal with this together. I would've thought that would count for something in this whole mess you have going on in your head. I get this a lot to take in, believe me, but honestly, Jack, you of all people, one of my closest friends, should see that I am trying my damnedest to see that we all get out of this safely. Honestly, this phone call was just to give you a heads up so if you are done chastising me or trying to vent your frustration or whatever it is you're trying to do, I'm gonna go now and possibly fight a whole bunch of betas who would rather I was dead. Have a good night, Jack." Then came the telltale click that told Jack Lyra had hung up the phone.

The growl that rolled out of him would've intimidated anyone, had any of his pack mates been around to hear it. He was both angry at Lyra for hanging up with him and for not telling him the dangers associated with them joining the family, even in the probationary way that they had. He felt that should've been something that had come up right away so they could've weighed the pros and cons with all the information; getting things on a need-to-know basis had gone way beyond insulting at this point. He was supposed to be her alpha, he was supposed to be her friend. All of that should've been enough but apparently it wasn't. He could understand her not thinking of it since Lyra was so impulsive but surely someone else would've thought of it and mentioned it to her before this. Eventually, he would get past the anger he was feeling about this whole situation that Lyra had put them in, not all of it was her fault. He knew that even if he did get over it their friendship was irreparably damaged; they would never be as close as they had once been ever again.

Those thoughts bothered him so much that they eclipsed everything else. Being werewolves together had made Jack and his friends closer, it created a bond, that until this whole mess started, Jack had thought would be unbreakable. But so much had happened so quickly that he wasn't sure he could ever trust Lyra like he used to.

Jack felt stuck between a rock and a hard place because he knew that now he was meeting with members of the alliance and it would be his job to tell them this new information regarding the beta wolves and the trouble they might be in. Feeling the weight of the position he found himself in, Jack locked up his office, shutting the door a bit harder than was strictly necessary, and made his way to the office of Pack J.

When he arrived to the meeting Mathew had set up, Jack was surprised to find out that it wasn't simply the seven alphas with the born werewolves in their packs. Everyone from the alliance seemed to be invited; there were still two or three missing but the majority of them were already there. That meant he would have to table his information about the beta werewolves because the last thing they needed was to let even more people know how large the werewolf community actually was. Something in him knew that if he shared this information with the packs that weren't invited to join the family, the repercussions would be worse than anything he could think of. A group of people surrounded Mathew and was standing in front of the corkboard Jack knew held the web of information they possessed about the lab assistants and the scientists they were working with. Seeing Rachel standing near the outskirts of the group, Jack made his way over to her; much to his surprise she looked up, saw him, and met him halfway.

"I see Lyra had a talk with you. I recognize that expression as the one I had when Graham and I held the same conversation earlier."

It was a relief to Jack that somebody else knew and that Rachel seemed just as conflicted with this new information as Jack felt. "Yeah, I was going to bring it up… but…"

"This party is bigger than you planned?" Rachel filled in.

Jack nodded by way of response but didn't say anything else; the expression on Rachel's face told him that she had been thinking the same thing. They stood there a moment as if both of them were at a loss for what to say, but at the same time weren't entirely sure that they wanted to join the group next to Mathew.

Before Jack could give his thoughts any more time, three more alphas walked in and Mathew cleared his throat loud enough to be heard across the room.

"Thank you everyone for showing up. Victor, if you will be so kind as to shut and lock the office door, don't worry, everyone, it's just a precaution, I don't expect us to have any unwanted guests," Mathew stated by way of greeting. "If you will all join me on this side of the corkboard, I want to show you the information we have found thus far about the scientists that seem to be showing extra interest in us."

Jack and Rachel exchanged concerned glances before heading towards the corkboard; when they were closer in range Jack could see that there was much more information filled in than there had been on the last version he had received. Some of the details he had read about in the files that were sitting on his desk but other pieces had been unknown to him. Before he could work up too much concern on that, Mathew started speaking again.

"As you can see, we have chased the funding for this little experiment, in part, to some extra curriculum searching we've been doing, to Garrison Inc., which as it turns out is a kind of shell company for the Oregon based Page Turner Enterprise. We have yet to figure out which of the three company founders is directly funding this project, if it is just one. But since we had enough information on exactly who was working on this project we wanted to get everyone together and let you know. It would seem the seven wolves showed different strengths than the lab assistants, which is what garnered their attention. It is as if they are using the lab assistants as their test subjects but they wanted the seven they've been going after in order to improve the lab assistants' capabilities. There also are some notes stating they have some of Lyra's blood somewhere, we don't know where it's stored, simply that they keep calling it the B site and they only took a few vials and therefore have been testing on it sparingly. This also lets us know that there is at least one, if not three, other buildings that they have been storing different information in with the idea that if we attack one site or they have to abandon one, the others still have enough viable information for them to continue their research. We've also learned one lab assistant, a..." Mathew shifted through the notepad he was holding, "Tory Pendleton, seems to not be involved at all. As far as we can tell she has had no contact with the other lab assistants, which I find curious as to whether that is her doing or theirs. Regardless, since we now have enough information to know that they are going to continue to come after those seven, if not more of us, as there are notes saying that is the next step of the plan, we are kind of at an impasse."

"The way I see it, we have four choices moving forward and I called this meeting so that we can make the decision as a group versus me being the only one with all the information and arbitrarily picking on everybody's behalf. The first is we continue to dig as much as possible and get all the information we can, but I'm not sure how much more we'll be able to get without knowing where these other sites are and we would be devoting a lot of resources to tracking all of these lab assistants in hopes that something happened. On the plus side to tracking all of them, we would know if one of them went after one of our own. This would also be sort of a delay tactic in that it would mean putting off making any real decisions until we had all the information we feel we can get. Though I'm not sure how long we could run using this much of our resources and connections before we burn out."

"Our second choice is to kill every person we know is involved with this process and hope that it stops the people doing the research and that there isn't anybody we've missed. It would also mean doing things covertly so that they seemed like accidents or they disappeared. Personally I'm not terribly fond of the idea of making ourselves into murderers. I really feel this is our most drastic choice but if the alliance decides that is the direction they want to go, I'm not going to stand in the way. I just don't feel that we really want to put ourselves in that category because while I want to do everything in my power to lay this to rest, I want to think that we would draw the line at murder.

"Our third choice is to burn down the building that we have found, collect everything in there first and hope that it delays the research enough to make a difference. But we already know that there are multiple sites and we don't know how much information is at each of the sites. Seeing as how we have already destroyed two that may or may not have been in use, it feels a little futile to destroy the building we know they actually use and have seen several of them going in and out of.

"Our fourth and final choice is to collect all the information we have gathered and turn it over to several of the officials that were in charge of the original project, ones that we know and trust, of which there are a few. And let them handle it. Inform them that this operation under this Garrison Inc. needs to be shut down. Now we wouldn't necessarily have a guarantee that they would do the right thing. And I can't say that I have the most confidence that they would, so as a backup plan to this we would leak the same amount of information to some press contacts that I have who would be sympathetic to our cause and give them a deadline to release the information with the company names and that sort of thing to put pressure on our government contacts to do anything. I have one particularly entrepreneurial press contact who will make a very sympathetic case for those poor college students who were unwillingly experimented on once and whom the government is not stopping a company from doing it a second time. I firmly believe with that kind of outcry they will have to show their hand and do something about it. I also think that if we go with this plan, it would be a good idea to have the reporter interview Lyra and or one or two of the others Pack L have been after to really hit the human interest story home. It would emphasize the idea that we are the victims and humanize us more than just a random number of college students. To be fair, I am partial to this forth idea because I think that it helps us come out looking good and while I have the spotlight to us, it adds enough of a spotlight that if someone went to make a move they would be risking themselves as well. I'm not entirely comfortable with us being out in the media and that whole circus but I think that it would help people be on our side, which I do believe is what we need right now. So those are options; I leave it open to the floor for the decision."

No one spoke right away as if no one wanted to be the person to sway everybody else or that's what seemed like to Jack. For all he knew, the others liked the second option and were afraid to say it out loud. He shared Mathew's sentiment about becoming murderers. While it might fix their problem in the short-term, he wasn't entirely sure that would be their best-case scenario in the long-term.

"If no one else is going to say anything," Bishop piped in, "from the options you've listed it seems going to the government and the media is truly our only option. I, for one, am not okay with murder or inaction and I really do not feel that giving away the information we know about that building by burning it down will help us any; if anything else it may make them more secretive and that's the last thing we need."

Charlie let out a heavy sigh, shoving his hands in his pockets. "My better half isn't going to like being part of a media circus. We got a lot of extra attention from the scientists and the last thing I want is to put her through that circus again. Only now it will be bigger, but if it is our best bet to keep our people safe, which it seems to be, I don't really see how we have much choice."

There were several mumbles and comments of agreement but no one seemed excited about the plan. It seemed, at least to Jack, as if it was the lesser of four evils for everyone involved. That wasn't terribly comforting to him; he knew Lyra would hate doing that interview but would do it for the good of the pack and for the good of her family. Even though he was angry with her, he felt a slight pain knowing how much this option was going to bother her.

"I agree, going public is our best bet," was all he said. He was dooming his littermate to being heavily in the public spotlight for something he knew she would hate and as angry as he was with her, he couldn't bring himself to feel entirely comfortable with that decision.

"With all due respect, Mathew, I would like to see if there are perhaps any reporters that we might be in contact with that are not necessarily your contact. I don't mean to sound as if I don't trust you. But I would feel slightly better if the plan didn't wholly rely on your dubious connections," Bishop ventured, keeping his eyes on Mathew the entire time.

Mathew raised one eyebrow in curious surprise but didn't say anything, simply nodded and Bishop pulled out his phone. At some point during this discussion, Bishop had come to stand on the other side of Jack and he watched as the other alpha pulled out his phone and flashed the screen so Jack and Rachel could see that it was Taylor he was calling before putting the phone up to his ear and walking out of the office.

No one spoke after Bishop left the room but when Jack did a quick scan it seemed as if at least half of the alphas in the room, himself and Rachel included seemed to not entirely disagree with the idea that not everything should rely on Mathew. Jack hadn't even been aware that it mattered to him that everything was being done through Mathew's connections until Bishop brought it up and now that the other man had, Jack found himself wondering just how much of all of this was only done because of who Mathew was and who he knew. Beyond that he felt a little spike of irritation knowing that Bishop was asking if there was a born a werewolf that was a reporter. He knew intellectually it was the best idea to have a born werewolf disperse the information because he or she would know what to leave out and what to put in to cover things on their end, but he couldn't help but be frustrated by the fact that they would be relying yet again on the born wolf family.

A few minutes later there was a knock at the door, Victor, who was the only second who seemed to be in attendance at this meeting, a fact Jack just realized, opened the door for his alpha.

Once it was shut Bishop addressed the room, "It would appear that on my end there are two reporters of decent reputation who would be likely more than willing to cover the story if we choose." He was looking directly at Mathew, challenging the other man to veto him and say that only his contacts would do.

Mathew inclined his head to Bishop with a professional smile on his face. "If you are willing to be the point of contact for one or both of those reporters, that would be fantastic. Before you leave today I will give you all the information that I have for you to pass along to them and please keep a copy for yourself just in case and this evening I will contact the government officials in question and give them a copy of the information, keeping one copy to myself in case we need it. I will then deliver USB drives with all that we have to each of your offices via my second tomorrow afternoon. Just make sure you or someone in your pack that you trust is there to answer when he knocks. If no one has anything else, I believe we are done and I wish everyone luck, as we are about to become a very public spectacle."

No one moved for a few moments, as if the weight of their decision was holding them in place. They were probably all feeling the same sense of foreboding that Jack did. Putting them in the spotlight was a bit of a gamble, especially if the government didn't act quickly.

Once people started to mingle, Jack looked for both Bishop and Mathew so that he could head the two men off privately and let them know what Lyra had told him. But they had quickly been monopolized by others, both of whom were also born werewolves so he couldn't very well broach the subject in front of those people. Giving a heavy sigh, Jack didn't feel like waiting around so he texted both Mathew and Bishop to give him a call later that evening at their convenience before heading out of the office.

Gretchen S. B.

All he wanted in that moment was to be left alone. He wanted to go to his apartment, lie on the couch, and zone out in front of the television and pretend for a little while that he wasn't the alpha of Pack F, that he wasn't a werewolf, that he was simply a man wanting some down time. He wasn't entirely sure he could pull it off, but he was darn well going to put an effort in.

When he got down to the parking lot he saw a Rachel heading to her own car several rows over.

"Rachel," he called, not yelling but saying it loud enough that she would be able to hear him with her advanced hearing.

Hearing him, she curiously turned over her shoulder; when she seemed to register that it was Jack calling after her, she stopped walking and turned to face him, letting him come to her. He didn't stop walking until he was less than a yard away from her, and even then he spoke quietly, just in case anyone else happened to be around.

"You didn't say much in the meeting. Are you comfortable with this whole idea? I can't make myself be fully okay with it and I'm not sure whether it's the media attention or the fact that I feel Mathew is putting a lot of faith in his government contacts."

Her brow furrowed and she pursed her lips ever so slightly before she spoke, "I like the idea of being in the public eye. I am a nurse, which means it isn't going to be too hard for them to hunt me down if they want to. As for the government contacts, while I'm prone to agree with you, I've also realized over the years that you should not underestimate Mathew. That guy has a lot of irons in the fire at any given time. And honestly with the born werewolves handling the media coverage we're kind of hedging our bets and balancing things out a little bit. It was a good idea on Bishop's part to do that instead of leaving everything in Mathew's hands. That being said, I do find it a little disconcerting that most of the things we've done so far have been funneled through Mathew. Bishop kind of brought that to my attention and I think I'm going to have to ponder on that to see exactly how comfortable I am leaving all of this in one man's hands. It's not that I find him untrustworthy but he is secretive and not just... I don't know; it makes me a little wary is all."

It made Jack relax little to know that somebody else was thinking the same thing he was. He and Rachel seemed to be on the same page about a lot of things, which made Jack feel a little saner in all of this chaos.

"I had the same epiphany. But I can't decide whether I'm more concerned about Mathew's secrecy or the born werewolves' secrecy. I think that I don't like my and my pack's fates being in anybody's hands other than mine."

Rachel snorted. "Well, yes, there is that. But in this particular case I think it is a necessary evil, seeing as how we don't have a lot of choices unless you really want to do the whole murder spree plan. I'm betting you don't. So we're kind of stuck in this limbo. Maybe having the world know that people are after us will benefit us. I don't know, all I know is this is the best plan that's been presented to help me and mine and that's ultimately, as alpha, who I'm looking out for." If they had been in any other situation Jack knew he would pursue the idea of dating Rachel. He knew that they would work really well together and were very similar in a lot of ways, but seeing as how they were both in charge of a great number of other people, neither of them could really afford to not have their head in the game right now. Part of him was sad and angry about that, that being a werewolf was yet again in the way of Jack living his life like a normal person. He pushed that thought aside and gave Rachel a sad, soft smile.

"Some days it seems as if being the alpha doesn't necessarily come with any perks, just a lot of responsibility."

She snorted again. "Noticed that too, have you? I'll see you later, Jack; I have to head to work. Because you know, I still have to be able to pay for food and my apartment." Then she waved, turned, and headed towards her car.

Jack watched her go with a plethora of thoughts and emotions swirling around his head. There was too much going on. Jack liked to tackle one problem at a time and the current situation they found themselves in had all sorts of things being thrown at them at once. There were too many fires on the stove for him to be able to put them all out at once. As he headed back towards his car, he knew that, try as he might, his efforts to try and escape for an evening were probably not going to get him anywhere.

Chapter 17

Taylor growled as he used his partially-changed claws to swipe across the chest of the beta wolf lunging at him. His adrenaline was spiking nonstop so the world almost vibrated around him.

Graham's father had been right; two beta families had banded together to try and overthrow the family so they could fight amongst themselves later. They'd struck at two in the morning when most of the compound was asleep. Since Taylor had drawn the night shift he'd been prowling the grounds when a call came over the radio that betas were attacking from two separate points in the compound. He had sprinted to the nearest point and thrown himself into the melee as more than a dozen betas had scaled the wall somehow. There were only four others from the family in that area, not good odds in their favor. Taylor quickly drowned out everything else and fought whatever came at him that he didn't recognize.

Right now he wasn't worried about the odds or made werewolves versus born wolves; it was about fighting for survival. Different beta groups had different rules when it came to fighting a family. Some killed anyone that fought against them, while others would simply subdue them and keep them much like a prisoner of war until they agreed to the new regime. Taylor would not let himself be killed or taken prisoner; he had to defeat whoever came at him by all means necessary and if that meant showing the made werewolf he had the ability of only changing parts at a time so be it. They were still a week and a half from the full moon so no one else in the area would be able to do what he was doing. Having those talon-like claws worked to his advantage as now his opponent, who was bleeding from the slashes in his chest, backed away and gave him a wider birth, eyes the size of saucers.

"The hell did you do that?"

The stranger was looking for an answer so Taylor just gave him a sinister smile; no answer was better than any answer he could possibly give. He bent his knees slightly and sprung, moving both arms in a clawing motion and slashed once more at the man in front of him, taking advantage of the other man's shock. It worked to his advantage as the man slid to the ground, injured enough that while he may live in the long run, he was going to be out of commission now.

Taylor turned away from him, as he was no longer a threat. Since they were outnumbered he needed to concentrate on the others around them first and foremost. Not two feet away from him he saw Jeremy, a wolf in the family the same age as Graham's eldest brother. Jeremy was grappling with a wolf Taylor didn't recognize. The two men were fighting over one dagger, Jeremy had his hand wrapped around the handle and the other wolf was trying to force Jeremy to let it go by digging into his wrist. Taylor reacted without more than one strategic thought; he bolted behind the beta wolf and slid his claws across the other man's throat. Not deep enough to kill him but enough to put them out of commission until their rapid healing could stop the precious, life-giving red liquid from leaving his body. The man crumpled to the ground and Jeremy stumbled from the force.

The other man looked at Taylor, eyes wide with surprise but knowing better than to bring it up now, he simply nodded his appreciation and both of them headed in opposite directions to fight off others.

There were four more people on the scene fighting now, which was good since a handful more of the betas had scaled the wall. Taylor was none too happy to see that the four that had joined them were Graham, Dylan, Lyra, and Zachariah, one of Lyra's twin younger brothers. He knew Lyra could hold her own or worse, take enough damage to survive, but Zachariah was only fifteen and was not going to be any match for anyone that came over that wall. As Taylor ran towards the young wolf, his twin brother Caspian was running into the fray. As Taylor watched, the two of them fought side-by-side, moving almost as one. Between the two of them they were holding their own versus the one beta they were fighting. It was impressive to see their movements and as much as Taylor wanted to watch to make sure the two were okay, they were far too outnumbered as a group for him to pay attention to anything else.

So he headed for the beta that would've attacked them from behind, growling as he ran so the other man would know he was coming and shift his attention from the twins. Granted, he would lose his element of surprise but if it kept attention off the twins it didn't matter in Taylor's book.

The beta growled at him menacingly before fanning out his fingers in a similar fashion to the way Dylan was. Dylan saw a flash before the man lunged toward him; he saw it barely in time to leap back a step. The beta was wearing some sort of hand guard with tiny knives on the tip of each finger as if emulating claws. It was a good move and he was probably cutting through members of the family at a quick rate but unluckily for him, Taylor was better equipped, as his nails were slightly longer than the blades on the fingertips.

He felt the tug as the knives sliced across his shirt, only grazing the skin underneath causing no more of a scratch than a paper cut. Growling, Taylor took advantage of the outstretched arm by taking both of his hands and digging the nails into the forearm as hard as he could and scratching down. He could feel the nails digging into muscle and shredding the flesh. There was a howl of angry pain from the beta as he yanked his arm back. Taylor released just in time to move his hands out of the way of the tiny blades that retracted from near his stomach.

Taylor only saw the beta telegraph his movements a split second before the beta was in the air; Taylor wouldn't be able to get out of his way fast enough so he curled and rolled so that the beta would only come down on his shoulder and side instead of on top of his chest. He felt those tiny blades prick his arm and one down the side of his back. He had gratefully gotten the beta's left-hand out of commission, which only left the right hand with its blades as a threat. Taylor spun himself out of the way as the beta hit the ground, then continued his movement, using the momentum to spin himself all the way and slide his leg on the backs of the knees of the beta, causing the other man to lose his balance, as he was still landing and fall backwards.

The beta let out a menacing screech that bordered on madness but before he could do much beyond try to use his useless arm to help him out, Taylor was at the man's head and kicked it hard enough to make him lose consciousness.

That would at least put this madman out of commission for about ten minutes, in which time Taylor hoped either help would arrive, or they would be able to take the number down more so that Taylor would have help fighting this man, because he was pretty sure the beta wouldn't make the same mistake again and when he woke up he would probably be surly.

Taylor looked around to find another fight; the adrenaline had him panting. He could feel the blood dripping down his shirt but ignored it as he surveyed the scene in front of him. There were still three others fighting but they looked to be all right so Taylor didn't need to intervene. There were no stray betas left, as a handful of other family members had come to join the fight while he fought the last man with the blades. The twins were now fighting alongside Lyra, them on one side and Lyra on the other. Lyra had done the same thing he had with her claws, slashing out at the man in front of her. As Taylor watched, she got one good in the man's side and he turned to look at her directly and Taylor could see he was losing a lot of blood. It was a matter of seconds before he would pass out so his body would be able to heal everything. As he watched between Lyra and the twins, dancing forward and backward, the man took a few more hits and managed to hit Caspian hard enough to knock him off his feet, leaving him dazed on the ground before the blood loss became too much and he himself crumpled in a heap on the grass. They were the last to finish up and once they had, the group of them stood in silence for a minute and all that could be heard was the heavy, labored breathing.

"All right, we need to restrain those that are still going to be alive and let the Luna treat them, once we've got them in cells that is," said Graham. "Does anybody have some kind of restraints?"

There were rumblings from several of the guys who had been on the night shift, Taylor himself had two sets dangling off the belt loops of his pants; he unclipped them and started by restraining the man with the knife gloves, then the one closest to him. Once they used the restraints that the night shift had, they were still several short. Graham got on his radio and let their dispatcher know that they were down five pairs and that they would need assistance moving the beta wolves into holding cells and getting rid of the several on the ground that were now deceased.

Since Taylor had a headset in he heard when dispatch came back over the radio and stated that there was no one to help at the moment, as the other side of the compound had not subdued those that came over the wall yet. At last report there were a dozen and a half more betas on that side of the compound. That they should stay put and guard the unconscious they had over there and wait until the other side could be subdued.

There were several curses and more than half of their number began to sprint to the other side of the compound. It left Taylor, Dylan, Graham, Lyra, the twins, as well as two others that had joined the fight to guard the unconscious.

The twins made as if to run but their sister grabbed both of them. "Um, nope. Mom's already going to be pissed that you were out and about this late, let alone fighting. You both know you're not supposed to be out here until you're at least eighteen. Both of our parents, as well as Luna, would kill me if I let you run headlong into another problem."

Both brothers tugged visibly but it was clear their sister wouldn't let them go. They both sighed. "Yeah, well, I guess it would be irresponsible of us to leave our sister outnumbered should the unconscious ones wake up," relented Caspian in a put-out tone.

Lyra rolled her eyes but didn't say anything else as she dropped both of their arms and made her way over to Taylor squinting at his scratches in the dark. When she reached him she gently pulled aside the scraps of cloth to get as good of a look at the cuts as she possibly could. "How bad are these?"

Taylor simply shook his head but realized she wasn't looking at him so he would have to respond verbally. "They'll be fine. They're certainly not deep enough for you to worry yourself with."

"Actually, little Luna, Saul over here could use your help. The one with the knives for claws just about gutted him," said one of the two men whose names Taylor didn't know, as they crouched above one of the men on the ground.

Lyra immediately turned and sprinted the two yards until she slid into a kneeling position right next to the man on the ground. "Lift his shirt for me, don't worry about being delicate about it."

The man on the other side tugged at the shirt; it was clearly stuck to the body but after a few hard tugs and some noises he managed to roll the cloth so that it lay on the part of his chest that wasn't wounded.

Lyra lifted her hands above her head, laying her left on top of her right. He could hear her using words but couldn't exactly figure out what they were as she began turning them so they were side by side, cupping in a down motion and moving until they met again, facing up, creating a circle. She did this multiple times before a soft blue glow appeared in the space in between her hands. It didn't matter how many times Taylor saw Lyra perform Luna magic, it was eerily awe-inspiring every time. She was doing what was called a Luna light; it was an ancient magic meant to replicate the light of the moon but in a much closer distance so the Luna would be able to see the injuries before her. Lyra's was not as strong or as bright as her aunt's but then she wouldn't come into her full power until her aunt to stepped down or died. She had enough abilities to be able to heal Saul enough that he could hold out until the Luna could get to him. Because the Luna was so precious she was usually not allowed to fight and would not be allowed to leave a safe haven until the fighting had stopped. Sometimes these precious extra minutes made the difference between life and death.

"Well, thank goodness he is unconscious," Lyra said, as she lifted her hands above the Luna light and gently brushed the top of it to bring it down so that was level with her eyes. Then she looked straight down at the wound and visibly tensed before taking both her hands and placing the space between her thumb and forefinger against each other, overlapping her left fingers over her right, placing her joined palms over the worst part of the wound, which Taylor could now see appeared to have ripped through an organ or two. She cocked out her elbows so that they were in line with her hands as she leaned forward. She then began ever so slightly swaying back and forth from her hips and speaking quietly in a language Taylor knew he would never understand. It was a minute or so before anything happened. Slowly, as they all watched the light, a light that matched the one just above her head emanated out from her hands and shone down on the wound; it grew brighter and brighter until eventually it began to hurt Taylor's eyes and he had to look away. If she had to make the magic that bright then Saul's injury was very bad. Especially knowing that she wouldn't be able to heal as much as her aunt would. At some point Graham had come to stand beside Taylor and the two of them watched in silence as Lyra did all she could for their family member.

She was still going, swaying faster and faster when a voice from dispatch came over the radio, "The intruders have been subdued. Assistance will be to you within the next five minutes with stretchers and such to take the prisoners into custody, do you require other assistance?"

Graham touched his radio in his ear. "We have the little Luna with us and she is working on someone who appears to be mortally wounded; I do not think that he can be moved before the Luna has seen him."

"Understood, Luna will be dispatched as soon as the prisoners are in custody and far enough away from your location."

Graham growled before answering, "Understood, over and out." He turned to Taylor. "How many do you think we lost this night?" Taylor simply shook his head, not looking away from the bright light Lyra was creating. "I don't know but I'm itching to call Bishop and find out if everyone on the outside is okay."

Graham simply nodded and didn't say anything after that.

Worry coursed through him as Taylor stepped away from the group and pulled out his phone. Sure, he was worried for the man on the ground Lyra was trying to keep alive, but more so he was worried about his pack. He hoped that no beta wolves had figured out who the made wolves were or that they were much weaker than their born counterparts and set up an attack. He would never forgive himself or the others if something happened to one of the made werewolves because of them.

Bishop picked up after the first ring. "Hold on a second, let me get to the office."

Then there was relative silence on the other end of the phone; Taylor could hear Bishop breathing. He could also hear Victor making some comment under his breath as the two of them walked from the meeting Bishop had mentioned they were at last time he called. Taylor was curious how his pack second had managed to talk himself into that meeting but there were more pressing things to discuss.

The fact that Bishop had put them on hold was a good sign, if he hadn't answered it all Taylor would've been worried. After a few minutes Bishop finally got back on the phone, "What's going on, Taylor?"

"The compound was just attacked by beta wolves. I wanted to check in and make sure that all of you guys were still okay that the damage thus far only extended to the born werewolf compound."

"Are all of you okay?" Bishop asked warily.

Taylor hesitated for a moment, simply because he was not used telling the truth. Even though he was more open with his alpha than the others were with theirs, he was still used to keeping their world a secret. "Casualties are as of yet unknown. I can only speak for Graham, Lyra, and I. While we're a little battered, overall we're okay."

He heard Bishop sigh over the phone. "That's somewhat good news. I will check in with the rest of our pack and contact you when I have an answer. If nothing is wrong I will text you; if there seems to be a problem I will give you a call."

Then the alpha hung up. Taylor slid his phone back into his pocket, relieved to hear that there hadn't been an overt attack, as far as they knew. Though to be honest, if one of them had been attacked they probably wouldn't have been in good enough shape to have called Bishop and told him what had happened.

Taylor made his way back over to where Graham stood watching Lyra keep the man on the ground stabilized. He was relieved to see that Lyra's expression was not quite as panicked as it had been before, which let them know that either the Luna was on her way or Lyra was confident she could keep the man stable until the Luna arrived.

It was answered for him when he stood beside Graham and the other man turned his head slightly. "The Luna is on her way, and should be here in the next five minutes or so."

Though he felt slightly insensitive, Taylor changed the subject, "Bishop and Victor seem to be okay and Bishop is contacting the others to check in with them as well. I think since Lyra has this in hand our best course of action is to hunt down Jesse and discuss with him the possibility of being our point of contact for breaking the news story about the lab assistants."

Graham turned more to face Taylor, giving him a thoughtful frown. "So they decided to go public with it then? I can't say it's necessarily what I would've done but I understand their reasoning." He then tapped his earpiece. "Has anyone seen Jesse recently?"

They knew the other man was on the compound, as they had seen him an hour or two before the attack.

"Yeah, I'm moving some of our uninvited guests into our less than hospitable guest quarters. You're more than welcome to come down and meet me," Jesse's deep voice came over the radio in response to Graham's question.

Graham simply looked at Taylor and nodded before heading towards one of the back buildings where they kept detainment cells for just such types of attacks. Taylor quickly caught up with him and the two men walked in silence. Neither of them was particularly thrilled about being in the media again.

When word had hit that hundreds of college students had been unwilling lab rats the media had a field day. It made international news and several intrepid reporters had even been able to pick some of them out from the blurry group photos that had been taken at the scene. It was only going to get worse now, since the scientists had decided to center on just the seven of them. Most likely, it would be the seven of them that would be sharing the spotlight with each other instead of having several hundred faces to blend into.

Jesse was waiting at the top of the stairs with a look of curiosity on his face when they entered the split-level building. "Is there a particular reason you two are looking for me?" Jesse's sandy blond hair, which was usually styled within an inch of its life, was currently disheveled and his pale blue polo shirt had rips in it, which told Taylor it was most likely being thrown out when the night was over.

As is usual for them, Taylor let Graham take the lead. After Bishop's phone call, he had filled Graham in on what exactly the alpha was thinking about doing. They hadn't had a lot of time to discuss it because it happened less than ten minutes before the betas attacked.

"How about we make our way to one of the main hall conference rooms before we discuss business," Graham proposed.

Jesse lifted his eyebrow higher before shrugging and moving his arms, telling Graham to lead the way. Being an investigative reporter for the Seattle Times gave Jesse a certain level of discretion when it came to information; that wasn't always the case with most of the family. A lot of wolves assumed that something said in the family stays in the family, but that didn't mean it couldn't be shared with other family members. They were lucky that Jesse wasn't necessarily like that. Lance, the other reporter, who worked for a more online-based news organization, didn't quite have the same tact.

Once the three of them had settled into the conference room with Jesse sitting across the table from the other two, he leaned back in his chair with his arms folded, his gaze darting between Graham and Taylor. "All right, you have my interest piqued. What exactly is going on?"

Taylor was somewhat surprised when Graham leaned back and motioned for him to take the lead. It wasn't Graham's style to advocate anything and the surprise showed on Jesse's face as well.

Going out of his way to maintain eye contact, Taylor took a deep breath before beginning, "Were you at the family meeting about bringing in the new werewolves?"

His question was answered by a scoff. "Are you kidding? Of course I was there. The family was all abuzz about the emergency meeting; I certainly wasn't going to miss that."

Nodding, he continued, "Good that means I can skip a lot of the explaining. The scientists that have been coming after the seven of us - we think we know what they're up to. They want to match the lab assistant made werewolf DNA, with those of born werewolves. As you know, that isn't necessarily possible, although to be fair I don't know enough about the science behind it to really make that statement. Anyway, we managed to find a sort of hidey-hole with a lot of their paperwork and information. So much so that we know what company is backing them. Though we don't know which exact backer is fronting the money, we have a pretty good trail. The alpha counsel has decided that the best course of action is to give all the information we have over to government contacts and hope that they take the businesses and scientists down."

"Really?" Jesse's voice dripped with disdain.

"Yes, we all feel the same way and that is where you come in. We want to leak all of the information that we have to the press."

Jesse leaned forward, putting his elbows on the table and a small smile began to grow on his face. "You want the public knowledge and sympathy to pressure the government into closing them down, just in case they wouldn't have done it in the first place. Not a bad idea. Just how much information are you going to give me about this?"

Taylor let out the breath he hadn't known he was holding and leaned back in his chair. "I'm going to give you everything my alpha sends me.

Technically, he's giving it to me in person so I'll be passing along however he gives it to me to you sometime tomorrow. We were also hoping that you might interview one or two of the seven of us thereafter. Give it a sort of personal touch. The thing is we would prefer if the source of the information, as well as the names of the interviewees, were kept a secret. We know this is going to give us a lot of media attention and prefer to keep them off our backs as long as we possibly can."

The blond man across from them didn't respond right away; Taylor could see the wheels turning in his head. He finally seemed to settle on something because he leaned over and pulled his phone out of his pocket, laying it on the table between them before tapping the screen so that it was hitting record. Both Graham and Taylor exchanged glances. But neither of them said anything.

"Going to ask you a few simple questions to get me started. To sort of frame the information I write. I will write these interviews down and then delete the recording so that you can't be identified by voice. The first question is how long have the scientists been trying to get a hold of you? My second question is at what point did you believe these attempts might be hostile? I think those two questions will do me for now but I will want to meet with you later once I've had a chance to read through all of the stuff you're going to give me."

He then waived Graham to go first.

Graham frowned. "For your first question, I would have to say between one and two months. I'm not one hundred percent sure. As for your second question, I knew that they were going to be a threat to us when they started to get hostile towards Lyra. While they tried to be nice to us males and convince us to join, they attacked her and attempted to kidnap her on multiple occasions. Once I found out that that was what they were doing I knew that they were not as benign as they wanted us to believe they were."

Jesse's eyes had gone wide when Graham had mentioned Lyra. Clearly the other man hadn't known to what extent the lab assistants had gone after her. He recovered quickly and then turned to Taylor when Graham finished speaking.

"About the same time as Graham. It's my understanding that they went after us at just about the same time. With the exception of Lyra, whom they kidnapped two or two and a half months before that in an effort to convince us to come look out for her, however, they didn't count on her escaping. As for when I realized they were hostile, I don't know why I thought this but we were at a multi-pack meeting, deciding on soccer teams for the year and they went after her aggressively to try and get her on their team and the way they did it, the tone in the woman's voice just sent off warning bells for me, which was only solidified when I found out how they had been going after Lyra."

When it became clear that both men were finished talking, Jesse tapped his phone to stop recording it. "I didn't quite realize they were being this aggressive, but then actually managed to abduct Lyra. I'm going to want to talk to her once I've gone through all that paperwork. Do you think that's going to be a problem?"

Graham shook his head. "Even if she has a problem with it, she'll do it anyway."

The reporter frowned but didn't respond to Graham's words. "All right, if you can give me some of that information tonight that be wonderful, otherwise first thing in the morning would be good. I'm going to do a mockup of the story tonight and if there is as much information as it sounds like there might be, this might be a multiple parts story. Going to run the mockup by my boss in the morning. I'm pretty sure he's going to approve it, then I'll be in touch with you guys. I'll let you see the articles before they run. But if they resorted to things like kidnapping I can understand why you'd want to be extra careful bringing sympathy on your side. I'll make sure the families mentioned and you guys are shown in the best light possible."

Taylor relaxed a little. He'd known Jesse would be the right person to go to but there was something about the other man basically confirming Taylor's expectations that made them relax. There was a sliver of hope inside him that maybe, just maybe, something would actually go according to plan.

"As soon as we leave this room I will call my office and ask him to send the paperwork to me ASAP or to leave it in the office for me. Either way I'll get it tonight or tomorrow morning; you should have all the information I can get you by early afternoon at the latest," Taylor stated, as he stood up.

Both Jesse and Graham followed suit. Jesse nodded before sliding his phone back in his pocket then all three of them left the conference room. Once they were outside they went two separate ways, Jesse back in the direction he had been helping round up the betas and putting them somewhere they could keep tabs on them, while Taylor and Graham headed toward Graham's father's house to see if there was anything else they could help get done. While they walked over, Taylor pulled out his phone to call Bishop.

"I did text you and tell you that everyone I could get a hold of was fine. There was no need to call and double check," Bishop said by way of answering his phone.

"I wanted to ask about the information Mathew gave you that I'll be passing along to the reporter. He's chomping at the bit to get it and I was just wondering if there's a way for me to get it tonight so that I can pass it on to them as soon as possible," Taylor requested.

There was a beat of silence as if Bishop was weighing his options. "I can hang around the office if you think you can get here within the next hour or so. Otherwise I can leave it here, tape it somewhere no one would find it so that you can get it at your leisure sometime tonight."

Taylor weighed his options; he was pretty sure with the betas' attack he wouldn't be able to leave in time to get to the office within an hour. "I think it's best to leave it somewhere since I don't know how long I'll be here, but I definitely want to get it tonight."

"Duly noted, I will stash it someplace and then text you the USB drive's whereabouts. I hope the rest of your night goes more smoothly."

Taylor couldn't help the soft smile. "Good night, Bishop."

The other man hung up without anymore of an answer. But then Taylor didn't really expect one, Bishop had never been one to say goodbye to people he was familiar with.

Once he was off the phone, he texted Jesse, letting him know that he would get the information to him as soon as he got it from the office. With that out of the way, Taylor could concentrate more on the problems at hand like exactly how many betas had banded together to try and take out the family compound. This particular strike seemed slightly bigger than usual, which meant that some of the betas might've been organizing, not exactly a good thing when the family was already facing a little bit of a crisis. Taylor stowed those thoughts away; speculating wouldn't do any good until he knew all of the facts. In order to get those they were going to need to talk to Graham's father, or barring that, listen in on some of the interrogations of the beta wolves that were still conscious.

Chapter 18

It was the longest he had been a wolf, by far. There was something madness inducing about being stuck in this unnatural shape. He had only ever changed when forced to and changed back as soon as he was able. This loss of control over his own body made him want to rip the throat out of any person that dared come near him, which meant of course that the only time anyone approached his cage was to deliver a sloppy meal. Not only was this a body he was not used to, but without his human body he couldn't communicate with anyone. It was completely isolating.

When one of the men in a lab coat finally came walking toward his cage he cursed himself for the excitement he felt. He was so eager to get out of the cage that even the sight of a lab coat made exhilaration bloom in his chest. The man in the lab coat, who appeared to be in his mid-sixties, kneeled down so he would be at wolf head height and smiled gently as if looking at an indulged grandchild.

"Now, I get the distinct impression that you might appreciate a chance to stretch those legs of yours. I do believe you haven't been taken out for exercise in a day or two. I hope you can understand why that would be necessary, seeing as how we needed to make sure that you were stable enough both mentally and physically to be let out. How about I call security and retake you out to have a good run, shall we?" The man stood up and turned, facing away before motioning to several security guards several cells away.

He couldn't help the humiliated grovel when he saw that one of the security guards was walking at him with a muzzle and leash as if he was some unruly household pet.

The lab coat clucked his tongue before looking from the security guard then back to him. "I don't think that's necessary, do you, 071? I do, after all, have this." He raised his wrinkled hand to show that he was holding the same remote the blonde in the lab coat had possessed when they put on the heavy collar. "Yes, he recognizes it. He won't give us any trouble at all. Wouldn't want to risk a shock or the now-fully-working quite accurately pitched dog whistle that the collar now makes. We had some trouble transmitting it at first but we have fixed the remote to make sure that it works absolutely fine now." He turned back to the security guard in question. "You may open the door, he will do as he's told." He then began walking away, simply assuming the others would follow.

There was an air of authority about this man that made him think this lab coat was in some kind of a leadership position. He bossed the security guards around more than the other lab coats had and there was an air about him as if he knew he was in charge. Even in wolf form, it made him wary to go with this man but he knew with the collar and remote he had very little choice. When the door was opened he slowly, hesitantly, walked out of the cell and headed in the direction the lab coat had gone. They went down the hallway he had gone down to receive the collar, past that room and a little ways further to another door where the lab coat stood, waiting to usher them in.

Once he was in the room, he could smell that other werewolves had been in here before. There were three distinct wolf scents that he could make out, as well as of bleach as if someone had cleaned something up and tried to eradicate the smell entirely, but they hadn't managed. Just under that bleach smell was the scent of blood. His heartbeat sped slightly; something unpleasant had happened in this space and now he was going to be trapped, not only in wolf form, but with five grown men and that stupid little remote.

He quickly tried to find some kind of hiding place, some kind of advantage. But there wasn't any. They were standing in a room that was made up mostly of a track about a third of the size of one you would see at a gym. It was lined with fake bushes and trees, as well as a wood fence on one side, only a few feet tall and a few feet long; it was incomplete and unnecessary as it took up almost all of one wall. On the opposite wall of the wood fence was a chain-link one. After taking the few seconds to scope out the room, he picked up his pace so he was a fair distance away and turned around to see the other men. The lab coat had closed the door and was standing a few feet in front of it with that same indulgent smile. There were now only two security guards, each one standing on either side of the closed door.

The scientist took two steps forward and it was all he could do to not jump up and try to rip that smile from the man's face. There was something about his eyes that said this man was used to doing unpleasant things and lacked the compassion to be bothered by them.

"Well now, we shall start this little exercise with letting you run around the track. I want you to get all of that pent-up energy out so go on; you will have about ten minutes to run as much as you can before we must start on your initial training." The lab coat then strode purposefully away from him and towards the wooden fence. A few moments later he was leaning against the wall that seemed to be to some kind of storage closet.

Not wanting to waste the chance at having some form of exercise, Parker began to run. As a wolf he could run much faster than as a human and he stretched his muscles to the brink, to the point where they protested and ached that he was trying so hard right off the bat. He ignored it; he'd felt worse pain than this and knew eventually he would overcome the pain and be able to move even faster, but he wasn't sure he could do that in the time allotted. He ran and ran and thought on nothing but making the turns as sharpened as he could. Trying to go faster and faster and faster, forcing himself to keep his breathing under control, concentrating on moving his paws forward with ever-increasing speed. Ignoring everything around him, the man, the experiment, the fact that he was no longer entirely human, everything except that track under his paws.

Then a piercing sound filled his ears and he tripped on his own two feet before tumbling over. He felt the wind trickle out of his throat before he could stop it and then the noise shut off as if someone had hit the alarm. His ears rang afterwards, even in the silence. The lab coat seemed to know exactly when the ringing stopped because his voice replaced it.

"I did give you a few extra moments because it seemed like you had a lot of energy to burn but it is time to start working on other things now." The older man walked slowly around the fence.

It seemed unnecessary, that high squeal of the noise. But then all of this seemed unnecessary. He stood his ground, watching the man walk toward him with what looked like an attack dog dummy, one that cops would use to train their animals. A feeling of dread began to seep out into his body. They were going to train him as some kind of attack dog. Only he was stronger, faster, larger, and more intelligent than any natural dog could be.

"First, let me explain to you what will be happening. We want to train you to be a kind of guard dog, if you will. We want you to be able to skulk, hide, jump, pelt, run, and attack like a good trained wolf. Only you will be using your human intelligence to get the better of the situation. The key here is to create the perfect mercenary, I suppose you could say; we want you to be the perfectly trained weapon in both human and wolf form. You have been chosen to be one of the batch whose job will be to help guard some of our more secluded and less important locations. If you do well in your training over the next day or two, because it does not seem to take more convincing than that, you will be given a job as part of security and if after an initial training, you do well, we will start training you in human form as well. Once you've perfected that, you will help us fund this endeavor by working on a team with other werewolves like yourself as groups of unstoppable mercenaries for hire. I know it sounds a little uncouth but something needs to fund all that goes on here and this seems the most likely choice. There are already groups chomping at the bit to take advantage of your expertise as it were."

The man was delusional. He spoke with this cheerful optimism only used by a zealot or someone who was criminally insane. He truly saw nothing wrong with the experiments that were being done to them. Experiments they had not agreed to or been informed about. He had no problem with the fact that they were all being held against their will after being told they would be helping their brothers and sisters in arms, when in fact it wasn't anywhere near the truth. And now he thought to train them to do his bidding. Part of him wanted to rebel, wanted to try to kill this man where he stood. But he knew his life didn't matter to these people. He had seen on four different occasions other subjects disappear and not come back, only to have their cell either left vacant or filled with somebody else. There were no qualms about killing those that went against what they wanted. His only option was to play along in hopes of escape. It was a bitter pill to swallow that he would have to act as the perfect little subject if he stood any hope of escape. The thought made him sick but he knew it was either that or force them to kill him. He would not spend any more time in that cell. He needed to get out of here; he needed to save all of these people that this insane scientist had taken against their will.

It was as if the man in the lab coat knew he was weighing his options because he stood there silently holding the dummy for almost a full minute before his smile widened. "There now, you are smart one. That is good; I think that will come in handy. I believe that intelligence of yours will stop me from having to excessively use my little friend here." He wiggled the remote before sliding it into his coat pocket. "Let us begin, shall we?" He turned and laid the dummy across the fence so the arms went over the top rung, holding it up as if it was in a slouch stance. Then he turned back, gesturing towards it while taking several steps back. "Now let's see how you attack."

Chapter 19

Lyra could feel her body dragging. It is as if she not had been going almost nonstop, reacting to the problems that seemed to be popping up back to back. She even called into work letting them know the manuscript would be late. She managed to make it into her other job; her coworkers were worried for her. Luckily, Hazel had led them all to believe that she had fought a bout of pneumonia, which made most people questioning why she had not been in feel bad for her. Others had been found to fill in on her classes for the rest of the session so Lyra had been told to go home and come back in a few weeks when she would for sure be at one hundred percent. The only thing was she wasn't sure when that would be the case.

Her aunt told her everything they knew about the drug in her system and about the suppressant Lyra must have every three days in order to stay out of death's doorway. None of the other methods Luna knew were working to clear Lyra's system; several of the family's chemists were working on it but no one knew when they would have something. Lyra didn't know if it was the drug itself or the suppressant but something in her system made her feel exhausted. She found herself barely having the energy to get through each day. Her adrenaline had taken hold on Sunday when the betas breached the compound, that had been the only way she had been able to fight and help out after, but once everything calmed down she crashed in her old room and didn't wake for twelve hours.

She had woken to find a voicemail from Jesse on her cell phone, letting her know he was going over the paperwork Taylor had given him and he would like to sit down with her for an interview.

The interview had been a little trying, not because of Jesse; she had known him for years. Having to describe being kidnapped and all her other associations with Pack L and the laundry list of terrible things that happened recently, she had been grateful when the interview was finally over. Even during the interview she knew it wasn't Jesse and his questions that were getting to her; it was the fact that they would now be back in the spotlight for everyone to see. People would know about the packs, something she tried to keep secret as long as possible and now it would be common knowledge, even to strangers. Worse yet was her concern for the plan the alphas concocted. They were trying to be preemptive, to get these people off their backs for good but she wondered what would happen if it didn't work. She worried that people just wouldn't care or the scientists moved ahead with a plan anyway, despite any public outcry. She wasn't just worried for herself though; she was concerned about what would happen to her now that she had that drug in her system. She knew that if things got worse, her family would close in on itself, taking the seven born werewolves with them, leaving the made werewolves to fend for themselves. She knew she was borrowing trouble thinking like this but she couldn't help it; it felt like they were all caught in a vortex where things simply became worse and worse the more they tried to get themselves out.

Jesse called her early Monday morning, letting her know that his editor was chomping at the bit to get this story published. With all the information Taylor had given him, he had enough stories that they could release over several days or even weeks. Jesse said the network had wanted him to write a story as soon as possible. Since Jesse had already prepared the first section of the story on Sunday in hopes his editor would be this excited, it had run this morning and he texted the seven of them to give them a heads up that even though he had not used their names they should expect some extra attention. He also apologized that he hadn't had time to run the story by them before it ran, but that he was working on an outline for the next three pieces and soon as he had them done he would be sending them to Graham, Taylor, and Lyra for their approval.

She and Graham were currently in the waiting room of the family's company. They'd been walking in when Jesse had texted them both to let them know he already had people requesting interviews with not only him, but his sources and his story might end up getting picked up by several larger papers. He hoped the increased exposure would help their cause.

The family's investment firm's waiting area had a large receptionist desk straight in front of the chair she was sitting in. To her right was a glass-walled conference room with floor-to-ceiling windows. Anyone in the lobby would be able to see what was going on inside. It was a way to show guests the business was doing well without throwing it in their faces. The conference room where the multifamily meeting would be held was actually farther back, where truly private business was done.

Right now he could see two women flanking an older gentleman, all with their backs to Lyra and Graham. Across the conference table sat her uncle and two of his most experienced executives. The three strangers probably had some kind of proposal they were trying to get her uncle to invest in. Graham's father was incredibly business savvy when it came to earning money. Her father and youngest uncle controlled other aspects at the various branches of the company, but they were not quite as successful as the oldest brother.

As the group in the conference room stood up, Lyra elbowed Graham and both of them stood as well, knowing that as soon as her uncle and his people walked out they would both follow her uncle straight to the back so they could all discuss, as a family, what exactly was going to happen, or what their plan was going to be for how to approach the multifamily meeting.

As the three guests, or clients, turned around, Lyra felt all the color drain from her face. Fear spiked through her system. She felt as if she'd been struck by lightning. She immediately gripped Graham's arm so tightly she probably left marks but she didn't care. She spun him around while he was still in shock from her grabbing him so that it appeared both of them were admiring the art on the wall.

"What, Lyra," her cousin whispered.

Lyra maintained her grip on Graham's arm as if it were a lifeline, the only thing keeping her from having an all-out panic attack. "Stay put; your father is meeting with Dr. Berman."

She could see his eyes widen in the corner her vision and then he discreetly looked past her towards the group walking out. She knew the moment he recognized the doctor because goosebumps raised on his flesh before he turned back to the paintings so the doctor would not have a chance to recognize them.

The doctor had gone missing, fled the police, but the man who caused all the problems they were having in their lives right now was sitting across the table from Graham's father. Lyra had no doubt he was here trying to further his experiment; she could think of no other reason for him to come seeking someone to invest in him. She felt her grip tightening on Graham's arm but couldn't control her fingers enough to loosen it.

Neither of them turned around, holding their breath the entire time, until they heard the elevator doors close, signaling that Berman and the two women with him were gone.

"What the hell is going on with you two?" The receptionist sneered in disgust from over Lyra's left shoulder.

Lyra turned slowly, trying to control her breathing but the overwhelming sound of her heartbeat in her ears made it hard for her to maintain stability. She felt Graham turning beside her. Her uncle's expression changed from disgust to concern when he saw their expressions.

Before he could say anything else Graham asked his question, "What was the name of that group you were just meeting with?"

Her uncle looked from one of them to the other suspiciously before responding, "I don't remember, it wasn't the best proposal. It was something to do with the Roman mythology, something like the Zeus Corporation or some the illusion of grandeur. Why?"

The last word held extra bite and she knew her uncle meant it to but that was probably more because of their reactions than it was Graham questioning him.

"Because, Father, the old man with delusions of grandeur is Dr. Berman. The man responsible for this whole thing."

Her uncle's face filled with rage and he snarled as he turned the receptionist. "What?! Call security; have them stop the doctor and his two assistants before they leave. If they haven't left already." Then he spun back to his two executives. "One of you give me information - everything on the company that just left. Then go to the research team, find out when they set up the appointment. Who they sat down with for the initial interview, and talk to whatever agent it was. Then I want to research everything you can get from these people. All of the help that you need, I want no stone unturned when it comes to finding out who it is we just met with."

The other men nodded curtly before both of them turned and jogged down the hall towards what Lyra could only assume was where the IT offices were. There were several werewolves in the IT department who were quite good at finding things that couldn't be found.

Her uncle turned to the receptionist. "We will be in the back conference room. Let me know if they are able to get the good doctor." Then he turned and stormed toward the back of the office.

Ruth nodded from where she stood with her phone to her ear. Lyra exchanged looks with Graham and knew he was thinking the same thing she was. They had no way of knowing if Berman had figured out their secret or if this was pure coincidence and he was purely pitching an idea. Without saying a word they both hurried down the hallway after her uncle.

When they caught up, he was swinging the wide oak doors open, not caring when they hit and rattled the walls. He then proceeded to spread out every piece of paper in the file he was given all over the conference table, as if worried he might miss something if even two pieces were stacked on top of one another. Graham seemed to have the same idea as Lyra, that it was best to wait and see what his father was going to do before moving further into the room and the doorway. Once he had spread out every single piece, he moved to the far end of the table and concentrated, scanning or speed reading each sheet as if absorbing all the information, or at least trying to.

"He said something about defense. That he was building some kind of model that would change the world. He skipped around the issue a lot, giving us it in pieces of information like it would improve safety, web entry, that sort of thing. But there were no specifics on what he intended to do, he said everything was in the proposal. Which is why we turned him down; he couldn't give us all the information and insisted on being secretive about it, there was no proof that our investment would be a good idea. So it has to be here somewhere. I was right on the name, it's Zeus Corporation; it has to be somewhere." He growled, shifting through the papers.

Lyra and Graham exchanged another worried glance before going to separate directions around the table, scanning the paperwork, looking for anything that would tell them what the doctor was up to. Whether this was just a ruse to get into the office or whether he really was looking for investor. The three of them made their way around the table in silence; scanning each document they came across hoping something somewhere would have the answer they were looking for.

After about ten minutes all Lyra had gotten was that Zeus Corp already had about sixty percent of the funding it needed to run its projects and that it was hoping the family investment firm would be able to give another twenty or thirty percent. There was no list of other investors, which from what she'd seen on other paperwork at the firm was worrisome. Her uncle never took on a project without all of the information.

Before the three of them could discuss what they read, Lyra's father and another uncle were standing just inside the doorway. When she looked up her father was clearing his throat to get their attention.

"Stephen, what is going on? It looks as if the wind blew through here and disorganized everything. Ruth tells us that a potential client did this, or upset you enough to put you in the state. Care to explain to us what exactly is going on?"

Lyra didn't wait for her uncle to reply to her father; she answered his question, "The client was Dr. Berman. He was looking for investors on the project he's working on under some random corporation. We're going through the paperwork, or we were, trying to figure out if this is a dummy corporation so he could simply get into the office or whether he really wanted the investment firm. We are trying to find out if it is the family he is after."

Her father began to growl and took more steps into the room. Her younger uncle had the presence of mind to close the conference room doors behind them but no one outside would hear their conversation, not that there was anyone but werewolves working at the firm.

Her father banged both fists on the table. "Do you mean to tell me the man that experimented on my daughter and nephew was in this building, in a meeting with you and you didn't know? How do you not have his face memorized and smeared into your brain?" The growl in her father's voice, under any other circumstance, would come across as a challenge to the head of the family but given the circumstances, Lyra was pretty sure her uncle looked the other way.

"I don't know either. I have been wondering the same thing since your daughter informed me of who he was. I should have known. I have no excuse for it. Now all I can do is try and find as much information on the man as possible. I've already dispatched people to look into the company and I'm assuming since you're not up there with him that security was not able to catch up with him and his young companions." Her uncle scrubbed vigorously at his face. "I can't believe we had him in our hands and I didn't recognize him. The nerve! From the looks of things, he's looking for funding to run some kind of experiment again. I would bet my life on it. There are keywords in here, such as 'protection' and 'possible weaponry'. It's a vague language but once you know what you are looking at, it all becomes clear."

Before anyone could say anything else that tension in the room launched higher as the conference door opened and presented Ruth in its stead.

"I'm sorry to bother you, unfortunately security didn't catch the man you are looking for. Also unfortunately the first two families are in the lobby waiting for your meeting. They were talking to somebody else on the phone, which makes me think the other families are going to show up early to catch you off guard. I assumed you would want a heads up." Without waiting for anyone's response she left, closing the door behind her.

Her youngest uncle ran his hand through his hair. "Just great. Luckily, you have people looking into the company, but I think it's time that we put these papers away, switch gears and discuss our game plan for this meeting." Even though he suggested it, her youngest uncle didn't make an attempt to start moving papers from the table. He knew better than to make any challenging kind of move while both her father and oldest uncle were this angry.

"Yes, you're right. Graham, Lyra, pick all this up and go put them in my office while the three of us talk. Take your time, so as not to worry the gentleman outside then go to Karen, my secretary, who should be at her desk, and let her know we will be needing refreshments set out early. Tell her she can wrangle whoever she needs to get it done, that we should look in no way hurried, but get things done as fast as possible."

Both Lyra and Graham nodded before stacking the papers on the table. Once they had them stacked and in the envelope, both hurried out and did as they were told. By the time they returned to the conference room, the three brothers seemed to have decided on a game plan, which was frustrating to Lyra because she knew both she and Graham wanted to be a part of the deciding process. She also knew not to complain about it because neither she nor Graham were members of the family council and therefore didn't get a say in things like this. Anyway, just because it concerned them didn't make a difference. Odds were neither of them would be sitting at the conference table for this meeting but in chairs in the corner against the wall.

As soon as the thought occurred to her she scanned the room and sure enough, two chairs were pulled away from the table, against the wall behind her father and uncles. Taking a deep breath, she swallowed her frustration and slowly walked across the conference room to sit in one of the two chairs. She knew better than to question any of them and if they really needed her they would let her know. She also knew that causing any kind of ruckus now would get her invitation to sit in on the meeting rescinded. So she bit her tongue and took her seat and nervously played with the bottom of her shirt, where her fidgeting would be out of sight of everyone sitting at table. Eventually, Graham seemed to come to the same conclusion she did, as a few seconds later he plopped down in the chair next to her. He waited more than a beat or two before grabbing one of her hands in his and gave it a reassuring, companionable squeeze before letting go again and putting his own hands in his lap. It was comforting because it was his way of saying, 'I know you don't like this, I don't like either but at least we're in this together.' And he was right; through all of this at least the two of them had each other to commiserate with.

Surprisingly, the meeting went off without a hitch. Her uncle had put her off kilter by opening with the surprise visit by Dr. Berman. He started by making the visit sound like a threat, glossing over the idea that Berman might just need an angel investor. He then moved on to explain how Berman's visit could be a threat to all of them, he downplayed the made werewolves entering the family on a probationary basis and instead made it sound as if the family was an added threat level to the made werewolves.

The other family leaders were divided on their response. Half did not like the idea that this doctor was sniffing around and offered any additional resources her uncle may need in order to make that problem go away. The other half stated that they wanted nothing to do with the situation and would not be having contact with any of the other families just in case this Berman had figured out what was going on. The second half figured isolation was their best bet to stay hidden.

Overall the meeting went in their favor, which was a relief because the last thing they needed right now, especially with the made werewolves and Berman, was a war between families. She had been rather impressed that her uncle was able to smooth it all over. After all the other leaders had left, her uncle mentioned that that was surprisingly normal, commenting on how usually multifamily meetings were split down the middle by the end, which helped them not have problems because if not resolved or close to fifty-fifty, no one was going to start an all out fight. He explained that having the majority was what led to problems.

Lyra knew that she should have left that meeting feeling somewhat relieved that at least one crisis had been averted. But the looming fact that Berman had somehow resurfaced was overwhelming any relief she could've found. She and Graham didn't talk the entire way back to the compound. It was as if shock had enveloped them both. All Lyra could do was hope that was just a coincidence, that he hadn't found out their secret, that he really was just looking for someone to give him money because if that was the case, they could talk to him. They could put a stop to anything that he would've done before he started. Those thoughts should've brought her a glimmer of hope but even that simple spark couldn't survive in this wall of worry and dread that surrounded Lyra.

Chapter 20

Parker was genuinely surprised that they were going to let him out of the facility so quickly. Not that he hadn't been there for what seemed like a long time but he had only been through the training with the old man, and one other guy four times. And they had already decided to let him leave and go on what they called a training mission. He knew odds were he wouldn't be able to escape this time but this would give him the perfect lay of the land so that he could better plan his escape. He knew he couldn't appear eager to leave because that eagerness would only work against him. So when he was pulled into that tiny room where they had attached the dreaded collar and that young blonde informed him he would be going out to do security, he was sure to keep his body tense as if the news didn't affect him at all.

The blonde turned away to face the counter, babbling about something but he couldn't concentrate on her words. Instead he concentrated on keeping his body language neutral so that no one would know what he was planning. When she turned and faced him again he saw that she had a needle with an unknown substance in her hand. That made him panic; not knowing what she was going to be injecting him with made his heart start to beat double-time.

"This is a kind of sedative. One can't be too careful about these things. We don't want you knowing the exact location of your assignment yet, since we don't exactly know if we can trust you to do your job. Don't worry, trust will, I'm sure, come with time but for now the sedative will do." Before he could react she plunged the syringe into his neck.

He had to fight his automatic response to bite her arm. He couldn't do anything to deter from his goal of escape and biting one of the lab coats would do just that. He locked his jaw and tried not to growl. It was only a matter of seconds before he began to feel the substance working its way through his body, making his limbs and head feel heavy. Then his legs began to wobble a little before giving out and his head drooped as he began to fall into a drugged sleep. Before everything went black he heard the blonde lab coat make a comment.

"Remember to tell them that the batteries on these upgraded collars currently only last eighteen hours tops, less with heavy use. Not that they should have trouble with this one from his record, but one of the others might give them a little difficulty. These batteries need to be changed out regularly to avoid complications."

He held on to that information, clinging to it as consciousness left him, praying that he would remember that tidbit of information when he woke up. He mentally repeated it to himself in hopes of increasing the chances he would remember it. That eighteen-hour deadline was his only hope of escape. If he could run out that battery, he would be free. He had no idea what the range of the collar was but it wasn't something he was readily willing to test. Staying outdoors, or out of arms' reach, for eighteen hours seemed relatively doable. If only he would remember that. He clung to that number as he felt his consciousness give out.

When he came to, a glance around the room told him there were no lab coats here. All of the men were wearing the same clothing as the security at the lab wore. Only these men weren't carrying the Tasers as the others had. These all wore black with multiple side arms and at least one visible blade. His nose told him before his eyes could see that there were two other wolves there with him. They were natural wolves but werewolves like himself. One of them, when he scanned that direction, was already seated and looking at the men in front of them warily, the other was still unconscious. He knew if he was in his human form, he'd be frowning but luckily that expression did not necessarily translate well on a wolf face.

Further inspection showed him they all stood in a rather small room, the size of maybe two storage closets. On one side of the room were the basic filing cabinets you would see in any office in America but the other side held shelves filled with different chemicals, as well as stacks of batteries in chargers that would fit in the collars around all three wolves' necks. There was no doubt in his mind that this was a room he should avoid being in again. Sure, the supplies could be brought elsewhere but he felt that not being in this location would certainly help his chances of success.

He heard a rustling to his right and turned to see the third wolf was stirring in a manner that stated he would be awake in the next few seconds. He watched as the other wolf's head rose and took in their surroundings before growling and fighting to get to his feet.

One of the men dressed in black stepped forward with a tiny remote in his hand. "I was warned you might be a little bit of a problem. Can't have you waking up testy." Then he pressed something on the remote

The wolf to his right fell as if his legs collapsed from under him and he felt for the other wolf as he heard the whimper. He knew the pain the other wolf was feeling but he also knew better than to rock the boat in what could be his only hope of escape.

The man with the remote chuckled, with a sinister smile that somehow made his face even uglier, more brutal. "Now that you're all awake, I'm going to be explaining to you what your job is here. You will each be teamed up with a guard to patrol the area around this building. Don't stray too far because each of those guards will have the remote to your specific collar and they can press that button faster than you can do anything. Not to mention the locals won't look too kindly on a giant wolf appearing out of nowhere. Your job is to be on silent patrol and eventually if you are good we'll let you roam the grounds on your own to fend off anyone who might get curious. But that won't be for a while; first you have to prove that you're not going to make yourself a nuisance." He looked directly at the wolf whose remote he held in his hand. "Don't think we're going to be giving you any leeway. We've been briefed on the sort of thing you're capable of and we've been instructed to terminate any of you, should you cause problems.

Don't think you'll be getting away with the same kind of thing the first batch did."

That statement made his blood run cold. How many of this first batch they mentioned had been murdered? And how many had been murdered simply for not doing what these men wanted them to do? A pit began to form in his stomach and he tried to console himself that as long as he could stay out of their clutches for those eighteen hours, he had a chance to survive.

"Now, you are all going to be good little dogs and behave as we walk you out of the building. It's daytime and the good folks that have work to do don't need to be bothered by the sight of you. They need to know that the work they're doing is going well and that the guard doggies are nothing to be concerned with. If any of you so much as shift your feet in a direction I deem inappropriate, I will press this button and will carry you out. Am I understood?"

He wasn't sure what was wanted from them by way of a response. But the wolf who had woken first seemed to understand what they wanted because he gave a howling bark. When the man apparently in charge nodded then looked toward him and the collapsed wolf, Parker repeated the noise. A few moments later the third wolf reluctantly did the same.

"Good, now that that's settled I'm going to hand off these remotes to the men who will be in charge of you and Jill be walking beside them all the way out and to your posts. Do not think any of them will hesitate to punish you if you act out."

He then handed the remote he was holding off to the man who stood to his left. Parker didn't look to see what the wolf next to him did because the next remote the man pulled out of his pocket had 071 written on the back of it and the placement of that remote took his entire attention. The bogeyman with sandy blond hair moved in and took it. He was sure from the look of the man that he wasn't the smartest man; he was the sort of guy who got through life on brute force and not much else. If his assessment was correct that lack of intelligence might work in his favor when he tried to escape. Not wanting to cause a punishment or appear eager, he slowly and cautiously stepped up beside the blond man who sneered down at him as he slid the remote into his right pocket. After a few moments the leader deemed them ready to leave the storage closet and he opened the door.

They walked out into what appeared to be a large lobby with a receptionist's desk facing a set of front doors. There was only a section of wall behind the young woman with black hair and it only took up as far as the desk did. On the other side of that black wall were openings that showed rows of desks and lab benches and perhaps two dozen people going about their workday. The ones closest to them stopped what they were doing to watch the parade of wolves. The receptionist, who couldn't have even been old enough to be in her mid-twenties, stopped her rapid typing to look up and watch them. The look about her eyes showed a certain fear that she tried to hide and he could see the company slogan behind her on the wall. It read 'Fredrickson and Company, enhancing relationships through enhancing nature'. He heard a snort disguised as a sneeze from the wall behind him. Clearly he had read the same thing Parker had. But Parker saw something else; the faces of the worker drones in the larger office space, something about them showed fear and curiosity that tugged at him. From the looks of the lab benches and how different they looked from the place he had just come from, he was willing to bet these people had no idea what they were part of. They probably thought these were simply trained wolves and nothing more. He didn't know why he was so sure of that but he is willing to bet that no one beyond the security team knew what they really were.

The group of them headed outside and proceeded to break off in different directions once they hit the parking lot. He looked back enough to see that the building they just left was a nondescript two-story office space with that same logo on the top of the building above the second-floor windows. The only difference being that they were a fairly good distance from the next building. He couldn't get a good look at it but he could see a driveway heading through the trees on the other side of the street across the parking lot. Though the building seemed to only be surrounded by trees on the other three sides. Which meant it was the perfect spot to be testing out the werewolves, as there wouldn't necessarily be close neighbors to notice.

The blond man turned right out the front door and Parker duly followed him; they went to the back right corner of the building before the blond man stopped.

"We'll stay around here until the folks inside go home then we'll take turns circling the property with the other two teams. After today we'll mainly be out here only at night. Though you might end up working through tomorrow as well, simply because the crates for you three haven't come in yet. Something about not being ready, I wasn't entirely listening. I'll be handing you off at the end of the night shift to a day guard then maybe I'll be able to get a quick nap in before I collect you tomorrow. Your job is to do is you were trained and monitor that tree line at the other end of the driveway. We watch that as well as the loading dock on the other side of the corner to her right. It's pretty quiet so there won't be a real opportunity for you to get yourself into trouble. I don't think I'll be stingy or compassionate should you need punishment. Now go on and monitor the tree line but stay within my sight. The moment I can't see you is the moment I press one of those buttons on the remote." The man made a dismissive gesture towards the tree line. It took all of his energy to not growl at the blond man so he settled for turning away and snarling so the other man couldn't see it. He walked to the tree line and began to familiarize himself with all the smells, memorizing and storing them just in case that information might come in handy later. When the blond man began walking towards the back of the building, he was careful to stay in his line of sight and move with him. He knew he wouldn't be able to catch everything and memorize it in the first pass but if he was going to be out as long as this man made it sound, there would be plenty of time for him to know every square inch of the area around the side of the building and hopefully around the other sides as well. It was just a matter of biding his time, he couldn't believe anything else, but part of him worried it seemed too easy to escape. Even if he wasn't supposed to know about that eighteen-hour rule, it seemed as if he could simply maul the man that held his remote in just the right spot to destroy the thing and then escape. There had to be a failsafe in place to prevent it; all he had to do was wait and watch to make sure he knew every angle and every possibility before he made his move. He had to give them no reason to send him back for retraining, he just needed to do exactly what they told him. That might be the one thing that could trip him up, so hopefully this building was as quiet as the blond man made it sound.

Chapter 21

Jack called a pack meeting after Lyra informed him about seeing Berman. He had been toying with the idea of calling one anyway because this second news article was apparently set to run tomorrow. The fact that they were going to run articles every other day told Jack just how hot of a topic they were. He had already had people corner him on his way out of work, trying to interview him since they knew, somehow, that he was one of the pack alphas. They didn't actually know about the whole werewolf thing but they did know he was a leader of one of the smaller groups, though he wasn't sure where they got that information. He went out of his way to pretend he didn't know what they were talking about; one of them had been embarrassed, the other hadn't believed him. When Lyra told him that she had seen Berman at her family's office, Jack had felt the world tilt. Having that evil man back in their lives, even momentarily, was life changing. If they had a lifeline or some way to find him maybe these problems could be over. They had enough information to know that the scientists trying to trap the born werewolves were most likely not related to Berman so the fact that he might be trying to start up his experiments as well was worrisome.

All of the pack had been there by eight o'clock. Lyra had skulked in about five minutes to and slid herself onto one of the barstools. It wasn't lost on anyone that she hadn't come in ahead of time and made something for the group; it was a statement of how wrong things were and just how far off the path of normalcy they had strayed. It reminded all of them of how far they were from their everyday lives that they had just been getting used to and Jack couldn't help but wonder if they would ever get them back.

Once everyone was there, and had welcomed Lyra back to the land of the awake, Jack stood just outside his office door, where everyone could see him, and waited until he had the entire room's attention.

"I know things have not been easy lately, I don't know how many of you have been bothered by reporters. I myself have already been in contact with two of them and I just denied everything. I'm not saying that you have to do that, feel free to do whatever is most comfortable for you; there's really no right or wrong way to do this. I just called everyone here so that we could touch base and check in, see how everyone is feeling about the article and give you a heads up: the next one is running tomorrow. Lyra tells me she's already read it and that it doesn't say anything incriminating or any have inkling to who any of us are. But she also gave me some very alarming news this morning that I will save her from having to share with all of you. She was at her family's office, waiting on her uncle, who when she and Graham arrived, was in a meeting. When the meeting got out she recognized the man opposite the table of her uncle as Dr. Berman."

He had to stop, as the entire room let out various shocked noises, not just shock but anger. Not even Justin or Syrus had jokes, even they were aghast.

It wasn't until then that Jack decided he wouldn't be telling the pack why Lyra was at the family investment firm. They didn't need to know right now that there were beta wolves that could hurt them. With all the media coverage, he was pretty sure the betas wouldn't go after them anytime soon because they too risked their own secrets getting out. Once the media coverage died down and the attention and spotlight weren't on them any more, he would bring it up and have Lyra explain to everyone exactly what danger her association put them in. At the moment, looking at how worn out and bad Lyra looked, he didn't want to put her through that.

He waited until the noise died down again before speaking.

"The family is scouring through all of the paperwork that he brought with him to see if he knows who all the werewolves are or if he knows about the born werewolves or if he really was just looking for an investor. We're hoping that it was the latter but just in case, I want everyone to be extra careful with where they go and who they see. I know we can't always be in pairs or groups so please, please be prepared at any given time to run or be on the defensive."

Seth leaned forward from where he sat on the couch. "So you're telling me that we currently have scientists, reporters, and the crazy scientists that did all of this to us out there and we don't know which of them knows who we are or is after us?"

Jack sighed. "That's correct. I know it's not good news but it's the only news I have. I am hoping to get a hold of several alphas later and see

271

if the council can get some kind of plan in place, but I'm not holding my breath. I think we have literally reached the time where all we can do is wade through the river and hope we make it out the other side."

With that, Jack walked into his office, signaling to the group at large that he was done talking. He didn't really have other information for them, even though he wished he did; this scenario sucked. He could hear various pack members making angry or worried statements. He heard Hazel say something about pepper spray and Justin say something in response. Instead of listening or joining in, Jack tuned them out and texted Mathew, Bishop, and Rachel, asking if anybody wanted to meet up and come up with a game plan. It was a false pretense though because as far as Jack knew, Rachel was probably the only one that knew about Berman and from what he knew about Graham, assuming he told his alpha wasn't necessarily a safe bet. They needed to know that the man was out there and it was Jack's responsibility to tell them.

Before he got a response from anyone, he felt Ryan's presence in the doorway just before the sound of the other man knocking on the doorframe reached his ears. He looked up at his second and frowned at the other man's blank face. "What is it, Ryan?"

The other man walked into the office and shut the door behind him. Since there was no other chair in the office, Ryan leaned his back against the door and folded his arms. "I wanted to let you know that I'm going to head out of town for a while. I don't exactly know how long it's going to be but my guess is at least two weeks. Where I'm going there's spotty cell service so you probably won't be able to get a hold of me, even if you want to. Feel free to call and leave a voicemail, I'll check it once a week, maybe twice. You should probably have Seth do things while I'm gone. In fact, I think it's best for the pack if I bow out and Seth becomes your second. I know this isn't the best timing but it's something that needs to be done."

Jack just stared at his second in shock. This was totally unexpected and couldn't have come at a worse time. Seth would step up and be his second but he was not proactive the way Ryan was. Seth would do what Jack wanted him to but other than that, he didn't like having a lot of interpersonal responsibilities. He felt anger; Ryan was just going to leave now that there was a revelation about Berman being in town and the news articles floating around.

"Do you really think that's the best move right now? The mad scientist is back and we don't know what his plan is so you're just going to leave?" Jack's voice had more bite and anger than he initially thought there would be.

Ryan's shoulders slumped ever so slightly. "Look, Jack, I am not asking for your permission. I am telling you what is happening. Despite the fact that you are the alpha, that doesn't actually mean you are in any way, shape, or form my boss or in control of anything I do with my existence. Consider this a courtesy. I'll see you in a few weeks." Ryan growled before standing up, yanking the door open, and storming out of the office.

As he walked past the bar, Lyra reached out to try and stop him, a worried expression on her face. Instead of stopping, he shrugged off her hand and kept moving. Jack could almost feel his pack falling apart. First Lyra and all her secrets and now Ryan bailing on the pack. Jack didn't know what was next but he knew it wasn't going to be good.

His phone screen lit up, distracting Jack momentarily from his thoughts. He looked down at it; it was a text from Rachel, stating that she was at work and had just started a shift two hours ago but that if the four of them wanted to conference call, she could sneak outside for about ten or fifteen minutes. As Jack was typing his response to the affirmative, Bishop beat him to it, agreeing that he couldn't get out of a prior engagement but could break away for ten minutes. No sooner had Jack hit enter and seen his words on the screen did Mathew respond with a message saying that he would call all of them in about five minutes.

Taking advantage of the break in time, Jack moved to slowly shut his office door so as to not make it obvious what he was doing. By the time his phone rang, he got back to pacing his office.

"This is Jack," he answered, as he hit the screen.

"Hi, Jack. I've got you and Bishop; I'm adding in Rachel now," Mathew responded.

Within a few seconds there was another click. "This is Rachel."

"Okay, Jack, what exactly was it you wanted to discuss? I know the article has gotten us some attention and Dylan tells me the next segment is coming out tomorrow. Is that what you wanted to talk about because I'm not quite sure that's necessary. Or was it something else?"

Jack took a deep breath before answering. Not one to beat around the bush, and especially since they only had about ten minutes, he decided to just come out with it. "The family is worried the beta wolves, werewolves that aren't part of the family but still live nearby, are going to attack, thinking that the made werewolves are a weakness. They already attacked once but everything seems relatively okay. Because of this, other families got nervous and wanted a multifamily meeting. Graham and Lyra showed up early to that meeting only to see their uncle in a conference of some kind with some potential clients, one of those potential clients was Dr. Berman looking for an investment in his company. We don't know for sure whether he came to them because he knows they're werewolves or if he came to them because their investment firm. The jury is still out and the family is looking into the business that he claims the money was going to. I figured you would want the heads up that he happens to be in town again, if he left at all."

There was silence on the other end of his phone for several seconds, making Jack think that the call had dropped. Then he heard Rachel cursing, in a whispered voice, over and over again before pausing. "Dammit, Jack, this is not the kind of news I needed today. Don't know why Graham didn't tell me this. Okay." He heard her take a breath. "Do we need to come up with a plan for this? Or should we see what information the family comes up with before we make any decisions?"

When Bishop or Mathew didn't answer right away, Jack stepped in, "I think we should see what the family comes up with first. Since they know his business operations, or at least what he's pretending his business operations are, I think our best bet is to see what they shake out. Especially since we don't have any of that paperwork and Lyra and Graham didn't think to make copies, as far as I know. Ultimately, I just wanted all of you to have a heads up and if you want to tell the other members of the alliance that's fine but I suggest you only tell them about Dr. Berman and not anything else like the beta wolves. I decided not to tell my pack about the beta wolves because I don't think they're going to be a problem for us while we have all this media attention," Jack added.

There was humming over the phone, it wasn't quite a growl. "This is not fantastic news," complained Bishop. "Unfortunately, Jack, I think you're right. Our hands are tied as far as Berman goes because we don't necessarily have a way to track him. Mathew, have you heard anything from your government contact yet? I know it's only been two days but with this added trouble, it would be nice to know if they have a plan to move in on those scientists."

"No, I have not heard from him. Though I cannot say I'm entirely surprised since, like you said, it is only been two days. I did warn him that we were going to the media to expedite the situation but I cannot believe that the media acting this fast made them all too thrilled. They could be dragging their feet because of the media or because of bureaucratic nonsense. I will call my contact as soon as we hang up and, providing he answers, see where they are in the process. Keep in mind the government isn't exactly known for moving quickly and we may be stuck in this limbo for a while," Mathew responded.

The phone was silent again; if Jack had to guess he'd say the other alphas were debating how much to tell their individual packs and which other alphas should be clued in about the beta wolves.

Bishop cleared his throat. "If no one has anything else, I really need to touch base with my second about all of this."

Rachel's snort came through the phone rather loudly. "Yeah, I've got a need to have a little bit of a discussion with mine as well."

There wasn't anything else they needed to discuss, as far as Jack was concerned. He didn't know if there really was anything more to say since they were kind of sitting in limbo, waiting to see how things shook out. "In that case, I will be the first one to say goodnight."

He didn't hang up right away; he waited until there were mutters from each of the other alphas and at least one click letting him know he wasn't the first to leave. Once he was off the phone, Jack rubbed and his sore head in a futile effort to get ahead of the migraine he could feel forming. He hated not having anything to do, nothing that would help the pack. He hated not being in charge and waiting on other parties to get things done. The worst part for him was that he didn't know if the other groups involved would do what they hoped or if they'd go in some other direction that would only cause more problems for the made werewolves.

Letting out a low growl, his arms fell onto the desk a little harder than necessary and he put as much concentration as he could into the files in front of him.

The ringing of his cell phone shocked Jack awake. He shot up in bed so fast that his equilibrium didn't quite catch up with them and he had to slam his arms on the bed to prevent from falling one way or the other. Once his brain un-fogged enough to realize that the noise really was his cell phone, he snatched it off the bedside table and squinted at the screen. It was a number he'd never seen before, which set his adrenaline running a little bit faster. All sorts of bad possibilities raced through his head as to who could've gotten his number. Was it someone in the government? Someone from Berman? Someone working with the lab assistants? Was it the media? He had no way of knowing until he answered. Part of him didn't want to but his own hand was already clicking the answer button and raising it to his head just out of habit before his brain caught up.

"Hello?" he answered gruffly.

There was hesitant breathing on the other side of the phone before the other individual answered, "Jack? This is Lyra's little brother, Peter. I'm sorry to wake you up but I figured that you would want to know this so I snuck your number off my sister's phone. Really, she left her phone on the counter so that I could see it and sneak the number, but that's not important. They found an address for

Berman's company and they're storming it right now. The council is kind of in a deadlock on whether to let you alphas show up and listen via the radio. That way you'd have some sort of idea of what was going on. Which is how we led to Lyra sneaking me your number so I could just call you and tell you it's happening. It'll be much harder for them to turn you guys down if you all show up. You should get here as soon as you can, the group's going in about five or ten minutes ago. I gotta go, someone's coming." Then the line went dead.

Jack was a little disoriented about that call. He appreciated what Lyra and Peter were doing by giving him a heads up, but was a little surprised that half the council was okay with them showing up; he would've thought that they would have been denied access completely. He didn't have time to mull on that though, he needed to call the other alphas and tell them what was going on.

He tried to think of the quickest way to let all the alphas know what was going on. The best method he could think of was a type of phone tree. If he put in a quick call to Bishop, Mathew, and Rachel that at least half of the alphas would know and those three could contact the others or more likely Mathew would contact the others.

Swinging out of bed and heading towards where he had thrown his clothes the night before, he quickly called Rachel and then before she picked up, added the other two alphas to the call so he could kill three birds with one stone.

Bishop picked up first. "This better be important, Jack, or so help me…" His voice came out as a growl.

"It is, trust me. Although I quickly put you on conference so we're waiting for Mathew and Rachel to pick up," Jack responded.

"At work, Jack, this has to be quick," Rachel answered.

"Okay, I assume if you are calling me and I hear Rachel's voice, something very bad has happened," Mathew's sleepy voice came through last.

Jack took a deep breath so he could say everything all at once. "The family found an address for Berman's dummy company and they're attacking it, or scouting it out, I'm not quite sure which, right now. The council is torn on whether to let us sit in and watch it or not. So Lyra secretly told her little brother to give me a call and let me know what was happening because it would be harder for them to turn us all down when we're on their doorstep. I'm on my way over there now and I think that any of the seven of us that can go, should. Obviously Rachel can't since she's at work but we can update her. Mathew, Bishop, if you two could call the other alphas and let them know what's happening, that would be great and unless anyone has any questions, I will see you in however long it takes all of us to show up."

"Well, that was fairly succinct, Jack and I appreciate the sneakiness of this plan. Bishop, I will call the other three. You and Jack just concentrating on getting to that door so they can't turn us down. I will see everyone in a bit and Rachel, we will update you when we have an update but if you would rather call one of us when you're off shift, that might be better."

"Will do," Rachel responded before Jack heard a click and he assumed she hung up.

There was a heavy sigh on the other side of the phone. "Is it too late to abdicate as alpha? I haven't gotten more than half a dozen good nights' sleep in the last year," Bishop grumbled.

"Yes, I think the ship has sailed on that one. I'll see you all in a bit," Mathew responded before there was another click.

Bishop didn't even respond; the last click hit and Jack knew he was alone on the phone.

Jack shoved the phone into his pocket and finished getting dressed. He wanted to be the first one to get to the compound, but since he wasn't sure how far away all the other alphas lived he was going to have to hurry. He figured if he could get there first, he had a better chance of convincing them to let them in since it was him that Peter had called. Worst-case scenario he would call Peter back and have Lyra's little brother sneak them out a radio or update them on what was going on. With a small blossom of hope that maybe things were finally headed in the right direction, Jack ran out the door.

Chapter 22

Graham was grateful that it had not taken much convincing to let him and the other six packs of wolves go on the raid. The council had wanted to go as soon as possible and it helped that all seven of them were on the compound at the time. He and Lyra had been paired together and were to go in in wolf form. He had thought it was strange when his cousin had changed before the vans had even left the compound. But she had given him a look that let Graham know he should change as well. Not questioning his cousin's reasoning, because clearly she had something in mind, Graham made his change right there next to her.

Once one of the men in charge saw that they were changing, he gruffly barked at them to go to the cargo van since it would be easier to pack them in there than in regular seats. Once the two of them were jammed in amongst the equipment the cargo van was holding, Lyra turned and looked him in the face.

Don't get mad, she started telepathically. *But I left my phone out for Peter so that he could look up Jack's number and give him a call, letting him know exactly what was going on so that he and the alphas could decide for themselves whether they were going to head over here or not. I figured it would be easier for them to convince the council in person than for the council to continue to debate and give up on it.*

When it had become clear that the made werewolves could not speak telepathically, as the born wolves could, it'd become an unspoken rule to not let any of the made werewolves know. Born wolves could only speak telepathically when in wolf form; no one was sure why. Speaking telepathically was the most private form of communication because you could aim it at one person in particular and there was no chance of someone else overhearing, no matter how good their ears were.

I think it makes sense. This affects them more than it affects the family, I think, so they should know. I already got a verbal chewing out from Rachel for not telling her about Berman at the family office. Thank you very much for that, because I know you are the one that told Jack who then told Rachel. But you're right; they need to know what's going on. Leaving them in the dark is only going to endanger them more. Let's hope they could convince the council to let them in.

Both of them had then sat in silence the rest of the drive to the address neither of them had really seen. Neither of them was the best with estimating time while in wolf form so neither of them had any idea exactly how long they were in the car. When the van stopped and they heard the driver holler back that they had arrived they both stood up and waited for the back doors to open.

Someone at some point had scoped out the layout, at least on the outside, of the building so Lyra and Graham were told to go around the left hand side to the back where there should be a set of cargo doors. There was also a team of two people in wolf form heading around the opposite side, as well as two teams in human form, with weapons; they would be flanking either set of wolves. The council was hoping that sending as many people in as they were would be overkill because if Berman's organization was much bigger than they thought, that would open up a whole new set of problems.

There was a small strip of the wooded area, which if they crouched, was a good hiding spot for Lyra and Graham to slowly move around the back. The wolf teams were being sent in first, almost as scouts to see if things really were as dead as they first appeared. The human team would be a minute or so behind them, depending on how fast they moved.

Graham was lying with part of his back against his cousin so that they could look to opposite directions. They were waiting to see if any guards were on patrol, because oddly enough, the only humans they could smell were rather faint.

A burly-looking guard with a gun turned the corner in front of them, coming from the back of the building, where they assumed the loading bay was.

I can't smell him. Do you smell anything? Graham asked his cousin, as a slight wisp of panic went through his body.

If they had developed some sort of drug or masking agent that put them one step ahead, who knew what else they had come up with.

I don't smell anything. All I smell is wolf, which is weird, since we haven't been here that long, Lyra responded.

Before they could discuss it further, there was the sound of a shot from across the building and the guard they were watching's radio burst to life with yells of shots fired. There must've been a silencer on the weapon, preventing the guard from hearing it. When his radio blared, he went running in. Both Lyra and Graham stood up to follow.

Before either of them could, there was a low growl from behind them; they spun in unison and much to their horror, there was a werewolf behind them, launching himself at Lyra. Graham instinctively backed up so that his cousin would have more room to fight without having to worry about him standing there. Having the two of them next to each other would only make things harder.

He watched as his cousin braced a split second before the other wolf landed, then she rolled out from under him before he realized she had moved from where she once was. Before he could recover from Lyra's sudden movements, she railed into his side with her head pushing them onto the ground. He was much faster than the made werewolves they knew but he smelled more like a made a werewolf than a born.

Graham took the opportunity of this new intruder being on the ground to surge forward; the unknown wolf began snarling and nipping at Lyra as she danced just out of his range.

They were lucky in that Graham and Lyra had fought in wolf form for years, as well as fought with each other; this made wolf seemed to not be in the practice of fighting in this form. Graham snuck up behind him and waited a split second as the other wolf raised his head to nip at Lyra again, then he rose up both his front paws and slammed into the side of the other wolf's head, forcing the fur-covered skull hard into the ground. He wouldn't kill the other wolf but it would render him unconscious for a while.

The adrenaline shooting through his body was hard to fight. His main instinct was to rip apart the wolf who went after his cousin. But the intellectual part of him knew the unknown wolf was worth more to them alive so that he could be interrogated. Fighting those urges was hard.

He knew that it was just as hard for Lyra, as he could hear her not-so-soft growl rumbling from her throat as she stared down at the wolf between them. Her chest was heaving with the effort to not pounce forward. All of a sudden the growling stopped and her head cocked to the side.

Graham looked down to the furry body where she was looking but he couldn't see was so interested in. *What?*

He's wearing a collar. You probably can't see it from your angle but from here, there's almost a metal plate of some kind on it with an engraving. I can't quite make it out.

She then eased her way down, clearly favoring one of her front paws, where he must have bitten her. She used her other front paw to brush some fur aside and sure enough, Graham could see what she was talking about.

071? What does that mean? I wonder if it's some kind of identifier, Graham mused.

I don't know, but I think we should move far from him because he may come in handy later. That being said, I'll check in with Dylan, who I believe should be in wolf form, if you want to check in with Taylor, and see how things are going on the other end. If they're fighting then that's more important than keeping this hostage.

He knew his cousin was right. As much as he wanted to stay and watch this hostage to make sure he didn't regain consciousness, since they didn't know exactly how strong he was, he knew they might be needed elsewhere. Even if Lyra was favoring one of her legs a little bit more than he would've liked.

Taylor? How are things going over there?

There was no answer right away, but that was to be expected considering how far away they were, there was a limit to how far telepathy will work. Before he got an answer, he watched his cousin stand up and test the leg she had been favoring.

We better go, Dylan says Taylor's injured and he's not so sure he's gonna win the fight with the two other werewolves he's fighting, she relayed, as she began dashing towards the building.

He didn't question it. Adrenaline shot through his body as they raced to help their friends. As they rounded the loading dock, they could see the other corner of the building and he could hear fighting noises as wolves growled and snarled at each other. Graham pumped his legs harder and quickly passed Lyra who, while she was running, wasn't running at her top speed. As he passed her he could see red matted fur on one of her legs. Running on it was probably doing even more damage but he didn't really have the time to stop and chastise her.

As they rounded the corner of the building the whole thing exploded. It was clearly from somewhere in the inside of the building because a split second before fire and debris shot out in front of him and bombarded him on his right side, he heard the explosion from somewhere in the building. Before he knew it, Graham felt himself flying in the air with no control over how he landed then his head hit something large and solid and everything went black.

The first sign that he was coming to was Lyra's human voice screaming, "I can help him. Let go."

Worried that she was talking about him, Graham forced his eyes open only to see Lyra was facing slightly away from him and Dylan had her around the waist. He followed both of their gaze; several trees seemed to be on fire. He couldn't see who Lyra was trying to get to but as he watched, she gave Dylan a swift kick between the legs, not actually hitting anything but using his flinch to break free and run straight into the fire.

Even though Graham's adrenaline was shooting through his system at lightning speed, he couldn't get his body to move enough to chase after Lyra and Dylan. All he could do was watch as Lyra ran headlong towards the flames rising in the trees. All he could let out was a shout but he doubted that she even registered it. He held his breath as she disappeared and Dylan quickly disappeared after her.

His breathing ragged, he looked down through the pounding headache that told him he was most likely going to have to deal with a strong concussion and focused on his legs. One of them was bent at an odd angle and he was sure that if he rolled up his pant leg, he would see the bone close to protruding through his skin. The fact that his cousin ran away from him, toward someone else made him worry even more about whoever she was going to help. There were only a select few that she would dive headfirst into trouble for, and then he remembered Taylor had been injured before the explosion. Fighting through the overwhelming pain in his head, Graham leaned to the side so that he could use his scratched up arms to drag himself closer to where his cousin had disappeared.

He hadn't made it more than a few feet before she and Dylan came barreling out of the wooded area holding a wolf. Both of them were covered in sweat and each had an arm with severe burns on it as if they had reached into the fire to grab the wolf he knew was Taylor.

They laid the wolf on the ground and Graham could see perfectly that the heavy burns had singed off the hair on the back third of Taylor. There was also blood matting the fur on one side of his head, behind one of the ears.

As he watched, his cousin knelt down in front of their burned friend and laid her hands about an inch from the severe burns and began whispering to herself. Graham knew what she was doing: she was using the magic that came with being a family Luna, magic that came from nature and passed intermittently through family bloodlines. A power that could heal almost anything on a werewolf. Not being a full Luna all Lyra could hope to do was stabilize him enough that he would be able to be brought back to the Luna to be healed.

He watched as the faint blue glow surrounded her hands and spread down the part of Taylor's body that was burned; the farther it got from her hands, the fainter the glow was. It didn't matter how many times he'd seen his cousin do this, he could only watch in awe every time. He watched helplessly as she tried to save their friend.

He'd been so busy watching Lyra he hadn't even noticed that Dylan had come to stand in front of them until the other man blocked his view of his cousin.

"I'm glad we are you are born wolf enough that your body shifted into human form while you were unconscious, that'll make this easier. If the changes Berman thrust upon us had changed that I am not sure I could adequately help you. I think we need to reset your leg before you really start healing so this is going to hurt. Get ready," Dylan warned, as he solemnly knelt down and put his hands about an inch from either side of Graham's leg.

He wasn't entirely sure that he would be able to feel anything in his leg through the throbbing in his head. But he braced himself just the same. Then the pain shot up from his leg as Dylan's hands touched his skin, and he noticed that the other man had somehow rolled up his pants. It told Graham just how out of it he was. Balling his hands into fists, he concentrated on watching his cousin; a split second later he heard the noises of his leg moving back into place then the pain an instant later. It didn't end like a quick jolt like the first wave had; it radiated up his body. Fortunately, it was a pain he could live with more so than his head so Graham concentrated more on the pain in his leg and it became slightly easier to focus.

"I don't think we're going to be able to find anything to work as a kind of crutch for you so you're going to have to use me and hop on the other leg. Can you tell if your other leg is stable enough to hold your weight?" Dylan asked from where he still crouched.

Folding up his leg at the knee to test the weight, Graham paid close attention to how the leg felt. When there were no immediate alarm bells he slowly nodded to Dylan, which brought his attention back to his head. "I'll be able to walk," his voice came out hoarse and pained. "But I have a pretty bad concussion from hitting what I assume was a tree."

Dylan nodded, his expression solemn. "It's okay then, we'll move very slowly, that way if you need to puke we'll be able to stop. I'm going to lift you up now because unlike Taylor and Lyra, you are still technically in the wooded area and I'd rather you not get set on fire." In one swift movement Dylan was kneeling on Graham's left side and snaking his arm around Graham's waist, gingerly picking him up.

About halfway through the process of standing up, the world spun and Graham had to stop the other man long enough for him to vomit up the entire contents of his stomach. The world was spinning so badly he had to slam his eyes shut afterwards just to prevent his stomach from roiling again. Luckily, Graham heard Boone run around the corner while his eyes were still shut.

"Boone, I could really use your help getting them back to the van and where the hell is everybody else?" Dylan called.

Graham could barely make out Boone's footsteps as he slowed to a stop near where he assumed Lyra was still working over Taylor. Then the footsteps picked up again and he felt Boone's arm wrap around his back and lift up his right side.

"Right now we're just dealing with damage. Out of the fifteen bodies we brought with us, one is dead, Taylor plus three others are worryingly injured, the other nine are now accounted for. The downside is that we don't quite know what triggered the explosion of the building. We're assuming it meant they knew we were here because it blew a lot of their people to smithereens. We have yet to find any that are alive. We found two made werewolves, who are much better fighters than the made werewolves we're used to, which is comforting. But both of them were taken out pretty soon because it seems they weren't terribly good at fighting," Boone reported. Graham concentrated on getting the words out as the two men basically did his walking for him. He could feel as they walked by Lyra, her energy pouring out enough that he knew exactly where she was even with his eyes shut.

"On the opposite side of the back end of the building, Lyra and I encountered one of the made wolves; we only knocked him unconscious on purpose in the hope that he would be of use later. Hopefully he's still there and didn't get injured in the explosion or the fire that's now consuming the building. The fire departments will get here soon; we need to clear out as soon as possible."

"That is the general consensus, you all are the last to be accounted for. Mainly because you're at the opposite end of the building and there's only one way back here. I already radioed in when I saw Lyra over Taylor's body. There are three people headed back to carry him to the vans; they're clearing enough space so that she can keep working on him as we drive back. I can't really reach my earpiece at the moment but give me a split second and I can radio in your wolf," Boone responded. A second later Graham could hear Boone talking into his radio, giving the approximate location of where he and Lyra had left the unconscious werewolf.

A voice came over the radio saying that they were on it and Graham felt himself relax. Hopefully they'd be able to get that other wolf and get information out of him now that the building was destroyed. The downside was he didn't know how Taylor was doing. His best friend from childhood was lying on the ground with Lyra frantically working on him; Graham knew better than to interrupt what Lyra was doing in hopes of getting an update. She needed all of her concentration for working on him if it was dire at all.

By the time they got about halfway around the building, Graham felt himself going out again. The darkness of his eyelids were somehow getting darker but knowing there wasn't much more walking until they reach the vans didn't help him in his struggle to keep conscious. Within a matter of seconds he stopped putting up a fight and everything faded out again.

"No, sir, we have no way of knowing whether it was someone on-site who set off the explosive in the building or whether it's some kind of failsafe to protect what's inside. It was a pretty thorough explosion though, as there wasn't much left of the building and even if there had been, we just barely got out of there in time to beat the fire department."

The voice then went silent; Graham wasn't quite with it enough to know who was speaking but there was little doubt in his mind that whoever it was was speaking to his father and offering a report of their failed mission. His head was throbbing less than it had been earlier but it was still painful, as was his leg. He could only assume that Lyra had taken a quick break while they loaded Taylor into the van to work on his head. Lyra wasn't as good as the Luna so she still left traces of her energy when she did any major type of work. He'd had her work on him just often enough to be able to identify her signature. He was grateful for his cousin's help but he was more relieved that Taylor was stable enough that she was okay taking a break from working on him.

"We only had one casualty and five injured. Two are severe, the other three will probably heal on their own but could certainly do with the Luna's help. We did manage to grab one of their guards. He was unconscious and in wolf form, which was weird, but he also has some kind of collar on. We don't know what exactly the collar does but you can definitely feel some sort of electricity coming from it. I'm sure our people will be able to get more information from it and him in interrogation. We're on our way back now, ETA is about thirty minutes out."

There was silence again but not as if the phone call had ended, as if the man speaking was listening to orders. "Yes, sir."

Graham stopped listening long enough to realize that he was propped up in one of the front single seats of the van. Not the very front but the middle row; moving as slowly as possible he straightened himself up so that he wouldn't be leaning on the door anymore. The last thing he needed was for them to hit a bump and injure his head further.

"It looks like Graham's awake again," came the voice he recognized as Dylan's from over his shoulder.

There was more rustling and the voice that had been on the phone seemed closer to him, as if the person had turned in their seat to face him. "Graham? Are you in a place where you can tell us what happened or do you need some more time?"

Even though his head was feeling better, Graham knew he wasn't quite coherent enough to form a report on his and Lyra's activities so he focused all his attention on a one-word answer, "Time."

There was a pause after his voice croaked out as if the voice in front of him had to think about the response. "Okay then, we'll wait till after the Luna has had a look at you. But I have warn you, there are three people ahead of you who need help more."

Graham simply grunted in response. This time his body was so exhausted he didn't fight falling back asleep. He knew that someone would be waking him up when they exited the van so he didn't have to worry about the concussion causing him problems quite yet. He also knew that it was just a concussion the Luna could pretty much heal that in less than ten minutes, the leg on the other hand, would take a few days.

Chapter 23

As the vans pulled into the circle driveway, Jack and the other alphas had been ushered into what appeared to be an open hospital room. The Luna and three others, Jack assumed were nurses, were scrambling around, and setting things up. Jack was relieved to see Lyra seemed to be relatively unharmed, other than a large bite on her leg that she had assured those on the radio would heal in a day or two if not sooner. Both Taylor and Graham were on the injured list and Taylor's status still wasn't entirely known. They had agreed not to tell Rachel about Graham until they knew for sure how he was doing. Which Jack felt a little bad about because he would've hated being out of the loop, but at the same time one of them was going to be talking to her later this evening anyway so it wouldn't do any good to worry her unnecessarily.

"Move," came a voice from behind the five alphas that had made it to the compound. All of them shifted to the left, away from the doorway and where all the action seemed to be with the Luna and her staff.

They watched in silence as three people were brought in on stretchers, really it was only two people and one wolf, which Jack assumed was Taylor. Then came Dylan and Boone helping a hobbling Graham then two other men helping a woman, none of them Jack remembered seeing before. The woman's side was a dark red spot, which led Jack to believe she had probably been bitten in wolf form and then changed.

Two others in all black fatigues scurried in after them and last came Lyra with her arms wrapped around her stomach. She stopped to stand next to Jack and the look she gave him was full of sadness and worry. In that moment all of the frustration and anger he felt towards her melted away and instead he reached out and wrapped his right arm around her shoulders and brought her in a kind of side hug, turning his lips up in as close to a smile as he could give her. Then the two of them turned and watched in silence as the Luna and her staff busied themselves assessing who in their care needed their help the most.

After a moment or two, the Luna looked up and over to them. "Lyra, I could really use your help over here. This man has shrapnel, or some kind of metal in his side. If he heals much more around it it's going to puncture one of his lungs. I need you to take it out while I work on one of the others."

He felt Lyra stir under his arm and start to move forward and Jack couldn't help the shock and worry that shot through him. He knew for a fact Lyra had no nursing or EMT training. He had no idea how she was going to help remove metal from one of the men's side. Or why one of the people he assumed were nurses couldn't do it.

Then Lyra looked over her shoulder at him and gave him a stricken look filled with sadness and worry before turning back and heading towards the man her aunt had directed her to.

That expression made him worry even more. He was missing something. There was some secret he wasn't a party to that he was about to find out about and Lyra was worried about his reaction.

He watched warily as she made her way to the body and stood at the opposite side, facing Jack and the other alphas. She then interlocked her thumbs so that her fingers on her left hand were on top of her right; she put her hands over the area the Jack could see was a hole in the man's side. She gave him one last sorrow-filled expressive look before closing her eyes and lowering her hands about an inch from the body. As he watched, a blue glow inched its way from her hands, expanding and contracting but slowly growing bigger as if it was warming up. It expanded so much that it encompassed the wound.

Then an outraged voice came from beside him, "Don't you dare look at her that way."

Jack turned his head slightly so through the corner of his eyes, he could see Dylan standing beside him where Lyra had been earlier.

"What a Luna can do is a gift that is so rare in our kind that less than half of the families worldwide have a Luna healer. It is a blessing, not the curse your expression tells her she is. If you wish to remain friends with Lyra, after this whole situation blows over you will school your face and hide your appalled expression." There was venom in those last few words, letting Jack know just how disgusted Dylan was with him.

Jack fought the expression he hadn't even known was on his face; it took quite a bit of effort but he finally felt it blank mere seconds before Lyra opened her eyes and looked at him. He must've done a good enough job because what she saw there appeared to relieve her. He watched her shoulders lower, releasing tension before she closed her eyes again; the blue light coming from her hands seemed to glow brighter and darker.

He watched in almost horror as the wound in front of her opened and expanded; as it did so, a piece of metal about the size of two fingers began to push its way out of the hole. Once about two inches of it were out, one of the Luna's nurses came to stand next to Lyra with a pair of tongs and grabbed it, removing the last inch from the man's body. Once it was removed, Lyra turned her hands so that her palms were next to each other, thumbs still interlocked but her fingers were now side by side instead of on top of each other. The blood that had come out of the wound with the object began to dry and Jack could only assume she was somehow using that glow to heal the wound. After another silent few minutes he watched the skin slowly close so that it only looked like a very deep scratch. If he didn't know any better, Jack would've thought that the wound was two or three days old. He was so shocked that Lyra could do that. It sped the healing process so much that he could understand what Dylan had said about those gifts being important or a big deal.

As he watched, Lyra walked over to her aunt where she was working on the prone wolf form. Her aunt quickly directed her to Graham who sat on one of the other beds. Lyra then made her way over and proceeded to talk in a low voice to her cousin, Jack assumed asking him what was hurt. Soon after, she had her hands, fingers splayed, reaching over the top of Graham's head and that blue light, not as dark or strong this time, glowed again.

Then his ears perked up as he heard voices in the hallway. If he could hear them he knew the other alphas could hear them as well, so he made no secret of the fact that he turned to face the people out in the hallway.

There was the head guard who had been testing them as well as two men Jack had never met before. The head of the guard had said something about a prisoner. Jack hadn't heard anything about that before and was curious as to why they had kept it off the radio, hoping it had been because he and the other alphas had been listening.

"Does that mean he's awake?" the old man said.

One of the younger, unknown men shook his head. "No, he's still unconscious, whatever knocked them out got him pretty good. I'm pretty sure the Luna could wake him up, or Lyra for that matter, enough for us to interrogate him. Our techs looked at the collar he is wearing. It seems to be doing something that stops them from shifting into human form. Or at least that's their guess. They're going to try and remove it before he wakes up. Then we'll be able to question him, hopefully he's cooperative. Even if he's not we'll probably be able to get answers."

Jack gave a quick glance to Bishop, who was standing to his left. The other alpha had been listening as well. Jack turned, knowing Bishop was following and they both walked into the hall and approached the three men.

They were met with frowns.

"With all due respect we'd like to be in on these interrogations since what Berman does affects us more than it affects you," Jack asserted, crossing his arms and giving as serious an expression as he could.

One of the younger men snorted but the head of the guard held up his hand and answered first, "While I see your point of view and may even agree with you, that's not going to fly. There is no way will be able to convince the council to let you sit in on that. Especially since you're basically on probation and no one on probation gets full rights and abilities to explore the compound unescorted. If you were full members of some standing it would be negotiable but there's no way it's gonna happen. I know you're going to argue but just save us some time and trust me. The best I'll be able to get you is an edited transcript, and even that will have to be approved by the council before I can give it to you." Then the older man motioned to the two younger men and all three of them headed down the hall.

The other alphas had followed Jack and Bishop out and the five of them stood in a small circle in the hall.

"Well, that's that convenient," whispered Bishop, "they'll give us a transcript but they have to approve what exactly the transcript says and how much information they're going to be giving us. While I trust our own to give us any information that we need, I'm still a little frustrated by the fact that we're going to have to put extra effort in to gain information that affects us."

The others all mumbled agreement. But no one seemed to have a way around it.

Cassandra flipped her long blond braid over her shoulder. "I don't know about the rest of you, but I'm getting really sick of being left in the dark with all this stuff that actually affects us. Hell, it's even worse for some of us because the born werewolf we have in our pack isn't part of the main family so we end up getting our information second or third hand. Not that I'm complaining, I appreciate you guys keeping us as much in the know as you can, but I'm really starting to want to hit someone." The last was said with a growl.

The group stood there, quiet for a moment as if no one was quite sure where to go from there. Jack understood Cassandra's frustration, as he at least had Lyra who was sneaking him more information than any others were getting. For the most part, it made him appreciate her a little bit more because even though she had kept this secret from him for years, she was trying much harder than the others to make up for it. That really seemed to mean something and that realization chipped away what was remaining of Jack's aggravation towards Lyra.

"I think perhaps this is not the best time or place to have this discussion. I would not be at all surprised if the walls here have ears," Mathew whispered.

If they had been in the company of other made werewolves, odds were not many people would've heard them but since they didn't know if the born werewolves truly could hear better Mathew had a good point. Without another word, the group of them headed back outside towards the front where all of them had parked.

As a thought struck Jack, he turned to Bishop who was walking beside him. "Do we need to stay? Do you know how Taylor is doing?" he asked, suddenly concerned for the other man more than he had been before.

Bishop shook his head. "I am pretty sure he will be fine, eventually. Though I have no proof of this, I know that if it wasn't true, Lyra would've been more concerned and she would've told me so. She doesn't strike me as someone to avoid the inevitable like that. Besides, I think I'm more in the way being down there, but if you would be so kind as to text Lyra and let her know that I would appreciate a call with an update when she gets the chance, that would be nice. But like I said, she would be more concerned if there was something that couldn't be healed."

Jack was surprised, but he nodded his agreement that he would pass along the message. He wasn't sure he could've been that calm if one of his pack mates had been injured and burned as badly as Taylor had been. But he could see the other man's point. While Lyra had been sad and most definitely upset, it was nowhere near as upset as she would've been if someone she was close to and cared about had been mortally wounded. He remembered the radio mentioning that Lyra had been working on Taylor on the way over; she must've been able to heal him to the point where she was no longer worried about his survival. Still, he wasn't sure he could take it as well as Bishop was; maybe that was because Bishop had only known Taylor for as long as they'd all been werewolves, whereas Jack had Lyra much longer.

Once they'd made it out to the circle drive and were standing by the closest of their cars the five of them stood in silence, all of them unsure as to what to do next.

Jack decided to break the silence, "Mathew, were you able to get a hold of your contact at the government?"

Mathew blinked once or twice at the subject change, as if he really hadn't seen it coming. "Yes, I was able to get a hold of him. I was going to mention it to everyone tomorrow morning, but now is as good a time as ever. And then I will update Rachel when she calls me this morning."

"He said that the powers that be were dragging their feet a little until the media coverage exploded like it has. When I informed him that there were several other articles going further in depth into the problem in the pipeline he was both frustrated and amused. He didn't like the media being involved but he was amused by the fact that what media coverage there'd been so far had gotten the ball rolling and he knew that it would only be a matter of days before the public would start to cry out for them to do something. After all, us poor college students have been through enough, as far as the public was concerned. But then as far as the public knows, we aren't werewolves and it was simple experimentation that may affect us later."

"While I didn't mention it to him, I cannot imagine that should the information leak that we have become werewolves, that the public would be as on our side as it is now. I think we would then become a threat, and monsters, and therefore be more of a problem than victims. So I think we need to be aware that somewhere down the line somebody might play that card. That if we continue to rock the boat they might let it be known exactly what we are. While I do not think that that is in our immediate future, I would be remiss if I didn't bring it up. That being said, I think the powers that be will probably more than likely to go after the scientists and lab assistants sometime within the next week. Much longer than that and they'll have to deal with a frustrated public on top of everything else."

Jack was glad to hear it. He honestly had expected the government to take its sweet time when it came to the lab assistants and the doctor that was after them. While he had been a little skeptical at first about them letting the media know what was going on, now he was more than glad that they ended up doing it and that they had gone through a reporter who was already a werewolf so he would be less likely to ask uncomfortable questions. But that line of thought added some questions for Jack.

"What about Berman? Should we be leaking the fact that he's still in town? Surely the public outcry would be just as large, if not more so, if people knew he hadn't run as far as everyone thought he had," Jack mused.

Mathew seemed to think about it as his brows scrunched towards each other and he folded his arms across his chest. "I do not think now is the best time for that. For two reasons really: the first being our best newspaper source is a born werewolf and I cannot see him being okay with leaking something that the family is currently looking into. I imagine that might get stopped. Even if it didn't, we don't quite have enough information right now, especially with the family not sharing, to give the general public more than a cursory idea of Berman being back. We could tell them about the company he tried to get to invest in him, but I have a sneaking suspicion that people would look into the investment firm and why they went after that, which I can't imagine the family would be thrilled about. Then they'd be looking into his business; the last thing we need is the media discovering what we really are, even if we could convince them that his newest experiments were the only werewolves and that we were just an early experimentation. We're then dooming the current experiments to the sort of attention we ourselves don't want. And I think until we know for sure that they volunteered for it, it would probably be best if we don't out them, and that really is a best case scenario because let's face it, eventually, some enterprising young reporter would figure out our secret and tell the world."

Jack and the others begrudgingly agreed. It wasn't necessarily something they wanted to hear, Jack was pretty sure the others agreed with him on wanting a simple way to get rid of Berman and all the problems he caused. But going to the media was probably not going to be enough. Mathew was right, they couldn't risk being outed for what they were and until they could protect themselves better that was the situation they were looking at.

No one seemed to have any more to say or any last minute upbeat comments to make; they were all in this waiting game together. Waiting for the media to stir up people, waiting for the government to step in on their behalf, waiting for the family to do something constructive because this raid hadn't garnered much, minus their current prisoner. Jack couldn't help the level of anxiety that was coiled around his chest. He had been terrified and horribly sad by the fact that Lyra had been in that coma but since she woke up, the world to gotten so much bigger and so much more dangerous in such a short time and Jack couldn't see a way out for them, any of them.

The silent acceptance of the current situation seemed to settle over all of them as they parted ways and each headed home, forced to sit and wait and hope for good news.

Chapter 24

Dylan hated interrogations. He understood them to be a necessary evil and a tool to get information from un-cooperating sources but he himself didn't really have the stomach for them. Which is why when it became clear that although Taylor was stable but would remain unconscious for some time yet, and that Graham was not in any sort of shape to view the interrogations and Lyra was too busy helping her aunt, Dylan volunteered to go and watch on their behalf. The only other pack werewolf that had any kind of authority was Boone, and even then it wasn't really authority but simply an understanding that eventually he would work on a security detail that gave him access to this kind of proceeding. Dylan knew that both Taylor and Graham would want their own set of eyes and ears at the interrogation and Dylan was the closest they would get so he didn't put up any kind of argument when Lyra asked him to go.

Now he stood in the far corner of the interrogation room next to Boone and two other men, watching the proceedings. There were two men doing the actual interrogation as well and then another three behind the two-way mirror to Dylan's right. The men in charge were behind that glass, including Graham's father. All of the men in the room were wearing earpieces so that they could hear any sort of commands the men behind the glass gave.

The man that sat in front of them was thin, as if he hadn't really eaten in the last few days and probably hadn't been fed well before that. He still held a lot of muscle on his form so he had probably been quite built at some point. His shaggy blond hair was long enough to fall into his eyes and his beard was unkempt enough to show that it'd been a while since he'd been allowed to shave. Dylan knew from how scraggly the hair on his face was that it probably wasn't by choice because odds were someone who put that much effort into their body would trim it before it got to the point it was at.

Dylan's theory had been confirmed a few moments earlier when they had first walked the man into the room and over the earpiece one of their tech guys informed them that the collar this man had come in with had been letting off some signal to the man's brain. They were lucky in that the explosion must've triggered something to drain the battery because with the battery so drastically low, they were able to remove it much easier than they thought would. Once they had removed it, even though the man was unconscious, he changed back to human form, but without any clothing. One of the Luna's medical staff had come down to give him a cursory once over and had decided that while the man would probably have a severe headache, she wasn't sure whether he would have a concussion or not, but other than that he seemed relatively unharmed. So they'd given him a shot of adrenaline and a painkiller for his head so that when he woke up, hopefully his body would absorb the painkiller fast enough. They'd then given the man a pair of sweatpants that looked about his size and led him into the interrogation room, waiting about ten minutes for the painkiller to fully kick in before addressing him. From the way the man sat with his eyes glued to the table, Dylan was willing to bet he was some kind of ex-military and he found himself wondering whether that would work to their advantage or whether it would mean that it was going to be harder for them to get any information from him.

The shorter of the two men running the interrogation, Cameron, slowly sat down in one of the chairs across from the man. "What's your name?" he asked as blandly as possible.

The man before them simply flickered his gaze at Cameron before looking down at the table again, saying nothing.

Cameron leaned forward making both his body and voice more aggressive, "I said, what is your name?"

The other man didn't even look up this time, just pretended as if Cameron didn't exist. The only change was his breath coming a little bit faster.

The taller of the interrogators, Ronen, sat down in the chair next to Cameron. "Let's try different question then. How is it that you became a werewolf?"

An expression of surprise and concern flashed across the man's face before it went blank again. There was no response beyond that.

Cameron pounded on the table but the man didn't even flinch. He then stood up, looming over the man and asked for his name again. There was still no response. Dylan watched in worry for the next minute or two as both the interrogators became increasingly aggressive; he knew what would come next. If they didn't respond, the interrogators would start to get physical, he had no doubt that that would throw the werewolf off guard because odds were both interrogators were much stronger than him or barring that, much stronger than he was used to fighting.

Then an idea popped into Dylan's mind and before he could ask for permission or think too much about it, he stepped forward, much to the surprise of Boone and the other men standing next to him.

"You're not alone here. We are, in fact, all in the same boat." He said it loudly but gently.

Both the interrogators looked at him angrily for interrupting them but the man still sitting in the chair slowly looked up at Dylan questioningly. The men on the other side of the glass seemed to have noticed his response as well because a quick voice he knew to be Graham's father came over other headsets.

"Stand aside with see what Dylan's going to try and do."

He wasn't sure if it was going to work, or if it would make a difference but Dylan wasn't sure he had the stomach to watch them torture the other wolf so he began the change. He did it slower than he normally would, which made it a little painful and frustrating. He forced his body to keep it at a pace where the man in the chair in front of him could see and understand what was happening. Watch as the bones and the muscles changed shaped and popped out of and into sockets. He kept his eyes on the man in the chair, focusing as if there was nothing else in the room, demanding the man see the connection between the two of them. As he watched, the man in the chair's eyes grew wider with understanding. When Dylan had completed his transition and shook his fur from where he now stood on all fours, the man's wide eyes finally moved from him to everyone else in the room and he spoke the first words anyone had heard from him.

"Are you all wolves? Did he do this to all of you?" There was a wonder in his voice and the disbelief that the world had in fact just gotten bigger than he thought.

Taking their cue from Dylan, both Cameron and Ronen moved around the table and slowly sat in front of the prisoner.

It was Cameron that answered him, "Yes, we are all werewolves. Though we were born that way and not made that way by your Doctor Berman."

The man in the chair growled aggressively at Cameron and everyone in the room tensed. "He is not my doctor. The man is a monster, a maniac with blind followers that are somehow convinced of his cause, whatever the hell that might be."

The room relaxed again. Ronan waited a beat before speaking, "So what is your name?" he asked more conversationally than before.

The man eyed them both warily for answering slowly, "Parker, Parker Holmes."

"Hello, Parker, my name is Cameron and this here is Ronan. The guy who changed into a wolf's name is Dylan. The three guys behind us are Boone, Moses, and Stewart. Would you mind telling us how exactly you came to become a werewolf, if you were born into it like us we would've already known who you were so we're just curious as to how exactly Berman is making werewolves." Cameron was trying his hardest now to be as nonthreatening as possible but Dylan knew he was only doing that to put Parker at ease. He was hoping Parker would see him not as a threat until they absolutely needed him to think of them otherwise, but Dylan could tell Parker wasn't fooled. He seemed smart enough to realize the situation he was in but he seemed willing to talk anyway.

"I guess, and I'll give you the Cliff's notes version because honestly, I don't really have the energy to give you much more than that. I haven't eaten in a little more than two days so the brain's not working at one hundred percent. Basically, I saw a flyer these people were testing equipment for the military that they had hoped would better protect the men and women overseas. Being freshly out of the military myself, I wanted to volunteer, anything I can do to help my brothers and sisters overseas, I'm going to do. It started out as mere fitness tests for all of us; everyone I met had been in the military within the last couple years and was there for the same reason as me. But the lab techs were giving us these vitamin injections that, looking back on it I'm positive weren't vitamin injections.

"One day when they had us doing a fitness test on treadmills, they gassed the room and when I woke up in a lot of pain, my body was changing into a wolf. There was a lot of transitioning between the two and the change seemed to make my metabolism go faster but they weren't really feeding us anymore than they would normally. Once they had gassed us they wouldn't let us leave the facility.

We were locked in these tiny cells so they could keep an eye on us and study us and poke and prod us whenever they wanted. I watched them take people in and out for experiments and of the dozen or so cages I could see, I know at least three that were led out to go somewhere and never came back. Whether they were sent on some kind of mission or killed, I don't know.

"A couple days ago, I don't know more precisely than that, you kind of lose track of time underground, they put this collar on, the one you probably found me in, that made me stay in wolf form. After another couple days I was loaned out, I guess you'd say, to be a security dog along with a couple other guys, at that building you guys raided. They hadn't fed us the entire time we were there so we weren't really working on one hundred percent, but they made sure the batteries were changed on those collars. They only have an eighteen-hour time. And they're basically prototypes, so I found out very recently they're prone to shorts, which is probably how you got it off. I'm incredibly grateful to you, by the way. That's all the information I have. I don't know what they injected us with, I don't know what was in the gas, I don't know anything about the collars, other than if you didn't do what it wanted, it would shock you or various other terrible things. It worked with a chip they said they put in my head near my ear."

He tapped the left side of his head halfway between the base of his neck and his ear. "I don't know exactly where it is but somewhere in there. That's really all the information I have. I know that I haven't been home in at least two months by my

Gretchen S. B.

calculations, but I could be off since I don't know what month it is." His voice grew more and more bitter as he spoke.

Ronan leaned back in his chair and watched for a moment as if waiting to see if Parker would say anything else before he responded, "I'm sorry about that. This isn't something that should be forced on somebody. Do you think you'd be able to tell us where the lab is?"

Parker's blond hair shook in front of his eyes as he moved his head back and forth. "No, when they moved to me I was heavily sedated and completely out so I haven't the foggiest idea where the lab is. I could tell you where the initial meeting place was; I remember that address where they're recruiting people. But that's it, I don't know if that is actually connected at all to the lab itself."

A voice came over the headset, one of the councilmembers, but Dylan wasn't quite sure which one. "Ask him if he's willing to stay and let us run bloodwork tests, more humane tests and if he's willing to work with us on finding Berman. We all know he doesn't have much choice but willingness would go a long way."

Cameron leaned forward on to the table, sliding his elbows in front of him, making it look like he was slouching more than he actually was. "Would you be willing to stick around, help us find Berman and his lab? Let us run some more humane tests on you, like bloodwork, to see exactly what Berman's come up with?"

Parker leaned forward, his eyes became slits and his lips formed a very small smirk. "You ask as if I have a choice. You and I, and everyone else here know I don't have one. But for what it's worth, I want Berman stopped as much, if not more, than you. I want the men and women that are in that lab free to go back to their lives. I told myself I would help them if I ever escaped and I'm going to honor that promise. So yeah I'll stick around and help."

Cameron leaned back, watching the other man thoughtfully. "To be honest with you then, we don't know if we can trust you, or how much of what you're saying really is the truth. So the accommodations we're going to give you aren't necessarily going to be nice, you'll be watched around the clock and we can't really let you leave."

A chuckle shook Parker's shoulders before any noise actually escaped his lips and he leaned back in the chair. "I didn't really expect anything else but I appreciate the candor. And really if I could get some food in the next hour, I'll be fine."

It made Dylan sad that the man before them was ex-military and had served his country, and had been experimented on and trapped, not fed for days and now he would be stuck in a cell again. Made him angry as well as sad. Luckily, he was in wolf form so his expression wouldn't really give him away.

"I'll make sure myself that you get food. And a werewolf's portion of food, not just human's," Cameron promised before standing up.

Ronan stood up as well and the two men that stood with Boone moved forward before Ronan motioned that Parker should stand up and the four of them escorted him back to the cell he would be staying in for the foreseeable future.

The cells weren't exactly nice but they weren't terrible either. The family had two sets of cells. The first was the dark and horribly uncomfortable cells they used for hostile guests, and the other the one, he was pretty sure they were taking Parker to, had a bed, a bathroom alcove that gave the illusion of privacy, and a television with some movies and books. It wasn't necessarily plush and the door was heavy-duty glass so that anyone walking by would be able to see what he was doing but it was probably better than what he'd come from.

Once the other men had left, Dylan and Boone exchanged glances; really Dylan looked at Boone. The other man shrugged before both of them walked out of the room and out into the hallway, knowing that once the men that were escorting Parker came back, there would be a discussion between them and the councilmembers that had been watching behind the glass. There wasn't a long wait before the entire group had congregated in the hall.

Graham's father spoke first, as was usually customary, "Well, that was not the most helpful of situations. On the plus side, he's letting us draw blood and run tests but is not much more useful than that." He looked at Cameron and Ronan. "Please tell me you had him write down that address that he was talking about?"

Both men nodded and Ronan stuck out his arm toward the head of the family handing him a small piece of paper. Graham's father reached out and took it before giving the address a cursory glance as if he had hoped it would be some address he recognized. Apparently he didn't because he handed it to Lyra's father with instructions to have the address investigated once they were done talking.

"Hopefully this address is one that they still use, or used recently enough that we'll be able to trace it back to something," Lyra's father said. "If this is their recruiting office we might be able to send in a spy or two just to see what's going on."

Dylan wasn't sure he was comfortable with them sending in a spy. On the plus side it would give them more intel; on the other hand, putting one of their own in danger didn't sit well with him, but then putting one of their own in danger wasn't exactly an anomaly.

There was some more back and forth on where to go from there but ultimately the men on the council decided that looking more into the dummy corporation Berman had fed them as well as this new address Parker had given them, to see if it was a real address or if he was setting them up, was the best course of action. Before leaving, the head of the guard mentioned that he had told the alphas he would try to get them a transcript of the interrogation. Graham's father frowned but approved the idea, as long as he himself edited the interview and ran it by him or his brothers before sending it to the office. The other man agreed before walking off towards the tech room where the recording would be.

Graham's father then dismissed all of them before walking away, he and his two brothers clearly about to go into a private counsel discussing the family's next move.

Dylan knew they wouldn't let him listen in, even if Graham or Lyra had been there, their chances wouldn't have been that good either so he turned to the opposite direction towards the infirmary so that he could check on Taylor and Graham. He wasn't more of a few steps away when he noticed Boone walking beside him.

Turning his furry head, he looked up at the other man.

Boone didn't even look down at him but seemed to realize the attention anyway. "I'm just as curious as to how they're doing as you are. There doesn't seem to be much else I can do right now and I'm not the sit-around-and-wait type. I fully intend to update my alpha about what's going on as soon as I know that everyone's all right."

Dylan was somewhat relieved to hear the other man say that because it actually had been his exact idea to update both his own alpha and Bishop since he knew Taylor would want his alpha to be updated as well, and since he was incapable of doing himself.

For the rest of the walk to the infirmary neither of them said a word. When they got there Dylan was concerned to see the Luna still bent over Taylor's body. The only plus side was somehow she had forced him to change. Changing from one form to the other when injured, even though exhausting, could help speed up the healing process. The downside was that now they could see how extensive his burns were. From the mid-thigh down there were third-degree burns covering his legs. They were shiny as if salve had been rubbed on them. His head though seemed to be doing much better, as all they could see was a slight bruising on his temple. Odds were under his scalp line there was a bit of a bump. He was still out though so Taylor had no way of knowing whether the Luna woke his friend up to change or that she had forced him to change while unconscious. He hoped for the latter because the burns looked extremely painful.

Lyra and Graham were on the next bed over, Graham was sitting up, and his leg was in a cast. The cast wouldn't be on more than a few days while his bones healed; it kept the bones in place so they wouldn't accidentally dislodge while healing. The back of his head had a large Band-Aid on it and a pillow behind it where he had hit the tree when he had gone flying from the explosion. Lyra sat on the side of the bed closest to them so that she could watch the Luna work on Taylor but still sit next to her cousin. The resident assistants were wandering around doing this and that but no one seemed in a hurry anymore. Only two other beds were occupied with people from the raid. Petra was asleep on her side but her entire middle was wrapped in bandages. And a wolf whose name Dylan didn't know but his face he recognized had both his arms in slings and big bandages around his chest.

While Boone headed over to the man Dylan didn't know, Dylan made his way over to sit next to Lyra's chair. Graham noticed him heading over first and his attention is what made Lyra aware that Dylan was heading towards them. As he sat next to her, leaning slightly against her leg, she set her hand in a comforting gesture between his shoulder blades.

She spoke while still watching her aunt with Taylor. "His head is pretty banged up, she doesn't know how bad it's going to be and I was more concerned with the burns on site so I didn't really check it out. We're not really going to know until he wakes up and my aunt doesn't want to wake him up until the burns are more healed, in at least a day or two. She's going to keep working on them because of how nasty they are but she only has so much energy, she's only got another fifteen minutes or so before she's going to have to call it a night. She'll keep working in the morning but I think his body is probably going to have to heal itself once she gets it to second-degree burns. She says physically in a week or so he should be fine, like I said she doesn't know if there was any damage from whatever happened to his head. And since you were there with him you're the only one that knows how he injured his head so she's not quite sure how exactly the damage occurred anyway. All we can do is hope that there isn't any brain damage. She's going to have people in here around the clock to watch him and Graham's stuck in here at least through the night so if he does wake up on his own, Taylor won't be by himself."

Dylan was relieved to hear that physically Taylor would be fine but he wasn't sure what to make of the fact that they didn't know about his mental condition. When they had been fighting, one of the wolves had surprised Taylor and slammed his head into some of the stone stairs of the building. The wolf hit him with enough force and rode him all the way down, causing his head to bounce in the same place several times. That had put Taylor out of commission pretty quickly and it also put him right in the building during the explosion. He could still see his friend's wolf body flying through the air when the explosion happened. It was not an image he would get out of his head anytime soon. That and Lyra running headfirst into the fire to save him. Dylan had wanted to save him just as much as Lyra had but since they didn't know how bad the fire was, he wanted her to wait so she could assess the situation. Thankfully Lyra hadn't waited because if she had Taylor might've had more of his body burned away. Dylan felt guilty about that, if he'd let Lyra go sooner would he have saved his friend some pain? He knew it wasn't something he should be thinking about, that he should just be grateful they got there when they did but if it'd been up to him things might've been worse and he wasn't entirely sure he could live with that. Once again, he was grateful that he was in wolf form so that no one would have to read his face or make him vocalize his thoughts because he wasn't sure he could say these things out loud. It was then he decided he would step outside, once he changed, to tell their alphas what had happened but he was coming immediately back into the infirmary because he would stand watch over Taylor just like Taylor would've stood watch over any of them. In that moment Dylan made it his responsibility to see to it that everything was done to make Taylor whole again.

Chapter 25

Lyra was exhausted. Her leg hurt but it was more of a dull ache, nothing she couldn't handle. When her aunt had finished with Taylor for the night she had looked at it and informed Lyra that her body would be healing just fine it would just hurt and that under normal circumstances, she could've healed it for her but she would rather be using her energy to help Taylor. Lyra had eagerly agreed, anything that was going to help Taylor, she wanted to do. And if it meant a few more days with her inconvenienced by her leg, she had no problem with that. Once they had that settled, her aunt had told Lyra it was time to take the suppressant again.

Lyra had almost forgotten that she was supposed to take the suppressant every few days; she was grateful that her aunt had remembered, because the last thing they needed right now was her in a coma on her way to death. She squeezed Graham's hand one last time and gave Dylan a pat on the head before getting up and limping after her aunt. Curiously, her aunt walked all the way back to her private office, grabbing all the stuff she needed to give Lyra the suppressant along the way. Lyra wasn't exactly sure why her aunt felt they needed privacy for the suppressant and a little bit of worry edged its way into her mind. Clearly her aunt wanted to talk to her in private about something but Lyra had no idea what.

Luna busied herself at her desk, motioning for Lyra to sit down in one of the visitors' chairs as she filled the needle full of the pale green liquid that would help keep the drug in Lyra's system at bay.

As her aunt was walking towards her she finally spoke, "With the most recent records your alpha was kind enough to share with us, we are couple steps closer to finding some kind of antidote for the poison you have. We're probably still a ways off but having paperwork on the chemical is definitely a help."

Keeping her mouth shut, Lyra looked away as her aunt injected the needle. Not because of a fear of the needle itself but of her aunt seeing the expression on her face that she was too tired to hide. She knew the voice her aunt was using; there wasn't a lot of hope at the moment, they weren't really any closer to finding a cure but her aunt was going out of her way to try and comfort Lyra with what little information they had gathered from the raid Jack and the other alphas had done on one of the labs. Lyra knew that while it had helped them come up with the compounds that were used in the drug, at least some of them, they weren't really any closer to a cure. She knew her aunt too so wanted to believe that they would come up with one and her aunt so wanted to comfort her that she didn't have it in her to show her aunt the doubt she felt.

Once she was finished, her aunt put the cotton swab on her arm and the Band-Aid over it. Once she turned away she said something much more interesting, "I overheard something that might interest you, or it would at least interest to me if I were you. After you all did your training tests I was walking down the hall coming to say hello to you and see if you wanted to go get coffee so that I could check on you, but I overheard a conversation amongst one of the wolves and one of the trainers. I don't remember his name but it's the one born of a werewolf parent who is in your pack. He seemed upset that he was so far behind the born werewolves and it wasn't a sense of pride or ego, it was almost as if there was something more that bothered him. Is there something going on between you two?" Her aunt then turned around suddenly so that she could get Lyra's split-second expression.

Lyra wasn't sure if anything showed on her face, she tried to keep it as blank as possible but she couldn't help it: her eyes had widened slightly and her heartbeat sped up as she remembered Ryan's declaration to her after the family meeting. "There's nothing going on between us, Auntie. What would make you think there was?" She tried to inject some sarcasm into the question but she wasn't sure she succeeded.

Her aunt narrowed her eyes slightly before responding, "Just a little of this and a little of that. Women's intuition mostly. Regardless, this bothered him enough that it sounded like he would be heading out of town for a while. I found that to be a interesting timing."

That time Lyra couldn't school her face; she was surprised that Ryan could even think of leaving when there was so much going on. A thought passed over her aunt's face before the older woman turned around again.

"I see that that is news to you."

This was why she had wanted to talk to her in private, while she was grateful her aunt didn't want to have this discussion in front of the others she wasn't entirely sure where her aunt was going with this so she decided to ask a slightly different question, "Did he say how long he would be gone or where?" She tried to keep her his voice as blank as possible.

Her aunt slid the needle into a small bag that she would end up throwing in the medical waste bin before looking up at Lyra again. "I didn't hear that part, they started speaking a little quieter, but it sounded like it would be an extended visit, not a day or two, and something about going to an uncle's house. I just figured it would be something you would want to know."

Knowing her aunt was done with the shot, Lyra stood up and headed out of the infirmary, waving off Graham's confused face as she walked by. While she was out she would call Jack as well so she'd have a bit of an alibi, even though it wasn't her real reason for storming out of the infirmary. It was already seven-thirty in the morning and while she had been exhausted from being up all night, the idea of Ryan abandoning them set a new course of adrenaline shooting through her. Once she was out of the hallway and out of hearing distance of the infirmary she scrolled through her contacts and called Ryan, putting the phone to her ear as she speed walked through the building. After three rings it went to voicemail. Not long enough for him to not have seen it; he'd clearly hit the ignore button. Growling to herself, she tried again; this time it went to voicemail faster. She tried a third time, only to be transferred to voicemail after one ring. This time she waited until the beep and left a message.

"Ryan? What is this I hear about you leaving town? Are you sure this is the best timing for that? I understand you might be upset with me or embarrassed or something but the pack needs you here. There is a lot going on; we need all hands on deck." Then she paused; part of her wanted to tell him that she didn't want him to leave, that she was counting on him being there and not just because he was the second. She relied on him to be more of a steady rock than Jack. He was always her ally when things got bad. When she and Jack fought, Ryan was always on her side. He meant a lot to her, and she was only now just realizing it. "Please at least call me and let me know you're okay," she pleaded before hanging up.

She knew he wouldn't call. But if he really was on some sort of out-of-town break from the drama that was happening he wouldn't be contacting anyone, least of all her. The thought made her sick, what if things got worse while he was gone, what if something happened? What if the suppressants stopped working and she ended up back in a coma without telling him how important he was to her? She'd only just realized it herself and he didn't know at all.

Knowing she still needed to call Jack, but not wanting to talk to him in such an emotional state, she sent him a text letting him know that once she heard what happened in the interrogation she would give him a call and give all the info she could. Odds were he was on his way to work or there already so he wouldn't call her back right away. That gave her a few hours before she had to talk to anyone. Not quite ready to go back into the infirmary and sit with her cousin and Dylan, Lyra ran, jogged really, since her leg didn't have it in it to run, into one of the wooded areas of the property.

Tears began to stream down her face, not just because of Ryan leaving, but the hopelessness of the entire situation. She hadn't wanted to separate her pack they had, in some ways, become closer to her than her family. Now one of them had left and they were facing more adversaries than ever before, she couldn't help but think it was her fault. She couldn't help but wonder if she could have prevented any of this. If there was something she wasn't doing that could make things better for everyone. As the tears streamed down her face, Lyra pleaded with the universe that things get better, that even if they couldn't get better for her, to at least get better for those people that she cared about because they deserved better than what was happening to all of them. After Berman's experiments, her pack deserved to live in peace, or as much peace as being a werewolf could give them. She didn't care what happened to her she just wanted those she loved to be happy and safe.

Chapter 26

The early morning sunshine seemed to burn spots through the trees as Ryan drove through the wooded area that made up much of his uncle's property. He had set out to his uncle's cabin at six hoping to hedge much of the rush-hour traffic.

About a half an hour ago when he had seen Lyra's name pop up on his phone display his hand had itched to hit the answer button. He wanted to talk to her, ask what could've happened that she was calling this early because he doubted it was because he was out of town. Something must have gone wrong somewhere or something happened. But then he thought on it a second and if it was something dire, Jack would've called or would call him; either way he wasn't ready to speak to Lyra so instead he hit the ignore button. When she called two more times it was easier each time to hit 'ignore'. When she left a message he couldn't help himself and listened to it. She sounded so sad and so concerned that he had to fight with himself not to call her back.

He knew with all his being that he and Lyra were matched but that in order to be a mate to a Luna he needed to be stronger than the average wolf. The Luna had to work outside of family rules sometimes and her mate needed to be strong in order to fight beside her. Ryan was starting at a disadvantage and he needed to remedy that and he knew his uncle could help.

Instead of calling her back he concentrated on the winding road that led to his uncle's, trying to absorb himself in the beauty of nature, though he couldn't quite manage it. Eventually, he gave up trying and turned up his radio when he heard more voices than music. Even though he knew he could concentrate and hear the hushed tones just fine, it was more habit to turn it up than anything else. Much to his surprise, it was a news report that he was actually interested in.

"This morning, warrants were issued for a Dr. Paul, as well as two other scientists and several of Berman's old lab assistants. As you may know, Berman was the one a few years back who did an unsanctioned experiment that ended up making a whole bunch of college kids sick on several college campuses. As it turns out, Dr. Paul and her cohorts were trying to kidnap several of the students to run experiments on them now, years later. If you haven't been keeping up to date, this news story has been going crazy in the press. But it wasn't until this morning that the government moved in and officially put in arrests. Half of the lab assistants and Dr. Paul are already in custody as I tell you this. In my opinion it's about damn time they did something. There's no way these scientists could've been operating this long without government knowing about it."

"Also as it turns out, the scientists were getting the funding from a billionaire in California, the CEO of PML Corporation. When reporters went to question him this morning he claimed he didn't know anything about kidnappings or attempted kidnappings. Which, let's be honest, isn't terribly likely. But as of yet it doesn't seem like the police will be issuing an arrest for him. He claims he will cooperate in any way necessary and that he was simply hoping that these scientists could help find a cure for one of his grandchildren who has a rare disease."

"I don't know about you, folks, but I don't know how credible it is that he didn't know what was going on, that he didn't sanction it himself. He was giving the money, after all. But at least the rest are happening for the people involved and it looks like they are confiscating all of the research these people did. They had three separate facilities hidden under various company names. Which seems a little too sneaky to be on the up and up as this billionaire says it was."

"Let's hear from you all. What do you think about this newest development with these college students and the scientists? Do you think no one knew? Or do you think it's some kind of cover up? We will hear from you at the end of this commercial break and I'll be updating you all morning as news comes in."

As a jingle started, Ryan turned the radio back down and felt his shoulders drop a little. At least this episode was over. The kidnapping would stop. Sure, they still had Berman to worry about but he wasn't their current active threat. These other scientists had kidnapped Lyra and tried to beat her up, he'd even fought some of them; to know that finally they wouldn't have to worry about them anymore was a huge relief. The small twinge of guilt he felt for leaving Lyra and the others lessened knowing that the threat was gone. Now he could concentrate fully on training with his uncle.

He pulled up to the house behind his uncle's bold black truck; as he shut off the car he heard faint growling, faint enough that he knew it wasn't in the immediate vicinity. He pulled out his keys and jumped out of the car so he could hear it better. As clear as day, he could hear in the distance two snarling and growling wolves that were clearly in the middle of a fight. Ryan smiled to himself and he knew that that smile was full of violent promise and not pleasant at all. A good fight was exactly what he needed right now so without any further thought, he left his car unlocked and hid the keys under the seat then began to change before running headlong into the woods towards whatever danger was waiting for him.

About The Author

Gretchen is a Seattleite that loves her home. She has a day job as a Program Coordinator a local university. She loves to read, write and create characters. As well as knit and binge watch Netflix. She is also on a sporadic book blog and internet radio show with some of her college friends. She currently lives with her husband and their mischievous Rotti mix, who always seems to find something new she shouldn't be chewing on.

If you enjoyed this book, please feel free to leave a review on Amazon, Barnes & Noble, or Goodreads. Reviews are always appreciated.

You can find Gretchen at:

Gretchens.b.author@gmail.com
Gretchensb.com
Twitter.com/GretchenSB
Goodreads.com/GretchenSB
Facebook.com/authorGretchenSB
Plus.google.com/+GretchenSB

68035576R00201

Made in the USA
Charleston, SC
01 March 2017